Pucked Over

A Sweet & Spicy Hockey Romance

Beth Anderson

Pucked Over

Cover art and design by Humble Nations

ISBN: 979-8-9854725-3-0

Published 2024 by Full Speed Publishing / Full Tilt Romance

Printed in the United States
First Edition
10 9 8 7 6 5 4 3 2 1

Pucked Over

Dedicated to all the ladies who also followed their dreams.

Chapter 1.

Stephen – October

The elevator came to a nearly silent stop on the top floor, Winning Towers' penthouse suite. *Nice*, Stephen Sloan thought, stepping from the car. He always got a kick out of how smoothly and quietly it operated. Maybe that was silly, but Winning Towers was one of Boston's newest, most luxurious buildings; everything should be the best for the fortune he paid for the condo. Not to mention that he enjoyed the little things in life—like a well-maintained elevator.

In fact, all machines should be kept in tip-top shape in his opinion, whether it was an elevator, a car, or the human body. At twenty-seven he still moved with litheness and grace that younger men, even men just beginning their careers on the ice, envied. There was a reason he'd been the Back Bay Warriors' starting center for six straight seasons.

Stephen shifted the bouquet—a dozen long-stemmed, pink roses—from his right hand to his left and patted his pocket as he crossed the thickly carpeted foyer. He could feel the awkward shape there, pressing against his hip as he moved, but it was reassuring to actually touch the ring-box. They said you should spend about three months' salary on an engagement ring and if he stopped to think about it, walking around carrying a two and a half-million-dollar ring was nuts. Just plain crazy.

He smiled—crazy was exactly right. He was crazy for Liza Gardner, and it was time to do something about it. They'd been together since sophomore year of college, and had lived together since Stephen bought the condo around the new year, but they'd never made anything official. The fact that they were together so long without doing anything to make it official was a subject of some teasing around the locker room. A sports team is on the road a lot and there are always opportunities and temptations. Plenty of the guys had girlfriends or even wives at home but gave in to those temptation—a little or a lot, depending on the person.

Not Stephen Sloan. He loved Liza Gardner and that was that as far as he was concerned. He loved her and he wanted to marry her. He expected her to bring the subject up herself at some point, but somehow conversation just never got around to it. Well, what good was talk anyway? It was actions that spoke loudest.

Sloan took out his keys, balancing his workout bag over his left shoulder and the flowers again in his right. He spent all week trying to figure out the best time and best way to pop the question. Finally, he decided the best way was the simplest: just do it. Go home early one night, surprise Liza, and then take her out on the town for a romantic evening to celebrate. He had no doubt she'd say yes. They'd been together for so long, they lived together most of a year—this would just tell the world what the two of them already knew, that they belonged together.

The key slid into the front door's lock as smoothly as the elevator operated, but he realized as he turned the key that it was unnecessary—the door wasn't locked.

"That's weird," he muttered.

One of Winning Towers' selling points was the fact that each apartment was completely soundproof. Inside your home, you'd never have to hear a thing you didn't want to. Stephen pushed the door open and was immediately assaulted by a world of sights and sounds he didn't want to hear, didn't want to see, and in fact never dreamed of in his own house.

R&B music was playing at a volume just below ear-splitting, but even so it wasn't enough to drown out the voices of what had to be fifteen people scattered around the entryway and living room. All strangers, though Stephen thought a few looked vaguely familiar.

The penthouse wasn't huge: four bedrooms, three bathrooms, a living room, dining room, kitchen. The front door opened into a sort of high-rise equivalent of the traditional New England mudroom, a short hallway with closets for coats and shoes.

Here, in the "mudroom," was the nearest of those strangers: a redhead in a completely sheer teddy sat, legs splayed, on the leather-padded bench in the entryway. She held a bottle of champagne in one hand—the bottle Stephen had purchased the night before in anticipation of today—and a half-full flute in the other. A nude man on all fours, like a dog, was at her feet. She laughed uproariously at something he said then squealed in pleasure as he pushed his face between her thighs, spilling champagne on the back of his head. He didn't seem to even notice.

"What the hell!" Stephen cried, the forgotten bouquet falling to the floor. He dropped his bag, stooped, took the nude man by the shoulders, and dragged him back away from the woman. "What the hell?" he said again. "What is this? Who are you people?"

"Hey, get your own!" the man retorted, slapping Stephen's hands away and resuming his exploration of the woman's body. The woman just laughed harder.

Drunk. She's drunk, Stephen realized.

The scene in the living room was similar, but on a larger scale. At least a dozen people, many of them fully nude, were engaged in everything from teasing to full-on intercourse. On the expensive carpet—*thank God it's Scotch-guarded* an absurd little voice in the back of his head murmured—on pieces of the sectional sofa, pulled apart and spread across the room so the couples—the trio in one grouping—could have the smallest measure of privacy. One couple stood pressed against the wall, the woman's legs wrapped around the man's hips as his buttocks thrust and strained. It was sexual bedlam of a sort that Stephen Sloan had never even seen in a porno flick.

"Where's Liza?" he said, more to himself than any of these depraved invaders. Except for the couple by the front door, none of them had even noticed his presence.

Sloan stalked the apartment, absently taking note of the wreckage. The kitchen was a hodgepodge mess of disordered snack foods and empty wine bottles. The dining room table was being used by a pair of enthusiastic blondes performing exotic acts for a mixed group of middle-aged men and women who were all clothed, but watched raptly as if there would be a test later on.

One of the guest bedroom doors was locked, and the soundproofing prevented any clues from escaping, but Sloan could guess what was going on. In the other guest bedroom were gathered a group of four—three women and a man—all nude but engaged in a heated political conversation. The surrealness of the scene barely penetrated Stephen's cloud of confusion.

Not counting bathrooms, there were two rooms left in the apartment: the bedroom converted into his gaming room, and the master bedroom. He had seen no sign of Liza, and he was certain of where he'd find her, but somehow, he couldn't quite bring himself to open the master bedroom door. He turned to the gaming room, flung open the door, wondering what new scene from hell he'd find. There was only one occupant: Mr. Belding, the building's head superintendent. He sat in Stephen's leather chair watching CSPAN on the 60" television.

Belding turned in his seat, saying, "Oh, Mr. Sloan. Hiya. I'll just, uh—" The older man stood, clicked the television off, replaced the controller in its slot on the chair's arm, then nodded politely and hurried past Stephen out into the hallway before disappearing around the bend towards the penthouse's front door.

"What the fuck…" This was the most bizarre thing of all.

Shaking his head, anger finally penetrating the confusion, Stephen Sloan steeled himself and threw open the master bedroom door.

The room was darkened, and the splash of the light from the hallway fell squarely across the king-sized bed, casting a buttery color over the three bodies writhing on top of the sheets. A slender, bald-headed man was mounting one woman from behind while she pleasured the other woman with her mouth. The second woman's fingers tangled in the first's hair and almost simultaneously, each let out of a moan of pleasure. The man's contribution was limited to strained grunting as he performed his work.

It took a moment, but Stephen recognized the man at the foot of the bed and the woman at its head: Paul and Melinda Doyle, a couple who lived two floors down. Both were avid hockey fans and when they learned one of their local super-stars lived in the building, they made a point of befriending both Stephen and Liza. The Doyles were a good deal older, at least in their early forties, but Stephen found them pleasant enough and he always appreciated the fans.

Or at least he thought he'd always appreciate them. He couldn't say that at this moment—in fact, he was boiling, his anger turning into true fury that melted away the last remnants of any possible doubt or confusion. The woman in the middle of the Doyles' sexual sandwich was Liza.

"Liza!" Stephen shouted and, gripping Paul Doyle by the waist, pulled him from the bed, using his superior strength to toss the older, somewhat smaller man practically out into the hallway.

"Oh, daddy, don't stop!" Liza squealed, not realizing what was happening. Melinda Doyle had though, and she at least had enough shame to look embarrassed at being caught in Stephen's bed.

"'Daddy's' already stopped," Stephen said, turning towards the doorway. Paul Doyle had picked himself up and stood just outside the room, embarrassment and fear mixed on his face.

"Stephen!" Liza said, rolling onto her hip to look at him.

"And if he doesn't get the hell out of my house, he's gonna be stopped permanently," Sloan growled.

The Doyles took the hint. Paul disappeared without even bothering to collect his clothing. An instant later, Melinda leapt from the bed and did the same.

"Stephen, you're home early," Liza said, a touch of wonder in her voice.

"And what do I find? A scene out of Bosch in my own damned house!" he yelled.

Liza winced, gathered her legs beneath her and swung them to the floor. She moved to Stephen, pressed her hands against his chest—even in this situation, she was aware of how muscular it was—and said, "Oh, Stevie, it's not that big a deal."

"Not that big a deal? Jesus Christ, Liza!" Stephen backed away, suddenly loathe to let her touch him.

"Look at it from my perspective," she told him, her lips curling into the pout he once thought so adorable. "You're always traveling for away games, leaving me here alone. I get lonely."

"Lonely!" He couldn't believe his ears.

"I get lonely," she continued. "And I invite people over, and I guess things get a little out of hand sometimes."

"A little," he said.

She took a step towards him. "Just a little. It's only sex, darling. It doesn't mean I don't love you."

Stephen backed away, the ring-box in his pocket rubbing awkwardly, uncomfortably against his hip. His face was hot, and his eyes began to burn.

"Get out," he said quietly. It took every ounce of willpower he possessed to keep from shouting it.

"What?" she asked.

"Get your things and get out of my house," Stephen said.

"Your house? You can't be serious," she scoffed.

"I'm serious, Liza." He turned towards the closet, opened it and pulled out the duffel he took on overnight trips. Tossing the bag at Liza's feet, he added, "Get your stuff together and get out."

Liza looked as shocked as Stephen had felt on first entering the apartment. Shocked and betrayed. He didn't realize how little he knew her until that very moment.

"What? You're—are you breaking up with me?"

"Do you really need to ask after all of—*this*?" Stephen gestured helplessly.

"You're serious," she said, awed. "You're fucking serious. Well, where am I even supposed to go?" she shouted. "I gave up my place to move in here with you and now you're kicking me to the curb? How dare you?"

"Me? *Me*?!" Stephen shouted. He thought she couldn't shock or upset him any further. He'd never before been so wrong.

She had a point though: he was the one with resources, enough money to go anywhere in the world and to do anything he wanted. Stephen always prided himself on his sense of fairness. Even in a situation like this, he wasn't going to abandon his core values.

He breathed deeply through his nose, let it out slowly, and said, "The end of the year. You can stay here 'til the end of the year."

Stephen picked up the duffel he'd thrown at Liza's feet, moved to his dresser and began stuffing things into it. He didn't even look at what he was taking, merely making sure he had some of the essentials. "I'm going to walk through that door January 1st," he said without looking at Liza, "and if you're still here, I'll call the cops and tell them you're trespassing."

He zipped the bag closed and marched to the doorway. He turned, but found he couldn't look at her. She was still nude, and he'd often spent happy, delirious hours admiring her lush body. Now it made his chest tight and his stomach ache.

"Got it?"

"Where are you going?" Her voice was soft now and the room was quiet. The loud music had stopped some time in the last couple of minutes, but Stephen only now noticed. Maybe the Doyles let the rest of the intruders know the party was over.

"Grandma Flora's, I guess. Remember," he told her, "January 1st. And clean the place up, will you? It's a pigsty."

Without waiting for a response, he left. In the small entry hallway, he paused to collect his workout bag and grind the roses into the tile with his heel.

Chapter 2.

Olivia – December

"911. What is your emergency? There's a what?"

Olivia Murray glanced towards her coworker, Deann's, station. Deann had just finished a call and was on the five-minute black-out period during which a 911 operator couldn't receive another call. It gave the operators a little breathing room and helped keep them sane. The call-center could be pretty stressful at times. Today wasn't too bad—there was maybe even time for a little fun.

"*Psst,* Dee!" Olivia half-whispered after muting her headset. She gestured to her phone, indicating Deann should join the call. Dee put down her cellphone, the text she was carefully crafting unfinished, and slipped on her own headset.

"There is a *man* here in the Shopright—"

"Yes, ma'am. I'm getting this down," Olivia said.

"There is a *man* here in the Shopright," the female caller said, "with his puh—his puh—"

"Yes, ma'am?" Olivia winked at Dee.

"With his *penis* out!" the woman finally finished, her voice edging towards hysteria. Olivia had never seen a penis worth getting hysterical about, but to each their own.

"Is he doing anything, ma'am?" Olivia asked.

"Well, he's shopping, I guess." The woman sounded confused by the question. That might actually be good; it kept her from being hysterical anyway.

"He's not touching himself or trying to make people look at him?"

"Good heavens, no! Thank God!" It seemed the caller hadn't even thought of those possibilities before.

Dee smiled and shook her head as she dropped out of the call. Her black-out period was almost over.

Olivia's call continued for several more minutes before a police cruiser responded to a call of a 7340—indecent exposure. Olivia offered to stay on the line with the caller, but she declined, saying she wanted to speak to the officers about "the penis man's punishment." Olivia couldn't control her giggle.

She glanced at the time and saw it was almost three; Deann was usually out at three to pick up her kids from daycare, but she'd agreed to cover the last two hours of Olivia's shift. Today was the second anniversary of her first date with Stan and she wanted to make it a special one. She'd already bought a new, curve-hugging dress, purse and shoes to match, and had a three-thirty salon appointment for the works: not just a cut and styling, but waxing (yes, even *there*!) and professional make-up. She shuddered mentally at the cost, but it would be worth it. She was going to knock Stan's socks off.

Olivia began gathering her things. "Dee, thanks again for this."

"Oh, sweetie, what are friends for? Besides," Dee laughed, "with my mom taking the kids tonight, Earl and I can have a little 'date night' of our own—except we won't be going anywhere."

"Win-win," Olivia agreed. She slipped into her coat, waved goodbye to the other ladies, all currently on calls, and headed out to the parking lot. It was barely three o'clock, but it was already getting dark outside. She sighed. She hated the long winter nights.

Though, she thought, remembering what Dee had hinted at, *there are a few benefits*. She smiled, thinking of the night ahead. It was going to be so perfect.

Olivia let herself quietly into Stan's apartment, excitement fluttering in her chest. She gripped the bottle of wine—Stan's favorite Ghost Horse cabernet; $280 a bottle, but worth it—imagining his face lighting up when he saw her.

Her auburn hair was perfectly coiffed, and the aesthetician had done the most amazing things with the makeup—things Olivia had no idea were even possible. She'd changed clothing at the salon, so the ladies there could see the whole effect and when she looked in the mirror, she literally almost didn't recognize herself. She had no idea she could be so *gorgeous,* and she hoped Stan would be happy. She couldn't look like this every day, of course, but today was special and she wanted to look nice both for Stan and for herself.

Stan's jaw would drop when he saw her. They'd share a glass of wine to celebrate two years, then have dinner at Enclave, the French/Vietnamese fusion restaurant that all the websites were ranting about lately. She had to make the reservation more than a month earlier. Oh, so much planning had gone into tonight. It had to be perfect. It just had to.

The apartment door clicked softly closed behind Olivia. The apartment was warm and cozy as always, but the lights were off, and something felt strange. Stan should be here; his car was in his reserved spot in the building's lot, and he almost always went right home after work, unless they were meeting up somewhere. Even though she got out of work early to visit the salon, she'd told Stan she was working late and wouldn't be getting out until at least seven, so he'd really be surprised when she showed up. In fact, their reservation at Enclave was at seven.

Olivia stepped further into the darkened living room. There were faint sounds coming from the far end of the apartment—the bedroom. The sound of movement, muffled voices and then a laugh. A woman's laugh.

Olivia's heart flip-flopped in her chest before sinking into her belly. Of all the ways she imagined this night happening, this scenario never once entered her mind.

Slipping off her new shoes, Olivia padded down the hallway towards the bedroom. Light seeped from the bedroom door, only partially closed. Steeling herself, already knowing what she would see, Olivia peered between the door and the frame. Entangled on the bed—the bed she'd slept in so many times; the same bed in which Stan had said "I love you" to her more times than she could count—were Stan and Sarah, the petite, perky-breasted twenty-three-year-old from next door.

Time seemed to slow down. Olivia's breath wouldn't come, and her heart had stopped beating. She understood what she was seeing but her brain didn't want to process it. It was a nightmare come true, a real-life horror story. A thousand things bounced around inside of her head: things she could say, things she could do. They smashed into one another, leaving her helpless and silent except for the gasp that escaped her lips.

Sarah noticed her first, locking eyes with Olivia from over Stan's broad shoulder.

And you know what she did? Olivia would later ask Dee. *The miserable little witch* smiled *at me. She actually smiled!*

Stan jolted, realizing something was wrong, that something had changed. He scrambled to cover himself—as if Olivia hadn't seen everything there was to see a hundred times before—when he noticed Olivia standing in the doorway, her face pale with shock and hurt.

"Olivia…" Stan started. His eyes were panicked, and his face reflected his guilt. Olivia started to back out of the room. He lifted a hand, as if he could reach her from across the room. "Wait," he said. "I can explain. It's a hormone thing and—"

She threw the wine bottle.

Sarah shrieked and Stan raised his arms over his head as the bottle impacted the wall behind them, showering them with shards of broken glass and rich, dark wine. The sheets were white silk, a house—and bed—warming gift Olivia had bought Stan when he took this apartment over the summer. The expensive fabric soaked up the wine, turning the color of old blood. She wished it was. She wished she could hurt Stan and his little bimbo's bodies as badly as his betrayal wounded her heart and soul.

Olivia was nearly to the apartment door when Stan caught up with her.

"Olivia, hold up. Please." He touched her shoulder, trying to stop her. She whirled on her heel, swinging her purse like a baseball bat, smashing it directly into Stan's face. His nose mimicked the wine bottle and exploded, blood gushing down his lips and chin.

"You fat bitch!" Sarah screamed from the hallway, naked as a jay. Her breasts really were perky as hell, Olivia thought, absurdly. "He's a fucking eight—you don't break an eight's nose!"

"I guess he'll be a seven now," Olivia said, surprising herself.

Sarah glared hatred at her. Olivia didn't understand it. She'd never exchanged more than half a dozen words with the other woman. Why did Sarah hate her so much?

As if reading Olivia's thoughts, Sarah sneered. "Still better than a four like you deserves, you God-damned oinker."

Was it simple jealously? Did you ruin someone's life over something that meaningless and petty?

"Oink, oink, bitch! And don't let the door hit your fat ass on the way out," Sarah taunted.

Stan suddenly appeared between them, face a bloody mess, the sheet he wrapped around himself before leaving the bedroom now forgotten and tangled around his ankles.

"I'm sorry, Olivia. Just go—please. I know this is my fault, that I fucked up—but don't make it worse. We can talk about it tomorrow."

"There's nothing to talk about," Olivia told him. She turned and took a step towards the doorway, then wheeled around as the anger temporarily took hold over her and lunged, her fist raised. Stan flinched, raising his arm to ward off a blow. It didn't make Olivia feel good—she wasn't really a violent person—but as hurt and angry as she was, she enjoyed the fleeting instant of power. She found her shoes, walked to the apartment door, put them on. She fumbled in her purse for a moment, then flung Stan's spare key at him, and opened the door.

"Bitch," Sarah called after her.

"Shut up," Stan said, tiredly.

In a daze, Olivia found herself in the building lobby. Her heart was thumping and her whole body felt hot. The last several minutes flashed through her mind and she was startled to realize the amount of anger she had inside of her. She'd never realized. She thought she was relatively happy. All it took was the one right—or wrong—trigger to make everything fall apart.

At least she hadn't cried in front of them. She could console herself with that much. Besides, there'd be plenty of time to cry later on—all night in fact, since she no longer had any plans. The thought choked her up and she felt the tears coming.

She took a deep breath, opened her eyes wide and shook her head, making her hair bounce.

"Screw them," she said aloud, lifting her middle fingers towards the ceiling. "I hope you're miserable together."

Forget crying, forget being alone tonight. She had a reservation at Enclave and there was no reason to waste it.

Chapter 3.

Wind whipped the streets of Boston's Back Bay area, slicing through Olivia's fur-trimmed coat as she walked, day-old snow crunching beneath her heels. Her breath fogged the air, mingling with the light flakes dancing beneath dim streetlights. The new outfit was sexy, but the material was thin and the skirt very short. Not ideal for New England winters. Olivia barely noticed the cold though; her anger kept her warm, fueling each step as she moved towards Enclave.

Tonight was meant for her and Stan. It was supposed to be a happy night, celebrating their life together and their love. And Stan had to spit on it—defile everything she thought she knew about the two of them. Well screw him. She'd made the reservation at Enclave weeks ago, and she'd damned well use it. No sense in letting an opportunity to dine in one of the hottest restaurants in the city go to waste. She straightened her spine, her new dress hugging her curves, making her feel defiant and confident.

She paused at a crosswalk, waiting for the light to turn red. Even on a dark, wintry night the city bustled, its narrow, brick-paved streets filled with people. There were others like her who were alone, but the majority seemed to be groups or couples, and as they moved around her, their very existence seemed to underscore her frustration. A teenage girl laughed and playfully hip-checked the tall, gangly boy with her before taking his hand. The sight, and the sounds, of the cheerful young couple stoked her sadness and defiance in equal measure. That might have been her once. That might have been her tonight if not for…

Just as she fought down another wave of anger, the flash of a larger-than-life image on a passing bus caught her attention. An underwear ad, one of those high-end brands few guys actually wore but which somehow remained a status symbol, a goal to achieve when you made it. The ad depicted a model whose jawline looked like it could chisel marble and whose eyes were fixed in an intense gaze, meeting those of some unseen viewer as if it were just the two of them, as if his body was for that unknown woman's eyes only and not an entire city's. His bare chest displayed a tapestry of tattoos, the hard muscles starkly defined beneath the ink and somehow catching the city lights just so as the stoplight at the intersection turned red and the bus slowed to a halt. Olivia didn't know much about photography, but she knew a work of art when she saw it.

Her anger flickered, replaced by something she wouldn't have thought possible. Her heartbeat suddenly felt stronger, louder, as if she could actually hear it. The light at the intersection changed and she realized she'd missed her chance to cross the street. But she couldn't help lingering a moment, watching the image as the bus rolled on, feeling a mixture of amusement and attraction and embarrassment. It was silly, it was just an ad on a bus, but whoever that guy was, he was the hottest she'd ever seen. She wondered if he was just a hot body or if he'd have understood her disappointment and hurt tonight, if he'd be the kind of man who could make the whole city fall away with just a look. She would look at him, absolutely, but would he look back?

The light changed again, breaking her from her thoughts. With a half-smile and a huff, she kept walking, feeling lighter, if only for the moment. For those couple of minutes, she'd forgotten all about Stan and his betrayal.

Olivia rounded the final corner and climbed the six brick stairs fronting Enclave. The restaurant was built in a converted brownstone and still had apartments on the uppermost floors. She wondered if the cooking smells ever got to the tenants. She knew they'd bother her.

She pushed the heavy, dark-wood door at the head of the stairs open. A gust of warm air wrapped around Olivia as she stepped inside, bringing rich smells of haute cuisine with it. She brushed snow from her shoulders and looked around. As mundane as the outside was, the interior exuded understated elegance—muted lights glowed from crystal fixtures, casting soft amber hues across dark leather booths and mahogany tables set with pristine white linen. The walls were hung with artwork that depicted scenes from an Asian countryside—Vietnam, she presumed. The low murmur of voices and the clinking of glasses filled the room. It was like a small world of luxury hidden on a side street, hidden from the cold Boston winter.

A tall, impeccably dressed maître d' stepped from behind a podium to meet her, bowing his head slightly. "Good evening, miss. Do you have a reservation with us tonight?"

"Yes, I do," Olivia said, smoothing her coat. Her heart skipped nervously. *There's still time—you can just walk right back out and save yourself some embarrassment,* she thought. She stamped that little voice down, pushing it into the back of her mind. *Go away,* she told it, determined that she was not going to waste this chance or let this night be a total failure.

"It's under Olivia Murray. Seven o'clock."

The older man glanced at his ledger, confirming her booking, then looked up with a polite smile. "For two?"

Olivia's jaw tightened, and she lifted her chin, meeting the man's gaze squarely. Her voice even, she said, "For one."

A flicker of surprise danced across the maître d's face, but he recovered smoothly, maintaining his professional demeanor. He could have been a stage actor covering for a partner's flubbing of a line. Olivia was grateful that he didn't question her. She didn't think her determination could have stood that. "Of course. Right this way, Ms. Murray."

She followed him into the heart of the dining room, past the tables of couples and groups of friends. She seemed to be the only person alone in the entire restaurant. That annoying little voice in the back of her mind imagined that the people at each table they passed were whispering and throwing her side glances. She told it to shut up.

The maître d' led her to a quiet table at the rear of the restaurant, by one of the few windows, a secluded spot with a view of the softly falling snow outside. From inside the restaurant, the outside world seemed remote, as if the world beyond were on pause—or maybe as if it wasn't real at all. The tall man held out her chair, nodding as she slipped off her coat, revealing the figure-hugging dress beneath. She hoped he'd at least snuck a glance; that's what the dress was for, right?

"Enjoy your evening, Ms. Murray," he said before slipping away.

Olivia settled into her seat, allowing herself a deep breath. Her nerves, her anger, her pain—all of it began to fade as she absorbed the warmth of the room. It might not last past the length of her evening, but it was a start. You had to start somewhere. With a defiant gleam in her eyes, Olivia scanned the wine list, determined to make the night her own, every bit as grand as she had intended.

A waiter approached, smiling politely. He greeted Olivia, offered her a menu, and stood poised with his leather notepad. "Have you had a chance to look at the wine list, miss?"

"Yes," Olivia said, glancing over the options one

last time. "I'd like a glass of the Castello di Ama chianti Classico, please."

The waiter smiled. "An excellent choice. I'll have that right out for you. Please, take your time with the menu." He gave a slight nod and backed away before disappearing.

Absently, Olivia unfolded and refolded her napkin, wondering what to do with herself. She was excited all week to try this place and—damn Stan and his little "friend"—determined not to let the whole evening be ruined, but sitting alone in a crowded restaurant, dressed to the nines and made up like a beauty queen, was more awkward than she imagined. With no one to talk to, she was left alone with her thoughts, and she knew herself enough to know those would turn dark again before long. The maître d' had been kind in giving her a window seat; he was giving her something to occupy her attention at least.

Olivia's eyes roamed the area around her. The restaurant was busy but not packed. This was probably the type that didn't really pick up until nine o'clock or later. At the table nearest was a trio: an elderly woman with elegantly coiffed silver hair, a young woman who couldn't have been older than twenty-two, and a strikingly handsome man around Olivia's age, twenty-seven. She noted them in passing, barely giving them a second thought before looking away, not wanting to be rude. Something caught her attention though and her eyes drifted back for a closer look.

Her heart fluttered. The man's features—those sharp cheekbones, intense eyes, and that strong, sexy jawline—looked familiar. Startlingly familiar. Her mind flashed back to the bus ad she'd seen just a few blocks away and the tattooed guy who briefly stole her attention. Was it possible? It couldn't be—things like that didn't happen in the real world.

Without being obvious, she studied him. The man

was dressed simply in a dark button-down shirt that hugged his broad shoulders, a sleeve of tattoos visible on one forearm resting on the table as he spoke. His voice was too low for her to hear but she imagined it was deep and smooth, rich like the wine she'd ordered. She could feel a blush creeping up her cheeks as she looked away, mortified that she'd been staring and embarrassed by what she'd been thinking. But her curiosity got the better of her; with a quick, inconspicuous glance, she looked again.

The handsome man laughed at something the young woman said, his smile crooked and easy, the kind that came naturally. Despite his youth, little lines appeared around his mouth and eyes when he laughed. *He must laugh a lot*, she thought. *Must be nice.*

Olivia tried to look away, but her eyes kept being drawn back towards the other table. It was crazy, but she couldn't shake the feeling that it was him. That the guy sitting fifteen feet away from her was the man from the underwear ad. Or at the very least, someone with an uncanny resemblance to him.

She sipped her water, telling herself to calm down, stop letting her imagination run away with her. It wasn't the man from the ad, that was just impossible. *So what?* the obnoxious voice in her head asked. *They could be twins and looks are all you know about the guy anyway.*

That was a point, she realized. The guy from the ad was the hottest she'd ever seen. Wasn't that what caught her attention? She thought back to the ad, the chiseled muscles of the guy's chest and arms, imagining the way the tattoos would ripple and move with his muscles. He must have been some sort of athlete. She felt her cheeks growing warm and picked up the menu, looking for a distraction, something to keep her eyes busy and away from that other table. This evening had been so hard and so strange and now it had certainly taken an unexpected turn. It seemed like almost anything could happen before the end of the night—like in a fairy tale.

"Cinderella..." Olivia muttered, wondering if the man at the next table might notice her too. Why not? She knew she wasn't any ten, but she wasn't a four like that witch Sarah had called her. Not the way she looked tonight.

At least a seven, she thought.

The waiter returned with Olivia's wine. "Are you ready to order, miss?"

Olivia realized she hadn't even glanced at the menu, despite having held it for several minutes. Her cheeks colored for a different reason this time. Without thinking about it much, she ordered the *salade viet de' vermicelles* hoping she'd like whatever showed up.

"Happy eightieth, Grandma," Stephen Sloan told the elegantly coiffed woman.

Grandma Flora smiled warmly, patting his hand as she chuckled. "Well, I appreciate it, honey. It's always a treat to be out with you kids." She turned her smile on Kylie Sloan. "Especially at such a fancy place!" She glanced around, clearly delighted by the soft lighting, the sparkling crystal, and the elegant atmosphere that made her feel a little bit like a queen on her special day.

Stephen grinned, squeezing her hand back. "It's the least I can do, Grandma, especially after everything you've done for me. I mean, I should be paying you rent at this point. After these last few weeks, I'm practically a tenant."

He laughed, but the mention of "tenant" cast a shadow over the table. They hadn't really ever talked about Stephen's stay at Grandma Flora's. They all knew why Stephen was staying with her—his split with Liza had hit him hard, and he needed time and space to get his bearings. Grandma Flora offered her home without a second thought, considering it as much Stephen and Kylie's home as her own. After everything he'd done for the family, all the money he'd spent on them over the last few years, providing him with a sense of stability was the very least she could do.

When, if, he wanted to talk to her about it, she would be there for him. Maybe his mentioning it now was his way of trying to ease into the topic at some point soon, but instead it slipped a tad of darkness into the bright space between them.

Kylie sensed the shift and quickly jumped in with her usual cheer. "Hey, don't be silly, Stevie. It's been just us girls in the house too long. We're happy to have someone big and strong to pitch in with all the chores. You know how many toilets the place has that need cleaning?" She flashed a mischievous grin, drawing laughter from both Stephen and Grandma Flora, who shook her head.

"Now, don't you two start!" Grandma Flora said, laughing. "I'm just lucky to have you both here with me. Now, I'd better eat up before this delicious French Chinese food gets cold." She picked up her fork, eyeing the dish in front of her with a look of satisfaction. It was a little spicier than she normally would have chosen on her own, but it was interesting, and she was glad that Stephen had taken her somewhere a little adventurous.

Stephen chuckled. "Actually, Grandma, it's Vietnamese. But close enough, right?" He winked at her, and she let out a little snort, rolling her eyes at his correction.

"Well, excuse me, Mr. World Traveler!" she teased.

Stephen started to reply, but suddenly, Grandma Flora's expression changed. Her eyes widened, and she started to cough, a quick, shallow sound that almost instantly became something much more serious. Her face grew red and her hands fluttered at her throat. Stephen's smile vanished at seeing something so wrong.

Kylie's eyes darted to her brother in alarm, her hand freezing over her plate. "Grandma?" she whispered, her voice thin with panic.

Grandma Flora clutched at her throat, gasping, her face turning so dark it was almost purple. She was choking and it was clear she couldn't breathe.

Before either Stephen or Kylie could recover from their shock, Olivia Murray appeared behind Grandma Flora's chair. Wrapping her arms around the older woman, she lifted Flora into a half-seated position, placed her fists just above Flora's stomach and pulled upward in a series of quick, firm thrusts. The restaurant went silent as people turned to watch, but Olivia stayed focused, her hands steady, thoughts single-minded.

Olivia worked for several seconds, feeling Grandma Flora's body writhing against her. The poor woman was panicking, and whatever was lodged in her throat didn't want to come free.

Normally Olivia was safely insulated from emergencies by a telephone line between her and the victims or their families and friends, surrounded by her own friends and her comfortable workspace. Part of her was surprised she had acted so quickly, without even thinking, but her body and her training had made the choice and there was no way she was going to give up now.

"Come on, lady," Olivia muttered, giving another thrust. "You're tougher than this." She'd heard what the guy had said a moment ago, and added, "Don't let this be your last birthday."

She worked for what seemed like an eternity, but finally a piece of meat flew from Grandma Flora's mouth with an audible pop and the raspy, gasping noises of the old woman dragging air into her tortured lungs.

Relief washed over Stephen as he saw Flora breathing again, her face slowly regaining its color.

"Oh… oh my," Grandma Flora whispered, her voice hoarse and awed. She sank into her seat, looking up over her shoulder at Olivia with teary eyes. She reached over and squeezed the younger woman's hand. "You saved me, sweetheart."

Kylie, already on her feet, quickly moved beside them, wrapping her arms around Grandma Flora, her own eyes shining with unshed tears. "Grandma, don't scare us like that," she said into Flora's ear, kissing her grandmother's cheek.

Throat tight, Stephen patted the old woman on the shoulder, then squeezed lightly. His smile was tight, hiding how rattled he really felt as he turned to Olivia. "I don't know how to thank you."

"I do," Flora said, twisting in her seat to look up at Olivia. "Unless the young lady is waiting for a date, I'd like her to join us. Will you, dear?" she asked, a hand on Olivia's arm.

"Oh, I don't know…" She hesitated. It was true that she didn't want to dine alone if she didn't have to, but she didn't want to intrude. These were strangers—one of whom she'd basically seen mostly naked, granted, even if he was just a lookalike with the guy from the ad—and it was a celebration of the older woman's birthday from the comment she heard—a family gathering. She had no right to butt in, especially not for only doing something that anyone would have. She'd just gotten there first.

"Are you waiting for someone, dear?" Flora asked.

"I'm not, but—" Olivia met Stephen's eyes for a moment and felt the heat returning to her cheeks.

"Then I insist," Flora said. "Stephen, bring the young lady's chair over, will you?"

Stephen Sloan smiled at Olivia, making her heart skip—just once—and went to grab the chair from her table.

A waiter appeared, his face pale and concerned. "Is everything all right, madam?" he asked Flora. "Do you need me to call 911?"

Grandma Flora, still slightly winded, waved him off. "No, no, thank you. Just a little more water, if you please." She gestured towards Olivia. "And if my hero here has already ordered, please bring her dinner to our table, will you, dear?"

The waiter looked to Olivia for confirmation and, helpless against this forceful little old lady, she nodded. Stephen returned with Olivia's chair and seated her before lowering himself into his own chair. He ran a hand through his hair, still processing what had just happened. He only then realized how fast his heart was beating.

"Now then, Miss Hero. I'm Flora Deming and these are my grandchildren, Stephen and Kylie Sloan," the older woman said, gesturing to Stephen and his sister in turn.

"I don't know about hero," Olivia told her, a bit overwhelmed by Flora's energy. "I just did what anyone would do."

"Nonsense!" Flora scolded. "You saved my life and I'm darned grateful. You've saved this lovely birthday dinner my grandson was kind enough to treat us to as well."

"Maybe stick to the noodles from now on though, Grandma," Kylie grinned, trying to bring back the levity of earlier. "Less of a choking hazard."

"Kylie!" Stephen snapped. "That's not funny."

"Oh, leave her alone, Stephen," Grandma told him. "All's well that ends well and the night's far from over. We've still got this yummy Vietnamese-French-Chinese food to finish. Oh, now before I forget: what's your name, dear?" She patted Olivia's arm.

"Olivia Murray," Olivia told them. Embarrassed by the old lady's attentions, she still managed to smile and nod at each of them, though she was quick to avert her eyes from Stephen for fear of making eye contact. She was sure he would know she was undressing him with her eyes.

The bus ad sprang to mind again and something almost clicked. Why did Stephen Sloan sound familiar?

Olivia's waiter arrived, bringing her salad and a

fresh glass of wine. Flora assured him that they didn't need anything else, then turned to Olivia and asked her something that Stephen missed, distracted by the loud chatter of a passing group on their way out of the restaurant.

He took the opportunity to study Flora's savior and saw a woman about his own age with a full, curvy figure, shown to effect by a red dress that was so tight it was like a second skin, but which seemed elegant rather than cheap or trashy. The color somehow accentuated the rich, reddish hue of her hair, which fell in soft waves around her shoulders, adding a warm glow to her complexion. He once heard that redheads shouldn't wear the color red, but somehow the vibrant color of the dress complemented her look perfectly, giving her a bit of a fiery edge as if she might turn saucy at any moment. Now she was a little uncomfortable, a little embarrassed at being the center of attention for three strangers—especially one she apparently recognized as a celebrity, he thought—but he was sure somehow, just a feeling as he watched the way she interacted with Flora, that she was usually comfortable with herself. He was certain Flora would win her over in no time. She always did, making friends wherever she went.

"Dear," Grandma Flora was saying. "Stephen, dear, you're being rude."

"Huh? What?" Sloan snapped to, unaware that his mind had been wandering and embarrassed at being called out by his grandmother.

"I know Olivia is a beautiful young lady, but you shouldn't stare." Her eyes twinkling, she winked at Kylie. The young woman tried, and almost managed, to suppress a giggle.

Stephen felt heat coming into his cheeks. "I wasn't. I was just thinking how lucky we were that she was here." He stabbed his fork at a tidbit on his plate. "Thanks… Olivia," he told her, before popping the food into his mouth.

Olivia smiled, liking the way he said her name. Before she could respond, Kylie added, "Yeah, Grandma's our favorite lady."

"Well, you're my favorite people too, both of you." Flora put a hand on each of her grandchildren softly, then turned to include Olivia. "And you, my dear, are the special guest for the night. Tell us all about yourself."

"Oh, you don't want to hear about me," she demurred, nibbling at her *salade viet d' vermicelles* to buy a moment.

"Oh, but I do," Flora teased.

"Let's start with you feel about tattoos." Kylie said, grinning mischievously again. She leaned across the table and tugged up Stephen's left sleeve, exposing more tattooed skin. A little tingle went through Olivia. "He likes to play it down off the ice, but he's kinda distinctive, you know?" The comment didn't make much sense to Olivia.

Stephen yanked his sleeve back down, throwing an annoyed look at Kylie, but she'd already moved on to another topic, chattering happily at Olivia. Like Flora, she made friends easily.

And Olivia, despite herself, found she was drawn to both of these women and told the three of them at least as much as she would any new acquaintance. She lived in Brookline now, but she had grown up in Vermont; she was a 911 operator and had been for almost four years. And yes, she loved her work. It could be stressful, but it was meaningful, and she loved her coworkers.

"Single, dear?" Grandma asked, winking at Stephen. He pretended not to notice, suddenly very interested in the wine glass in front of him.

Olivia hesitated. Flora couldn't know, but she got the feeling that somehow, some weird way, the old woman *did* know. Maybe it stood to reason: Olivia was alone in a fancy restaurant, dressed to kill. That she had been stood up was a pretty reasonable assumption. Mentally, she sighed. If only it was that simple.

"I'm single," she told Flora. "Very recently, in fact."

"Well, isn't that nice?" Her smile was positively beatific, like the happy little Buddha on a marble plinth by the restaurant's entrance.

"So I wonder," Flora continued, "if you have any plans this weekend, Olivia, dear?"

It was Thursday night. Normally, she'd leave Friday night and the weekend, if she wasn't working, open to make plans with Stan, but obviously *that* no longer applied. What did she used to do on her own, before she and Stan started dating? She was a little startled to realize that she couldn't remember.

"Not yet," she said, noncommittally, poking at her food. It was delicious, but the serving size was huge and as much as she liked her new acquaintances, she was leery of stuffing herself in front of them. Kylie was so slim and pretty and Stephen was… well, he was hot as hell.

"Do you like hockey?" Kylie asked.

"Oh," Olivia said, a little surprised by the question. It wasn't something she would have expected from a young girl.

"I guess I know a little about it. My boy—my *ex*-boyfriend followed all the local sports teams. I've been to a few games of just about everything, I guess."

"Well, that's perfect," Flora said. "It just so happens that our Stephen offered to get Kylie and I tickets to the Back Bay Warriors game Saturday night. I'm sure he could get one more, couldn't you dear?" She turned her beaming smile on Stephen. "Yeah, sure," he said.

"Then it's settled," Kylie said, the younger and older women trading off as if they'd planned it. "Here," she dug into her purse and produced her cellphone, holding it out towards Olivia. "Airdrop me your deets."

Olivia smiled at how easy-going these two ladies were. It was hard not to want to go along with them. "I guess I could use a night out and hockey would be a change of pace."

"We're big hockey fans," Flora said.

Kylie and Olivia exchanged contact info and Olivia was about to put her phone away, but Kylie interjected with, "Bro," and gestured towards Olivia with her head. Stephen made a face, a kind of resigned annoyance, at his younger sister, but fished his phone from his hip pocket and tapped it against Olivia's. It happened so quickly, and Kylie had arranged it so smoothly, that Olivia was in awe of the younger woman. She wished she could be half that slick.

"Well, now." Flora clapped her hands. "If that's all settled, what say we find out what a Chinese-French dessert looks like?"

Chapter 4.

"Hey, Sloan!" Ken Johns called, his voice carrying a teasing edge. "You've been single—what? Two months now? Don't you think it's about time you started enjoying the finer things in life? You know—puck bunnies!" He waggled his eyebrows exaggeratedly, like Groucho Marx, earning a laugh from Jake Archer, leaning against the lockers with his arms crossed, clearly in on the joke.

It wasn't much of a joke, but it had kept these two entertained for a couple of weeks and on a Saturday night, they were both in especially high spirits. The joke had bothered Stephen at first, but now he let it roll off his back. He was used to years of locker room talk and this was just one species of it.

Stephen finished lacing his skates and looked up at the shadow that fell across him. "Yeah, man," Jake chimed in, his grin widening. "Seriously. I counted, like, eight different girls wearing your jersey. I bet half the ladies out there tonight are here just to see you, Mr. Star Center. And from what I *hear*, some of them are aiming for a, uh, closer connection." He smirked, nodding toward the stands on the other side of the wall, as if the fans were waiting just for Stephen's attention, as if they were beating against the wall, trying to get to their hero.

Stephen rolled his eyes, though he couldn't help but chuckle at their antics; playing along was the best way to settle these two down. It wasn't any fun if it didn't seem like teasing. Shaking his head, he said, "Thanks for your concern, guys, but I think I'll survive without that kind of attention. I've got enough going on without adding groupies to the list."

"Oh, come on," Ken pressed, dropping onto the bench beside him. "It's been—seriously, what was it now? *At least* a couple of months since you and Liza called it quits. She was one tasty little snack, I'll absolutely grant you, but *you've* got to admit that freedom has its perks, right?"

"Look, Liza had her cake and ate it too, man," Jake said. It wasn't a tease this time. He actually sounded concerned for his teammate. "That's what you said, basically, right? Having some fun and taking care of yourself isn't, like, being disloyal or anything. There's nothing to be loyal to."

Jake was right; Stephen knew he was, but the situation with Liza wasn't even finished. She was still living in his house, wasn't she? They were still connected and until that connection was finally, completely broken, he just didn't see how he could even think about starting to date again. Not when his wounds were still so fresh that they were practically open and bleeding.

"Guys, I appreciate it," he began, looking down at his skates. "But I'm not ready for a relationship is all."

"Who said anything about a relationship, man?" Ken slapped his shoulder then gestured towards the wall separating the locker room from the stands. "You think those girls expect anything more than a cheap thrill?"

It was the wrong thing to say; Stephen felt himself getting angry. He knew his friends wanted to help, but they were treating his life like it was a game. It was true that all of their lives revolved around hockey, a game in itself, but it wasn't their entire lives, and Stephen didn't treat his life off the ice the same way he treated the sport. If Ken and Jake or anybody else wanted to, that was their business, but Stephen had other priorities.

Stephen forced a smile, trying to keep things light. The last thing he needed was conflict with teammates just minutes before hitting the rink, but he felt the twist of that anger and it made his voice tighter than he intended. "Fun's not really on the agenda right now, guys. I've been staying at my grandma's, trying to sort my head out. Parading puck bunnies through Flora's house doesn't exactly appeal, you know?"

Ken seemed ready to back down, to leave it alone, but Jake wasn't about to let up. "All right, all right," he said, putting his hands up in mock surrender. "We get it. But remember, they're out there tonight, and they're all yours for the taking. Probably already making bets on who's going to get the ol' wink and smile from the great Stephen Sloan." He gave a dramatic sigh. "It's a shame—a sin even—to waste your kind of prime bachelor talent."

Stephen stood. Ken patted his back and said, "If you change your mind, let us know. We've got intel on all the best prospects out there. Like that girl in the blue mini last week—you know, the one with the tig ol' bitties?" He grinned. "She was making eyes at you the whole game."

"Yeah," Jake laughed. "That skirt was so damned short, you know she wore it hoping you'd warm her up." He nudged Stephen with his elbow, and the other man rocked side to side on his skates dramatically, trying to match his friends' playfulness.

"Thanks for the uh… support, guys," Stephen told them. "But I'll be fine."

A couple of the other guys trundled over and made some comment to Ken about the opposing team. Relieved that the topic was finally switching from himself to game strategy, Stephen turned his attention back to his skates, making sure the fit was perfect.

Even as he focused on the match that was about to start, his mind raced through the conversation with his friends and then, unexpectedly, flickered back to Olivia—the mysterious woman in the red dress who'd appeared at the very second when Grandma Flora had needed a hero. She'd been watching him during dinner, hadn't she? He shook his head, trying to dismiss the thought. He was here for hockey, he reminded himself.

Still, as he finished adjusting his skates, a small smile tugged at the corner of his mouth. That dress had looked very good on her.

Chapter 5.

Olivia wove through the bustling, jostling crowd outside the arena, her heels clicking along the pavement as she carefully maneuvered around excited fans decked out in Back Bay Warriors jerseys and scarves. A number of them carried cardboard signs with their favorite players' names on them, often with messages and even hand-drawn emojis. She counted more hearts than any others, but there were a few eggplants too. She laughed when she saw the first one and then kept an eye out for more.

She had texted Kylie earlier to make sure they'd meet near the box office, so all four of them could be sure to find seats together, but making her way through the crowd was turning out to be more of an adventure than she'd anticipated. Usually at these kinds of events, she had let Stan take the lead and simply followed in his wake. She hated that part of her wished he was here now.

Finally, Olivia spotted Grandma Flora, bundled up in a cozy wool coat, a Back Bay Warriors hat pulled over her ears and a matching scarf wrapped around her neck. The elderly woman stood to one side of a huge mural depicting the emblem of the Warriors, alongside the Bruins and the Celtics logos. She was telling Kylie something as the young woman caught sight of Olivia and waved. Relieved, excited to see her new friends again, Olivia grinned and picked up her pace.

"Hey, ladies!" she called, pitching her voice to carry above the din of the crowd. She gave Kylie a quick hug and offered Grandma Flora a warm smile. "Thanks so much for inviting me tonight. I'm glad to see you two again. I hope I'm not too late."

"Not at all, dear." Grandma Flora's eyes sparkled. "You're right on time. And here—" She held up an envelope. "I had the box office hold these tickets so we could all sit together." She opened the envelope and distributed tickets to Kylie and Olivia.

Olivia smiled, glancing around as she took the ticket. She thanked the older woman and then added, "I thought Stephen would be here with you two. Is he running late?" It crossed her mind that maybe she'd misunderstood Flora at the restaurant. She had told Olivia that Stephen promised to get her and Kylie tickets to the game, but had she said Stephen himself would be coming too? She didn't remember, but didn't think she had. A flicker of disappointment passed through her.

Kylie chuckled. "Oh, don't worry, we'll definitely see him inside," she said, mischief dancing in her eyes. Olivia was beginning to recognize that look of her new friend's. "He's just getting himself into the right headspace for the game. He takes these things pretty seriously."

Grandma Flora patted Olivia's arm reassuringly and smiled up at her. "Yes, dear, once we're in there, you'll get your fill of him. You're in for quite the show. He's always been our star at these games."

Olivia had the sudden mental image of Stephen, shirtless, his body painted in the Warriors' colors, maybe with a letter emblazoned on his chest, standing in a line with half a dozen other shirtless guys spelling out their hometown team's name and cheering at the top of their lungs. She cringed at the thought of such a beautiful guy doing something like that—it was more Stan's kind of thing, but even he wasn't that big of fanatic.

She realized Kylie was watching her and flashed a little smile at the younger girl. Kylie grinned back and then giggled to herself.

Oh, well, she thought. Even if Stephen did turn out to be one of those true fanatics, that wasn't the worst thing in the world. He was a little gruff at dinner, but no guy whose grandma and sister cared as much about him as these two ladies obviously did for Stephen could be anything but decent. And there was still the fact that he was absolutely gorgeous. It was funny how much he really did look like the guy from that ad on the bus, she mused.

No matter what happened though, Olivia was looking forward to the evening. It was a long time since she'd spent a Saturday night out with friends, and it was a refreshing change from her usual routine. She wondered what Stan would think of her going to a sporting event without him. She hoped the seats were really good ones; maybe he'd see her on TV. She laughed at the thought.

Kylie laughed, too, looping one arm through Olivia's and the other through Grandma Flora's as they began heading toward the entrance. "Beats a night of bad TV, right?"

As they shuffled through the crowded lobby, Grandma Flora turned to Olivia with a playful gleam. "Stephen will be glad to know you're here tonight. He may not admit it, but he could always use a little help in the cheering department." She paused, lowering her voice conspiratorially. "And between us, blondes are just no good for him." She winked, giving Olivia a knowing smile, and momentarily touching Olivia's reddish hair.

A slight blush colored Olivia's cheeks, but the image of a Warriors-painted Stephen came back to mind. It wasn't the worst thing in the world, no, but she really hoped that wasn't what was happening here. "Well, I guess I'll do my best then," she said.

Moving along with the crowd, they entered the rink and found their seats, surprisingly close to the ice. Olivia hoped the tickets weren't too expensive as she settled in between Flora and Kylie. She glanced to a corner of the rink where one of the teams was beginning to warm up. She didn't like to admit it, but her favorite part of hockey was always the squats and stretches the players performed on the ice. She had no idea what they were actually called, but some of them looked like they were… well, humping the ice and it was interesting and fun to imagine those muscular bodies beneath the uniforms. Her blush from earlier returned and she glanced quickly at her friends to see if they noticed.

They hadn't. Both Kylie and Flora were surveying the stadium, people-watching. There were already thousands in the stands, and it seemed like half of them were crowding the ice, calling to their favorite players, asking for autographs or souvenirs or selfies. She knew sometimes kids gave players little gifts of candy in exchange for autographs. She didn't know where the custom came from, but she found it charmingly innocent.

Less innocent were the dozens, maybe hundreds of girls, parading around the cold rink in skimpy clothing, holding up signs with messages like "KENNY, I'M YOURS <3" or "MIKE B, DO ME, BABY" and that eggplant emoji. Puck bunnies, she thought they were called. Unaccountably, she felt a twinge of jealousy. Maybe it was that those girls were so uninhibited. No matter how she felt about a particular athlete or celebrity, she could never let herself do something so embarrassing.

They're just showing their love, that little voice in her head said. She hadn't heard it since that last disastrous night at Stan's and was surprised to hear it now. She supposed the voice had a point. It wasn't embarrassing if those girls didn't think so. She shrugged and decided to each their own.

Olivia relaxed in her seat. Flora turned to her and began chattering, but the redheaded girl only half-listened and gave Flora little encouragements. She already knew Flora well enough to realize that she didn't need a conversation partner so much as an audience. It was relaxing and reassuring to be here with Flora and Kylie though. She felt at home with them, despite knowing them for less than forty-eight hours.

It was a good thing too, because if she hadn't been completely at home with her new friends, it would have felt strange sitting here without Stan, who'd always been the one to drag her to games. But she didn't feel out of place. She smiled, leaning back in her seat as the lights dimmed and the pregame excitement filled the air, wondering when Stephen would show up.

Chapter 6.

The first strains of upbeat music pulsed through the air, growing louder—she was surprised to recognize "Enter Sandman" by Metallica. She wasn't a fan of the band in particular, but who didn't love that one song at least? The crowd certainly did and as the electric guitars wailed, Olivia felt the energy of the crowd ramping up around her. She glanced at Kylie and Grandma Flora; both ladies grinned, eyes trained on the ice as Kylie whispered something into her grandmother's ear. Olivia realized for the first time that Kylie's mischievous look was shared by Grandma Flora. No guessing where Kylie got it from then.

The music surged louder, and the Warriors stormed onto the ice, greeted by thunderous applause and cheers. The players' skates slashed across the rink, moving with a speed and intensity that surprised Olivia—it was like they were an army battling the ice itself and determined to pummel it into submission. She leaned forward, her eyes wide, and tried to follow the blur of players whizzing past their seats. Olivia wasn't used to this kind of atmosphere, but she had to admit—it was exhilarating.

One player in particular flew down the ice, gliding with a fluid grace that caught her attention. He zipped by, and as he neared their section, he turned, giving a quick wave to their side of the stands. Olivia caught a glimpse of the name and number on his jersey—*Sloan #7*. Her heart skipped a beat as realization dawned.

"Wait—that's Stephen?" she blurted, her voice carrying a mixture of surprise and awe.

Next to her, Kylie started giggling and Grandma Flora took Olivia's arm, giving it a squeeze. "Well, what did you think, dear?" she asked. "How else would we get seats reserved for the players' families?"

Kylie nudged her with an elbow. "Get it now? That's our boy. We promised you'd see him inside, didn't we?" She laughed again.

"I didn't…" Olivia began, faltering. She had no idea, but it all made sense. The ad on the bus—that sexy, absolutely stunning guy. She remembered thinking at the time that the model's muscles didn't look like they were just for show, that he must be an athlete of some sort. Athletes did that sort of thing all the time, didn't they? Stephen Sloan's name even sounded vaguely familiar when they were introduced. Her heart fluttered; the guy she met didn't just look like that gorgeous, half-nude man modeling underwear—he *was* that gorgeous man!

It made so much sense that now that she actually felt dumb for not realizing.

"Don't feel bad, dear," Flora said, leaning briefly against Olivia. "Stephen's not one to call attention to himself away from the game."

"Yeah, and you're not a puck bunny or anything. How would you know?" Kylie chimed in. "He is pretty popular though." She gestured around, and Olivia suddenly noticed that at least a dozen people nearby were sporting Warriors jerseys with *Sloan* emblazoned across the back, all bearing the same #7.

Stephen made a return pass, waving again—this time clearly to the three ladies though Olivia wasn't sure if he could actually make them out or not. As his form retreated, gliding swiftly across the ice to rejoin his team-mates, she couldn't tear her eyes away.

I can't believe that's him, she thought, remembering the guy from the restaurant when they'd first met. He was sexy as hell, well-dressed and groomed, and when with his sister and grandmother, when Olivia first observed them, seemed at ease and easygoing. When she joined them, he pulled back, becoming reserved, almost shy. That wasn't at all how she pictured professional athletes acting. Weren't they all supposed to be, if not full of themselves, at least confident and outgoing?

Grandma Flora, beaming proudly at Olivia's wide-eyed expression, said, "Stephen's been a star since college. He actually never finished his final year. He was a first-draft pick. I understand they have rules about that sort of thing now, letting students finish and holding the spot or something like that. Well, anyway, the Warriors drafted him, and he's been with them ever since. They let him keep his #7 even. That was very important to Stephen. He's been #7 ever since he was a little boy." She laughed. "I suppose he considers it his lucky number. At any rate, he's been very successful with the Warriors and now he's just about as beloved around here as any boy in Boston could be."

"I'll bet," Olivia agreed. Boston loved its sports heroes more than any other city she knew of.

In the center of the ice, Stephen and a player from the opposing team faced off. Stephen leaned in, his gloved hands gripping his stick firmly. Olivia imagined him locking eyes with his opponent, a determined look on his handsome face, the chiseled jaw set like stone. The referee held the puck high, drawing every eye in the arena. He gave it an instant, bringing the tension almost to a breaking point, and then, with a swift flick of the wrist, dropped it to the ice.

As soon as the puck hit, what seemed like chaos exploded across the ice. Sticks clashed, bodies leaned in, and Stephen fought for control, his movements quick and sharp, the strength of his arms and legs propelling him into a kind of armed struggle against the opposing team. That's really what hockey was, Olivia realized—it was a battlefield. The players carried what amounted to weapons and even wore a sort of armor. The thought sent a pleasant ticklish feeling through her and despite the cold temperature of the arena, she began to feel a little warm.

At last, with a decisive, powerful sweep, Stephen won the puck, flicking it back to his teammate, Jake Archer, who skated it down the ice. The crowd erupted, cheering as the Warriors took possession and, in what seemed to Olivia like an organized mob, rushed the puck toward the opposing team's goal.

Stephen was already in motion, gliding along the boards and cutting around defenders with practiced ease. A defender swooped across his path but with skill that seemed almost superhuman, Stephen deftly ducked around him without slowing even a fraction. The puck moved from stick to stick—from Stephen to Jake to Ken to Mike B and back again—as the Warriors executed sharp passes, weaving around their opponents. Stephen positioned himself near the goal, ready to receive the goal-making pass, his skates digging into the ice as he prepared to pounce.

An opposing defender came charging in, trying to cut off the play. Stephen braced himself, meeting the other player with a solid shoulder-to-shoulder hit that sent a ripple of excitement through the crowd. Even from a distance, Olivia felt like she could almost *feel* the impact and she experienced a pang of sympathy for Stephen. She instantly realized how silly that was—this was part of hockey, and she could tell just by the way Stephen moved that he loved every second of it.

There was a moment of struggle as Stephen and the other player pressed against one another, trying to gain dominance, but it was over almost as soon as it began. The opposing defender stumbled, but Stephen kept control, deftly skating backwards, eyes darting from the puck to his teammates and back again.

Finally, Ken shot past the last defender in his path and scooted the puck in a straight shot directly to Stephen. With a quick pivot, Stephen pulled it close, cocked his stick back, and released a blistering slap shot toward the goal. The puck rocketed across the ice, past the goalie's outstretched glove—missing by less than a fraction of an inch it seemed—and into the top corner of the net. The red goal light flared, and the arena exploded with cheers.

Olivia was on her feet before she realized it, clapping and cheering with the crowd, her heart pounding with excitement, shouting, "Go, Stephen!"

Stephen's teammates piled around him, smacking his helmet and shouting their congratulations as the scoreboard ticked up the first point of the game. The hometown fans began chanting "Num! Ber! Sev! En!" as he skated back to the bench, giving a quick wave to Olivia's section, his eyes bright with adrenaline and a grin on his face visible even through his helmet and mouthguard.

The puck dropped again, and the action resumed, each shift as fast and furious as the last. The players moved with a fierce intensity, the puck darting across the ice in rapid, dizzying patterns. The Warriors defended hard, blocking shots and checking opponents, and attacked even harder. The sound of bodies hitting the boards mixed with the scrape of skates and the echoing cheers of the crowd drove them on.

As the game continued, the tension grew by the minute, and Olivia found herself captivated, unable to look away. Each play was a blur of action, strength, and skill, and she was beginning to see why Stephen was such a favorite among both the fans and his teammates. The Warriors worked together, but it was clear even to an amateur how they rallied around Stephen, how each of their plays centered on his being the point of their sword as they attacked the other team. He moved with such confidence, and his focus seemed razor-sharp. Olivia could only imagine the hours—the years—of practice and dedication he'd poured into his game to reach this level of skill.

"You okay?" Kylie asked, surprising Olivia. She realized she was sitting on the very edge of her seat and that her heart was racing. She inched backwards, reseating herself more squarely. She smiled at the other girl and said, "It's just—wow." Olivia watched plenty of sporting events with Stan, but she'd never been invested like this before. She'd never actually *cared* what happened or who would come out on top.

Kylie grinned. "I know, right?"

As Olivia's focus returned to the game, Kylie leaned behind her and shot Grandma Flora a thumbs up. They shared another one of those mischievous grins.

Chapter 7.

From the moment the game began in that familiar haze of adrenaline and focus, Stephen moved into his happy place. He didn't like that expression—it seemed so silly and juvenile—but that's what Kylie once called it, back when he was still in high school, and she was just starting middle school. The hockey rink, specifically when Stephen was in the middle of a game, was his happy place. And silly as he thought the expression was, he really couldn't deny it. He never felt as alive as he did when he was on the ice, putting hard-won skills and muscles to the test against a worthy opponent. It didn't matter if the Warriors won or lost—okay, it did; obviously he wanted to win, but sometimes you do your best and it still doesn't happen—he enjoyed every minute of every game.

As he lined up at center ice, he could feel the hum of the crowd surging through him like a physical sensation, all of those eyes on him, every person in the stands waiting as eagerly for the puck to drop as he and the center from the Stamford Stallions were. He could hear a murmur of voices, but it was distant, far more distant than just the space between the ice and the stands as he tuned out everything inessential, narrowing his world to the ice and his opponent in front of him. His eyes locked with the Stallion center's, then shifted to the referee's hand, waiting for the drop. The moment the puck left the ref's grip, Stephen lunged forward, digging in and snapping his stick down, fighting to push the puck to his team.

The puck shot back to Jake, his defenseman in the current lineup, and as it did, Stephen was already skating hard, cutting through the neutral zone, his legs pumping as he pushed himself, trying to get ahead. The cold air hit his face, sharp and bracing, faintly stinging even after all these years, and he could feel the tension in his muscles ease as his body found the familiar rhythm. He scanned the zone, watching his teammates move the puck up the ice, weaving around the opposing defense, as he set up in position near the net, ready, his eyes darting between his teammates and the goal.

One of the Stallion defenders closed in on Stephen, charging at him with breakneck speed, but Stephen planted his skates, bracing himself for the impact. They collided with a bone-jarring impact that Stephen felt in every inch of his body. The boards shook behind him as the Stallion pressed, trying to push him out of position and away from the Stallion goal, but Stephen held his ground, muscles tightening as he pushed back. Adrenaline sang in his veins and his soul soared. This was living! This was the only thing he wanted to do with his life. The clinch broke and the Stallion player stumbled, losing his balance. Stephen skated backwards, keeping his control and freeing himself up to receive the puck.

The puck moved closer, and Stephen, only half-consciously aware of it as he kept track of all the moving pieces on the ice, felt his instincts kick in. The puck slid to his stick, and in a single fluid motion, he spun, wound up, and let a shot rip. He heard the slap of the puck against his stick, felt the impact travel its length up into his arm, then the split-second arc as the puck traveled through the air, and finally the unmistakable *whoosh* as it sailed past the goalie's glove, just barely outside of his reach, and hit the back of the net.

For an instant, time slowed almost to a standstill, as if his brain was catching up to the lightning-quick pace of his actions. Then it was over, and the red goal light flared. The crowd erupted, chanting his number as the really diehard Warriors fans always did when he scored a goal, and his teammates swarmed around him, slapping him on the back, shouting over the noise. Stephen felt a grin spread across his face. He had no idea how many goals he'd scored in the course of his career—he'd have to check the fan websites, and wouldn't that be funny? Looking himself up like that—but he never lost the thrill of the goal, and he never stopped appreciating the pounding energy of his teammates, or the cheers of the crowd. He loved it all, he loved *them* all because without all of these people, he wouldn't be here, playing this game that he loved more than anything else.

And it was just starting. They were a step closer to winning, but the game had only just begun. Skating back to the startling line, he glanced toward the stands, a habit he hadn't shaken after all these years, even though he couldn't really see individual faces in the crowd. He knew that Grandma Flora and Kylie were up there in the section reserved for players' families. He wondered if Olivia, the woman from the restaurant who'd joined them after giving Flora that life-saving Heimlich maneuver, had joined them. Kylie and Flora had invited her, and he'd made sure three tickets were available at the box office, but he wasn't sure if she planned to use hers—and he wasn't quite sure why the question worried him so much.

Chapter 8.

"Lose somethin', bro?"

Stephen turned to find Mikey Bukowski gesturing with his chin, leaning on his stick nonchalantly. "You been starin' up there at the stands every chance you get tonight."

"Maybe that tig bitties girl is back," Jake joked.

"No, it's nothing," Stephen said, brushing them off. "Just wanted to see if I could spot my grandma and sister."

Mike and Jake shared a look, but that was all. There was a game to play.

Nervous energy crackled in the air, rolling off the fans up in the stands and the teams themselves. The Warriors held a 2-1 lead going into second period, but the Stallions put up a tough defense and even tougher offense, attacking the Warriors' defenders like their very lives depended on it. Ultimately, second period ended with the Warriors scoring one additional goal and the Stallions scoring two. Third period would decide it all.

Lining up for the puck drop, facing off against the Stallion center for the final time, Stephen could feel the intensity of the other team rising, a wave of mental pressure that was almost a physical force, as if they were pressing their collective willpower down on him. His legs were beginning to ache from the exertion of two hard-fought periods, but that was nothing. He'd been tired before and he'd be tired again. He brushed the fatigue aside, tightening his grip on his stick. He met the Stallions' center's eyes for an instant, then flicked his gaze towards the stands. *Stop it*, he told himself. *Focus.*

The puck dropped and the Stallions came out with maximum aggression, winning possession almost as if the puck had been drawn to their sticks. They moved the puck up the ice like a machine built just for that purpose, closing in on the Warriors' goal with an ironclad defense of their scorers, leaving no gap the Warriors could exploit, no room to swipe the puck.

Stephen could sense his teammates' frustration boiling over—he wasn't immune to it either. Something about the Stallions had changed since the second period and now, in the opening minutes of the third and final period, he was already hard-pressed to come up with tactics on the fly that could deal with them.

Lost in thought for only a split second, he was slammed into the boards by a Stallions forward, the hit hard enough to make his teeth rattle. He bounced back quickly, pushing through the pain, shaking his head to clear it.

That was when he saw it: a Stallions forward broke free from his own team's protective shell, guiding the puck before him with absolute precision as he streaked down the rink with nothing but open ice between him and the Warriors' goalie. A painful jolt of urgency shot through Stephen and he pushed off, skating with everything he could muster to close the distance. His entire body was sore, his muscles burned, but he zeroed in on the puck, calculating his timing down to the millisecond.

The Stallions player was just crossing the blue line, his stick poised for a shot. Stephen made his move—one of desperation he would have admitted if anyone had asked him. With a quick burst of speed, putting every ounce of energy he still possessed into the motion, he lunged forward, stretching his stick out just enough to make contact with the puck. The blade of his stick met the puck with a sharp *clack*, nudging it off-course and out of the Stallions player's control. The stands erupted in cheers, and a round of "SLOAN! SLOAN!" chanting kicked off.

The Stallion forward stumbled, surprised by the sudden interference, but Stephen was already on the puck, sweeping it away and pivoting in an arc to shield it from the other player. His heart hammered as he looked up, quickly scanning for an open teammate to relieve the pressure. He knew he'd barely managed to prevent a scoring chance, and he couldn't let it go to waste. Mikey B was the only opening he saw; he forced what he knew was a sloppy pass up the ice. It was another move of desperation, but it worked. The goal was safe—for now.

The clock ticked down and as the puck shifted possession again, the extreme physicality of the game escalated. The Stallions wouldn't let up the pressure, and the Warriors were struggling to keep up. Stephen wondered where their energy came from. It was as if the Stallions had somehow had a night's sleep between the second and third periods. Every time the puck shifted, it was a battle that tested the Warrior players' endurance. Stephen kept finding himself caught in a series of skirmishes along the boards—were the Stallions targeting him specifically? It wouldn't be the first time a team had gone right for him. His body slammed into another Stallion player, trying to cut him off from a pass Ken was readying; their sticks clashed, and it got heated, almost coming to gloves before the Stallion broke off, his purpose accomplished in ruining Ken's chance to pass.

With just under eight minutes left, the Stallions broke through the 3-3 stalemate that had lasted all period. There was a turnover in the Warriors' zone, leading to a quick pass to a Stallions forward parked angled with line of sight to the goal. Stephen watched in frustration from the far side of the ice as the puck snapped off the Stallion player's stick and sailed past the Warrior goalie's outstretched glove. The horn blared, and the scoreboard flashed a 3-4, favoring the Stallions. The Stallions' fans erupted. They were the minority up in the stands, but enthusiastic enough that their cheers almost drowned out the groans from the Warriors' side. Stephen felt a stinging sensation in his belly. The Warriors were behind.

He skated back to the bench. Waiting for the reset, he gulped water and glanced up towards the stands. He knew he couldn't make out any one individual person at this distance, so why did he keep looking? Grandma Flora and Kylie were up there somewhere; he knew that was well as he knew his number or skate size. They never missed a home game. Who else might be though…?

He shook his head and turned to the scoreboard. There were fewer than eight minutes left in the period and a sense of urgency began to fill him. The Warriors needed to get the lead back, and fast.

"Hup, hup!" Coach Gilman called, waving his arm in a big sweep, as if he was pushing the Warriors from the back out onto the line. A minute later, the puck dropped, Stephen dug deep inside of himself, trying to find that extra reservoir to tap into, the way the Stallions somehow had. Exhaustion weighed on every muscle, but he pushed himself to skate harder, faster, as he and the other Warriors battled for control. At five minutes, Stephen managed a pass to his winger, Ken, and set himself up near the net, hoping for a rebound. The Stallions' defense was relentless though; they cleared the puck before the Warriors could get a decent shot.

At just under two minutes, the Warriors were scrambling. The Stallions had the lead and all they needed to do was defend and run down the timer. There was a moment when it looked like the Warriors might make a miraculous comeback, but the Stallions seized control in the neutral zone, pushing forward with an intensity that caught the Warriors off-guard. Somehow, they had managed to do that over and over again tonight. It was the same team the Warriors bested last season without much issue—so what was the difference now?

Stephen raced back, but just as he reached the

defensive zone, the Stallions' top forward faked a pass, cut sharply to the inside and released a quick wrist shot. The Warriors' goalie managed to slap it away, but all that did was keep the Stallions from increasing their lead.

The clock fell under a minute. Stephen's heart sank. Something went out of the crowd, at least on the Warriors' side. It was clear how this game was going to end—there was simply no way to come back from it. The Stallions' fans roared as their center regained possession of the puck. With only a few seconds left, they made another attempt on the Warriors' goal. Again, the goalie batted it away, but it was only a gesture of defiance.

The final buzzer sounded. The fans in the crowd either cheered in victory or moaned in defeat. Stephen skated off the ice, his shoulders heavy with the weight of the loss. It had happened before, but it was never easy to accept. The Back Bay Warriors had lost a home game.

Chapter 9.

The final buzzer sounded, and the scoreboard locked in the end verdict: 3-4 in favor of the Stallions. Waves of sympathy washed over Olivia. She searched the ice for Stephen and spotted him skating slowly off to one side of the ice. She wasn't sure, but she thought his shoulders slumped just a little as he joined the rest of the Warriors in their line to shake hands with the opposing team. It was a tradition Olivia didn't understand when she first came to games with Stan, but now she appreciated it—it was a way for the teams to acknowledge each other's skill and hard work, no matter who won or lost. She thought it was a nice gesture, a touch of class and civility in a game that could sometimes get pretty brutal.

As the players on each team shook hands, Olivia's eyes remained on Stephen. She couldn't help but wonder how he would handle the loss; he struck her as the type who might take it personally, who would put on a stiff upper lip, but replay every missed opportunity in his mind, even if he'd played to his absolute utmost.

Grandma Flora let out a soft sigh, breaking Olivia's thoughts. "Well, they gave it their best, but some nights just don't end the way you'd like them to," she said, trying to sound upbeat, but her disappointment was clear.

Kylie nodded, her expression sympathetic as she glanced toward the exit where the team would eventually emerge. "Stephen's never been great with losses," she told Olivia. "He'll snap out of it, but he's the kind of guy who carries the weight for a few days, all bummed like he's the only one responsible for it all."

Olivia listened, feeling like she'd gained some insight into Stephen Sloan. She saw how powerful his drive was tonight, the way he'd thrown himself into every shift, fighting for control of the puck, never holding back or going easy even when he must have been exhausted and sore from the exertion and the battering he took, even when it was clear that winning the game was slipping out of the Warriors' reach.

"It's not just a game for him, is it?" she asked, mostly to herself. Flora put a hand on Olivia's arm and said, "No, dear. It's a lot more than that. Hockey is his purpose."

"Well, I realize I don't know that much about the game, but I thought he was amazing," Olivia offered. "I mean, that last steal he made—I don't know about, like the strategies and stuff, but I could tell that was pretty impressive."

Grandma Flora smiled warmly, giving Olivia's hand a gentle squeeze. "He'll be glad to hear that, dear. Sometimes a little encouragement is just what he needs after a night like this."

The crowd began to thin, and Olivia, Flora, and Kylie stayed seated, watching as the fans trickled toward the exits. Olivia's mind wandered again, wondering what Stephen's mindset would be. Kylie said he'd carry this for a while. She just met the guy, but still, a part of her hoped she could find a way to help him move past that, to get over the disappointment as quickly as possible. She remembered his smile the first time she noticed him, back at Enclave. It was a sweet, happy moment between a family, and she wanted to see that smile again—as soon as possible.

Stephen wiped the sweat from his brow and the back of his neck with the towel a coaching assistant had given him. Clenching the towel, he paused a second to look at the Warriors emblem woven into the downy fabric.

Win or lose, he was proud of the team and proud to be a member of it, but this one stung. It really did.

Down the hall, just outside of the locker room, was the expected row of reporters waiting to get their soundbites and quotes and photographs. His body was still in fight or flight mode, still coming down from the game's intensity, and his mind kept replaying those critical moments from the third period. He knew he was looking for answers that would be meaningless even if he found them. You can't change the past and once a game has been played, that's it—it's been played for keeps.

The first reporter, a distinguished-looking Black guy Stephen recognized, but whose name he couldn't remember, stepped forward, microphone extended. "Stephen, tough loss tonight. You guys really dominated the Stallions last season—beat them 5-1 last match up, if I'm not mistaken—but they came out swinging in this game. What do you think went wrong out there?"

Stephen nodded, steadying himself before responding. "Yeah, they really showed up tonight," he began. His voice was steady, but there was a hint of frustration he couldn't quite keep out of it. He was disappointed in himself for that, it wasn't professional, and he was better than that, wasn't he?

"We weren't as tight offensively as we needed to be," Stephen said. "Especially in the third period. They capitalized on some mistakes, and, you know, they took advantage of those chances. We played hard, but they played harder, and they made the big plays when it counted."

He paused, glancing down at the floor for a moment. "We'll talk about it as a team, but I imagine that we're going to take a good look at what happened tonight, and when we do, I know we'll learn something and come back stronger. We've got a lot of talent on this team, and we're not going to let one game define us."

The reporter nodded, satisfied, and stepped back.

But before Stephen could retreat into the locker room, another reporter jumped in, voice loud and pointed. "Stephen, if I can change gears for a second—what's going on with you and Liza Gardner? We haven't seen you two together in months. Is there any truth to the rumors that you two are done?"

Stephen's jaw clenched, and he felt a sudden prick of irritation as he turned. The reporter was a woman he'd never seen before: small, blonde, curvy. She reminded him a lot of Liza and that made him even more annoyed, remembering the way the two of them had parted back in October. He had come off the ice still processing the loss of the game; his mind was focused on his team and the events of the night. Talking about Liza with a stranger who just wanted to pick over the corpse of his failed relationship was the last thing he wanted right now. His gaze hardened as he looked at the reporter, carefully weighing his words.

"Liza and I…" he started, then paused, his voice measured. "Liza and I have been going through some changes in our lives, and we're both doing what's best for us right now. I appreciate your interest, but tonight is about the game, and about the Warriors, and what we need to do to keep moving forward as an organization."

Silence fell over the hallway. A couple of the reporters shifted uncomfortably, while others scribbled quickly on their notepads, or let their thumbs dance across smartphone screens. But everyone was watching Stephen for any further reaction. He held his ground, his expression calm. His eyes firm, his jaw clenched faintly belligerently, sending clear signals that this was all he was going to say on the matter of himself and Liza.

After a beat, another reporter cleared his throat and asked a follow-up question about next week's matchup, smoothly steering the conversation back to hockey. Stephen heaved a mental sigh of relief, shifting back to talking shop, focusing on the Warriors and the work he knew he needed to put in. When that reporter was satisfied, Coach Gilman appeared at Stephen's elbow, saying, "All right, folks, let's give Stephen a chance to hit the showers." He clapped a hand on Stephen's shoulder and gently pushed him towards the locker room doorway.

Grateful for the save—from experience, he knew reporters would happily keep a player talking for hours, if you let them—he entered the locker room and began stripping off his gear. He let out an audible sigh now, relieved to be free of the constricting equipment's weight. If only the weight of the lost game, and the even heavier weight of the question about Liza, were as easily shed.

Chapter 10.

Olivia shivered slightly as a gust of cool evening air swept across the back of her neck. She stood outside the arena with Flora and Kylie, waiting for Stephen to emerge. The excitement she felt watching him play was still fresh in her mind; images of Stephen on the ice, how powerful and competent he seemed in his element, mixed with how she'd seen him in Enclave when they first met—first sweet and easygoing when he was with his family and then a little standoffish and gruff to hide his shyness when she joined their birthday celebration. She couldn't forget that bus ad either—she wasn't sure she'd ever forget that very first image of Stephen Sloan, even if she didn't know who he was at the time. Now her heart fluttered at the thought of seeing him again up close and personal, face to face.

But then again, standing among a throng of fans and friends hoping for a glimpse of their local hero, that small obnoxious voice of insecurity crept into her thoughts.

You don't stand a chance against those puck bunnies, girl. Give it up.

"Bug off," she whispered to herself, pitching her voice low enough that no one heard her.

She glanced down at her outfit, tugging self-consciously at her coat. There had been plenty of gorgeous women in the stands tonight—beautiful, glamorous women wearing jerseys with "Sloan" emblazoned on the back, calling Stephen's name and holding signs with personal messages, each of them clearly hoping to catch his attention. She'd even heard a few of them giggling and whispering about him as they waited by the player's entrance, making comments about his body or wondering how he was in bed—things like that. She wanted to believe she was above such juvenile chatter, but a lot of them were very pretty and she couldn't help but wonder if Stephen noticed them.

What's it matter? Why would he notice you? that voice of doubt said, sending a pang of uncertainty through her. Stephen was famous after all, plus handsome, talented, rich, adored by fans. What did she have to offer compared to all that?

Then there was Liza Gardner. Olivia had spent a few minutes in the restroom after the game, nervously searching Stephen's name on her phone, trying to learn more about this man she was so drawn to, but didn't really even know. She'd gotten to know Flora and Kylie pretty well in such a short time—but Stephen? He was still a mystery to her in so many ways.

Googling him, she hadn't expected to see so many photos of him with a petite, beautiful blonde by his side. Liza was the picture-perfect celebrity's girlfriend: elegant and poised, with a kind of effortless charm, but a hint of wild sexiness that she couldn't hide no matter how she was dressed—not that she seemed to try. She was glamorous in every image Olivia saw of her, and Olivia had read enough to gather that Liza had been with Stephen for years and there was a blurb about them moving in together earlier in the year. Yet, at dinner, it was clear that he wasn't living with her; he was staying at his grandma's house. It didn't add up, but she couldn't bring herself to ask Kylie for details. *It's none of my business,* she reminded herself, though the question lingered at the edge of her mind.

Olivia turned to Kylie, thinking maybe she would ask the younger girl if they could get a chance to talk some time the next day or so. She would need to find a way to ask some of these questions without sounding desperate—

she didn't want her new friend to think she was only using her to get close to Stephen. That had probably happened before and Olivia already valued Kylie's friendship too much to risk it. Before she could say anything to the other woman though, a long, lanky figure approached from out of the crowd, smiling easily with a casual confidence that let him cruise right through the masses and up to the three women. Olivia thought she vaguely recognized him from one of the action shots splashed across the colossal TV screens ringing the ice.

"Mrs. Deming! Kylie!" he called, opening his arms in a playful greeting as he stepped up to the trio, then wrapping them around Grandma Flora, lifting the little old lady into a bearhug. "So glad to see you, girls!"

"Randy Roberts," Flora said, trying to sound stern, but not able to resist a giggle. "You put me down this instant!"

Grinning, the tall, charming man with the boyish grin set the old lady gently on her feet. "Sorry, I couldn't help myself."

"You always did know how to make an entrance," Kylie said, smiling. "And I swear, you're the biggest flirt on the planet."

"Not for long," Randy grinned. "In fact, that's why I wanted to talk to you folks. Wanted to make sure my favorite fans remember you're invited to the shindig! Second weekend in January, don't forget!" He flashed a grin, eyes twinkling.

"Don't you worry, we'll be there," Grandma Flora replied, smiling warmly. "We wouldn't miss it for the world."

Kylie rolled her eyes with a grin. "Like you'd let us forget, Randy. Besides, I already bought the perfect dress, just for you," she teased, playfully flicking his shoulder.

Randy placed a hand over his heart, feigning a swoon. "Well, if I weren't about to get hitched, I'd be trying to sweep you off your feet, Kylie. And you too,

Flora—if your grandson hadn't warned me away from you. Something about how I'm trouble…?"

Grandma Flora let out a delighted laugh, swatting his arm. "Oh, don't you sweet-talk me, Randy. I could be your great grandma." It was true that Randy seemed a little younger than Stephen, but Olivia thought that was an exaggeration.

Randy laughed too, and then turned to Olivia as if just noticing her. She'd been watching the exchange with a mixture of amusement and a little surprise. She didn't know people actually acted this silly in real life. Her eyes met Randy's and his seemed to light up with curiosity for an instant.

He leaned in slightly, giving her a crooked smile, turning on the charm again. "And who do we have here? A new member of the Stephen Sloan fan club?"

Grandma Flora patted Olivia's arm. "Randy, this is Olivia. She's a friend of ours. She came along tonight to cheer on Stephen."

"A friend of Flora's, huh?" Randy said, giving Olivia a playful wink. "That means you're practically family. Any friend of Flora's is a friend of mine. She just about raised me you know."

"Oh, stop it, you fool!" Flora laughed. To Olivia, she said, "He's just joshing you, dear."

"Only kinda-sorta," Randy said. "Flora is basically the team's grandma, not just Stephen's.

"Anyway, nice to meet you, Olivia." He extended a hand, and Olivia shook it, feeling a blush rise to her cheeks as he gave her hand a gentle squeeze. For a second, she thought he was going to lift her hand and kiss it, like one of those hokey old movies, but he refrained.

"Nice to meet you, too, Randy," Olivia managed, smiling a little shyly, both flattered and caught off-guard by his charm.

"I don't know if you caught all that before," he told her. "But it just so happens that I've got a wedding coming up in a few weeks. Flora and Kylie are already on the guestlist, but since you're friends with the girls and Stephen, I'd love for you to come too," Randy said, still grinning. "No pressure, no need to dress up or bring a gift—just come along and have a good time."

"Oh, I don't know," Olivia replied hesitantly. "I mean, I don't even know your fiancée, and I'd hate to intrude…"

"Oh, nonsense!" Grandma Flora interjected, patting Olivia's shoulder. "Randy's right—if you're a friend of mine, you're a friend of his, so you're welcome. He said so himself, didn't he? Don't be shy. Besides, who doesn't love a wedding?" She smiled warmly. "It'll be a great way to get out and enjoy yourself."

Kylie nodded enthusiastically. "Yes! Weddings are a blast. And knowing Randy, this one's going to be wild—I can practically guarantee it."

She glanced at Randy, who gave her a huge, theatrical wink, then, clasping Olivia's arm with both hands, she said, "You *have* to come!"

Randy gave her another warm, encouraging smile. "I promise we won't bite. And seriously, I want as many people there as possible to celebrate. You only get married once, right? I mean—well…" He broke up into laughter at himself. "Okay, so maybe not true for everybody, but it is for me. I love Amy and this is a once in a lifetime deal for me, so I'm throwing the ultimate bash. Besides, you'll have Flora, Kylie, and Stephen to keep you company, and they can introduce you to everyone else. What do you say?"

Olivia felt the walls breaking down. Randy was so over the top boisterous and friendly it made her want to accept just to avoid disappointing him. Not just that, Flora and Kylie seemed to genuinely want her to come too. Before tonight, it had been so long since she'd done something spontaneous, something social and fun—maybe the hockey game was just the start of something new and wonderful, a whole new way to be Olivia Murray.

And then of course Stephen would be there… the idea of spending more time around Stephen—and meeting his friends—was more appealing than she wanted to admit to herself.

"All right," she said finally. Smiling, she added, "You know what? I'd love to come."

"Now that's what I'm talking about!" Randy declared, clapping his hands, his eyes twinkling with satisfaction. "It'll be a night to remember, I promise you that."

With a final wink and a quick goodbye to Grandma Flora and Kylie, Randy strode off to join a few other teammates waiting a distance away. One of them waved in a "hurry up" gesture and Randy's tall, rangy form broke into a trot to catch up. Olivia watched him go, a warm buzz of excitement spreading through her. An invitation to a famous hockey player's wedding, a night out with her new friends… and, most of all, the prospect of seeing more of Stephen. This was definitely shaping up to be a new chapter in her life. Was it really less than three days ago that she broke up with Stan? She remembered the scene in his apartment, and the way she found Stan and that perky little witch Sarah… but already the pain was fading, and she began to wonder how much Stan had even meant to her to begin with. In fact, those feelings she once had were starting to feel so distant it was like they belonged to someone else entirely.

The question remained though: if those feelings were gone, if they didn't even seem to belong to her anymore, how did she feel now? And once she sorted out that much out… what did she want to do about those feelings?

Chapter 11

Olivia's thoughts were interrupted by Kylie nudging her with an elbow; the somewhat smaller girl was grinning and pointing toward the arena's side doors. "There he is!" she said brightly, as Stephen finally appeared, wearing his Warriors jacket, his duffel bag slung over one shoulder. He looked tired, utterly worn down from both the exertion of the game, and likely, Olivia thought, the loss in the end. Despite his obvious weariness, Stephen's face lit up with a smile as he spotted his grandmother and Kylie, lifting his hand to wave. It really was touching how close this family was, Olivia thought.

"Hey, Grandma, Kylie," he called as he approached, giving each of them a hug before turning to Olivia. His smile softened a little when he saw her, and Olivia's heart fluttered nervously.

"Olivia, hi," he said, his voice friendly but maybe with a hint of something deeper. "Thanks for coming out tonight. Wasn't sure if you'd make it."

Olivia felt her cheeks flush. She smiled back shyly, trying not to let her nerves show. She suddenly felt like a teenage girl confronted by the school's star jock. In a way, that was what was happening wasn't it? She laughed mentally at the idea of herself in a cheerleading uniform. It helped lift the tension.

She smiled more openly and said, "Of course! I mean, I didn't understand half of what was going on out there," she admitted with a laugh, "but I think you're amazing. I mean, the way you played… was amazing."

Stephen's mouth quirked into a lopsided grin, then he chuckled. "Well, I'm glad I made it look good at least. It was one hell of a rough game tonight," he added. "I underestimated The Stallions. We all did, and it cost us. They really had our number this time." He shook his head. "I just don't get what was so different from when we played them last season."

Kylie jumped in, giving him a supportive nudge. "You'll figure it out, Stevie. And either way, you played great. All of the Warriors did, and we were all cheering like crazy every time you got close to the net. It doesn't matter if you lose one dinky little game, right? There's still a lot of the season left."

"Yeah, well…" Stephen seemed uncertain how to respond to his sister's encouragement. It was all true, and he'd probably heard it before, Olivia imagined, but it seemed like he had trouble accepting it. Was this what Flora and Kylie meant when they told her that Stephen took these things a little too personally?

Grandma Flora gave Stephen's arm an affectionate pat. "You know we're always proud of you, win or lose. You're always number one in my book."

"Actually, I'm number seven, remember?" Stephen smiled at his own joke.

"Ever since you were a little boy," Flora agreed.

Kylie said something then, and Stephen recognized the tone as a question, but the words didn't register. Flora responded, saving him the trouble, and he let his gaze drift back to Olivia, who watched him with a mixture of awe and awkward shyness. She seemed to want to say something to him but was apparently trying to find the right words.

Olivia wasn't sure of the right way to phrase it, to tell Stephen that she appreciated his skill, his dedication. She wanted to tell him how impressed she was with his character—she never before realized how much you could tell about someone by the way they played a game. That's what hockey was—a game—and she'd always thought of it and all other sports as just kids' games that adults were paid absurd amounts to money to play. Enjoyable to watch for millions and millions of people, sure, but still just games. It wasn't until tonight, watching Stephen, having someone to follow and cheer for, that she realized just how appealing sports could be. And in watching Stephen specifically, she felt she learned a lot too about what kind of man he was.

Before she could muster the courage to say what she was thinking, he leaned in, his voice soft. "Seriously, it means a lot that you came," he said, his tone earnest. "Hockey isn't everyone's thing, and I know tonight didn't go too well—I wish your first time seeing me on the ice wasn't a loss, but that's the way it goes sometimes, I guess. Well, not guess—I know it is. It's part of the job. But either way… what I'm trying to say is it's good to have you here." He smiled. "I'm glad to see you."

Olivia's heart raced, and for a moment, her self-doubts faded. Maybe he didn't care about the puck bunnies in the stands, and maybe the rumors she read online about him and Liza being finished were true. She didn't know for sure, but Stephen Sloan was standing there, looking at her, his warm brown eyes meeting hers, and she felt like he saw *her*, Olivia Murray.

She smiled, a surge of renewed confidence flowing through her. She was starting to feel the way she did back at the salon, when the stylist showed her the final results of her makeover. "I'm just glad I could be part of your cheering section," she told him. "I know the game didn't go the way you wanted it to, but I had a lot of fun. You guys definitely had me on the edge of my seat the whole night."

Stephen smiled broadly, his eyes crinkling at the corners—one of those things Olivia first noticed about him when she saw him up close, in the restaurant. It was a good look for him, it added character, she thought.

"Good. Let's see if we can keep you cheering next game, too.

"You know…" Stephen began, sending Olivia's heart racing again. "I wanted to thank you again too, for what you did for my grandmother."

"Oh, no, I just—"

Olivia tried to protest but Stephen cut in. "No, I mean it. She's really important to me. She basically raised me, and she's always been my rock. I don't know what I'd do without her. She and Kylie… well, they're the two most important people in my life and you saved Flora's life, so… thanks."

He paused, seemingly embarrassed now, at a lack for words. He wasn't used to opening up to people outside of his family.

Olivia could sense how hard it was for Stephen to say that. He was a titan on the ice, but away from it, she was just now realizing, he was simply another guy who sometimes wasn't quite sure of where he stood in the world.

She put a hand on Stephen's arm, smiled softly at him and said, "You're welcome and I'm glad too. I really like Flora and Kylie. I wish it could have happened a nicer way, but I'm really glad to have met them—and you."

Stephen smiled, feeling something that he wasn't quite sure he could identify. It began in his belly and seemed to spread throughout his body, comforting and soothing. "Me too."

They stood there, the silence that fell between them now a comfortable one as the bustling crowd began to thin out. For the first time that evening, Olivia allowed herself to actually imagine what it might be like to spend more time with Stephen outside of the rink, away from the questions and the doubts. And not with Flora and Kylie, with Olivia butting in on their family trio, or in a big group setting, like Randy Roberts's wedding. She was imagining just the two of them, Stephen and Olivia—two people who could possibly make a connection deeper than just a chance encounter in a restaurant or as a sports star and a brand-new fan. Maybe even as a man and a woman…? A delicious little tingle went down Olivia's spine as Stephen glanced at her, the hint of a smile still on his face, and she dared to hope he might be thinking the same thing.

Chapter 12.

Monday, 11pm:

Olivia stifled a yawn as she sipped her coffee, leaning against the breakroom counter as the clock ticked just past 11:30 p.m. Tonight was the first night of her once-a-month week of graveyard shifts, and the full moon hung brightly outside the window, casting a strange glow over the parking lot. It was just her luck to be on graveyard duty for the three nights of the full moon. She threw a knowing look at her coworker Deann, just pulling up a chair beside her, a mischievous grin already forming on her face.

"Here we go again," Olivia muttered. "Full moon Monday. You know it's going to be one of those nights."

Deann snorted. "When isn't it 'one of those nights?'" She laughed. "I get you, though. You weren't working graveyard during the full moon back in August, right?"

Olivia shook her head then sipped coffee. "Uh uh. Thank God. Full moon plus the dog days of summer?"

"Well, you must have heard about it—that guy who called in convinced he was turning into a werewolf?"

Olivia nearly choked on her coffee, laughing at the memory. "Oh, God, yes. He was dead serious, wasn't he?! He wanted someone to go out to his place and keep an eye on him."

Across the room, one of the newer staff members, Jenny, raised an eyebrow, looking from Olivia to Deann in confusion. "Wait—keep an eye on him? You mean, like, restrain him or something? Lock him up?"

"No!" Deann shook her head, laughing. "He didn't even bring up the possibility of hurting anyone—that was the funniest thing."

"Or maybe the saddest?" Olivia suggested, grinning.

Dee continued, "He just wanted someone to make sure he didn't tear up any of his new furniture. Apparently, he'd just spent a fortune on it, and he was worried he'd wolf out and ruin it."

Olivia chuckled, rolling her eyes. "Poor guy."

"Well, he was so serious about it," Dee said, "that I had to pretend to take notes and everything. He was getting frantic and I even considered really having the PD do a wellness check on him, but I wasn't sure if that would be playing into the fantasy or whatever."

"So what ended up happening?" Jenny asked.

"Well," Dee glanced at Olivia, then back to Jenny. "I told him to close his blinds really tight and give us a call if he showed any… furry tendencies."

Disbelief on her face, Jenny wasn't sure whether to laugh or not—she was new enough that she considered this might all be a joke. "Well, I'm not sure what's crazier—that he actually thought he'd turn into a werewolf, or that you kept a straight face through it all and treated him seriously."

"Oh, I didn't," Dee laughed. "I kept having to mute myself so he wouldn't hear me. But, yeah, for real—you haven't seen anything yet." Deann grinned teasingly. "There's something about the full moon that brings out the strangest characters. By Wednesday, we'll have had at least one ghost-hunter, a handful of 'psychics,' and maybe even a vampire or two."

"Don't forget aliens," Olivia sighed, taking another sip of her coffee. "But I guess we'll be ready for all of it. At least as long as there's coffee on hand."

The three of them shared a laugh before filing

back out onto the floor and settling into their workstations, headsets in place, computers ready to receive and direct calls. The center was already busy, calls going off constantly, and it would only get busier as the night wore on. Probably wouldn't begin to slow down until around four o'clock or so—that seemed to be when the full moon people wore themselves out.

Despite the night ahead of her, Olivia felt a warm surge of camaraderie though. Working the graveyard shift was tough—sometimes even lousy, like full moon nights—but she really did love her job and her coworkers. Even Jenny, still in her second week and technically still in training, was becoming precious to her. And it was partially because of nights like these, full of bizarre stories, ridiculous laughter, and shared experiences that made her love this place so much.

Almost the instant Olivia signed into the phone queue, her line buzzed. Instinctively, she scanned the call info scrolling across her computer screen as she answered, "911, what's your emergency?" with her usual calm.

A woman's shaky voice on the other end answered, "Hello? Hello?"

"I'm here, ma'am," Olivia responded. The voice was middle-aged, scared. It could be anything, Olivia thought: a prowler, an abusive spouse, a disturbance in a neighboring apartment. "What's your emergency, ma'am?" she repeated.

"Oh, thank God. I was afraid they might be blocking the phone signal or something."

"Ma'am," Olivia said, putting the soothing quality into her voice that she always used for situations like this, where the caller seemed too upset to even explain the situation. "I need you to take a deep breath, slowly, in through your mouth."

There was a pause and then she heard the woman's intake.

"Good. Now let it slowly out through your nose.

I'm going to count, okay? One… two… three." Olivia heard the woman slowly exhale. If she was able to follow instructions, she'd be okay, Olivia thought.

"Now, ma'am—what's your emergency, please?"

"There's…" the woman began, her voice small, as if trying not to be overheard. Olivia's heart fluttered, fearing the worst. She imagined the poor woman huddled in a closet or beneath a bed, trying to escape the sight of an intruder—or worse, a partner on the warpath.

"There's this light," the caller finally said. "It's green—like neon green, but sort of emerald? It's unworldly, I've never seen anything like it, and it's shining right into my bedroom, like a spotlight right through the blinds and focused on the bed. It's eerie, like I'm being targeted and I'm—I'm afraid it might be… the aliens."

Olivia rolled her eyes, simultaneously muting herself so the caller couldn't hear her sigh. It was definitely a full moon tonight. She glanced at Dee's workstation, to her left. Her friend winked at her and said something to her own caller about having a patrol cruiser swing through the area.

Olivia bit back a smile, unmuted herself, and leaned into her soothing tone, prepared for any sort of response. This kind of caller might be talked down or they might escalate. At the very worst, Olivia might need to have the police perform a wellness check.

"Ma'am, I can assure you," Olivia told the woman on the other end of the call, "there's no reason to worry. There is no such thing as aliens as far as I know and as long as I've been doing this job, I've never heard of anyone being spirited away from their bedrooms."

That last part wasn't strictly true—she remembered a kidnapping last year in which a little boy was taken from his bedroom in the middle of the night, but that was part of a messy custody battle during a divorce. The mother had broken into her ex's condo and taken the boy, but she was most certainly from this planet.

"You don't understand!" Olivia's caller hissed, her voice dropping to a whisper as though the aliens themselves might hear her and retaliate for her bringing an outsider into things. "It's so bright, and it's pulsing! It's almost…" Her voice became slow, as if she were falling asleep. "It's almost… hypnotic. I just… I just know they're here to take me. I've listened to Giorgio Tsoukalos's podcast…"

Olivia took a steadying breath. "All right, ma'am. I understand. Please remain calm and listen to me. Before I dispatch officers, can you do me a favor? Can you try to see if you can figure out where the light is coming from first?"

"I *know* where it's coming from!" the woman snapped, coming out of the daze she'd seemed in.

"I understand, ma'am," Olivia reassured her. "But I can't have officers going in unprepared."

The woman hesitated, but Olivia could hear her moving around, the muffled sound of sheets and creaking floorboards. "Okay, that makes sense, I guess," she said after a moment.

"I'm… I'm going to check," she whispered. "I'm getting out of bed now, keeping low to the floor. I'm almost at the window… Oh God, it's getting brighter! It's so bright now."

"Just take it slow," Olivia encouraged her, keeping her voice steady and reassuring, calming. Her eyes flicked towards the call-length ticking upwards on the corner of her computer screen. If she couldn't talk this lady down soon, she might really have to send police out, just to ensure this woman didn't hurt herself or someone else. Anything was possible when someone became this confused and upset.

"When you reach the window," Olivia told her, "carefully pull back the curtain, and take a look. I'm right here."

Voice trembling, the woman told her, "All right…

I'm at the window. I'm… opening the curtain now…"

There was a pause, and Olivia braced herself, biting her lip lightly. She wished she could laugh—to an outsider, this was probably ridiculous, but she knew that to the caller it was very real and terrifying.

"Oh, for heaven's sake," the woman finally grumbled, all traces of fear vanishing from her voice. "It's the new sign from that all-night dry-cleaning place across the street. I forgot they put up that hideous thing over the weekend."

Olivia released a small laugh of relief, forgetting to mute herself this time. "Mystery solved, then?"

She was afraid the woman would take offense at her laughing, but the caller seemed not to even heard her. She told Olivia, "Yes, I guess so, but honestly, who needs a sign that big or that bright?" The caller huffed. "It's practically an otherworldly torture device. I'm going to call the city council tomorrow."

"I think that's a good plan, ma'am," Olivia said, smiling now. "You have a good night, and remember—we're here anytime you need us, but please make sure you assess the situation thoroughly before calling."

Olivia disconnected the call, shaking her head. She was relieved it worked out, but if that was any indication of the night ahead of her, she was in for a doozy. Chuckling, she recorded the incident notes in her log, not entirely sure how much she should bother writing. Maybe just chock it up as another full moon alien invasion and let it go at that.

Chapter 13.

The night was long and busy, but finally seven a.m. rolled around. Olivia let out a long, relieved sigh, stretched her arms above her head, and stood from her desk. It felt like she hadn't moved from the chair for hours and hours, but in truth, it had been fairly slow after about 4:30. Just as she predicted, the people affected by the full moon were dropping off to sleep about then, wearing themselves out, and the remainder of the shift had been pretty routine.

"Good job tonight, sweetie," Deann told her, weary but cheerful.

"You too, lady," Olivia answered. "See you tonight."

"Oh, God, yes. Round two." Dee smiled, picked up her bag, said her goodbyes to the rest of their coworkers, and left. A moment later Olivia did the same.

Olivia stepped out of the building into cold, crisp morning air. The city was just starting to wake up, the sky still being painted in soft shades of pale pink and blue by the sun rising over the rooftops. She pulled her coat tighter around herself—the old pink one she'd had since college, not the fur-lined one she wore for going out on the town—and savored the cold brushing her cheeks. The feeling was a refreshing jolt after hours under the fluorescent lights of the dispatch center. In a couple of weeks, she knew she'd be sick of winter, but for now, the weather was still a novelty.

The streets were quieter than usual as she walked to her car. The early hour seemed to provide the city with a restorative moment of calm, as if the rising sun was trying to make up for the full moon bringing its usual collection of strange calls and surreal moments. Olivia breathed deeply, thinking back over the night. It was a bit hectic in the moment, but with the first night behind her, she could smile about it—it was just part of the job, and she made it through the night intact.

Now she was ready to go home, kick off her shoes, take a long, hot shower, and sink into bed for a few precious hours of sleep before doing it all over again.

First though, she had a stop to make.

Olivia reached Revere, the small, working-class town north of the city, and a few minutes later pulled into her dad's driveway. The familiar sight of Jack's modest frame house brought both a sense of comfort and routine and a sense of nostalgia. It wasn't the house she grew up in—that was up in Vermont—but not long after she moved to the city, her parents retired and chose to relocate to be closer to their only child. Once, the house had been neat and tidy, but with the passing of her mother, Francine, her father had begun to let it slip—just as he had himself. Now, the house still looked all right, but the aluminum siding was a bit dingy, in need of washing, and some of the paint on the porch was peeling. She'd once asked Stan if he might be able to help her dad out with some repairs one weekend, but somehow, he'd managed to divert the conversation without ever giving her an answer. She'd almost forgotten about that and even now, it annoyed her.

She grabbed the bag of groceries she'd picked up on the way over and let herself into the house, the door sticking a little before she gave it a nudge with her shoulder. The house was quiet, but she knew her dad was already up, probably sipping his first cup of coffee in the kitchen and waiting for her, as he always did on these mornings. It was a tradition that after the first shift of her monthly week of graveyard duty, she came over to Jack's and made them breakfast so they could take some time to catch up.

"Hey, kiddo!" Jack's voice greeted her warmly as she walked in, his gruff face lighting up when he saw her. He normally had what Olivia jokingly called "resting bitch-face," but smiling changed his entire demeanor, reminding her of big, gray teddy bear. Even in his early sixties, Jack was a big guy and one of the best huggers she'd ever known. He set down his coffee and stood, taking the bag of groceries from her and placing it on the kitchen counter before giving her one of those hugs. She allowed herself a moment to lean into him, relishing it. This wasn't her home exactly, but sometimes it felt like it.

"Survived another full moon nightshift, huh?" Jack asked.

"Barely," she replied with a tired smile. "I'm glad to see you, Daddy." She opened the grocery bag, pulling out eggs, bacon, and bread. "Scrambled okay?"

"Sure, honey." Jack reseated himself at the kitchen table, finishing off the remains of his coffee, watching his daughter bustle about the kitchen. She must have been tired from a long night, but here she was, taking care of him. "Take your time," Jack said, settling back in his chair but keeping his eye on her.

"I'm fine, Daddy. I'm more hungry than anything right now." She gave him a small, tired smile over her shoulder.

Jack watched her for a moment, leaving her to her tasks. When he sure she was in the flow of things, and he wouldn't distract her, he started, "So, about Christmas... You got plans lined up already, or do I need to start finding a gift for that fella of yours?"

Olivia hesitated, her hands still for a moment as she cracked an egg into the bowl. She hadn't expected him to ask about Stan—she had thought of Stan, of course, but Jack never really liked him and avoided bringing him up at all, unless he couldn't help it. Usually on these mornings, his name never entered the conversation. With the holiday almost here though, she supposed it was inevitable that he'd ask. He didn't like Stan, and didn't try to hide that fact, but he was always civil, and he made an effort for her sake to be kind to him on holidays and his birthday.

Deciding it was best not to make a big thing of it, she said, "Actually… no, Dad. You don't need to worry about Stan this year." She kept her tone light, as if Stan no longer being in the picture wasn't the slightest concern.

Jack looked at her sharply, his bushy eyebrows lifting. "No gift for Stan?" he asked, trying to mask the curiosity in his voice. "Does that mean you two…?"

Olivia nodded, made an *mhm* sound and flashed her father a small, tight smile as she poured the beaten eggs into the hot skillet. "We broke up last week. Some stuff happened, and it doesn't matter what, I don't want to go into it—but, bottom line, it's over between us."

Jack's face softened, though she caught the glint of satisfaction he couldn't quite hide. She could just imagine he was thinking *good riddance,* but he had the grace not to say it out loud. Instead, he cleared his throat, reaching for his coffee. He realized the mug was empty and stood to refill it from the pot on the counter by the stove.

"Well," he said slowly. "You know how I feel, so I can't say I'm disappointed." He kept his tone as neutral as he could manage, a skill he learned from years of conflict resolution as a policeman. "I never thought he was much of a match for you. But I know these things still hurt, so I'm sorry. If you want to talk…"

"Honestly, Daddy, it's okay. It hurt at the time, but I realized after that it was going to happen sooner or later and it's better now than drag it out through the holidays, right?" Olivia stirred the eggs, then shifted to the griddle and flipped the bacon, releasing a fresh wave of warm, savory smell that filled the room.

Jack grunted, took a sip of his refilled coffee and realized he had forgotten cream and sugar. He didn't bother, though, simply watched her cook. Finally he said, "Good riddance, then."

Olivia's back was to him, so he couldn't see her smiling as he voiced exactly what she'd imagined him saying.

"If you're okay with him being gone, then I say you're better off without him," Jack added. He was quiet for a moment, then said, "And you know, I meant it: I'm here to talk, even if it's just to complain about ex-boyfriends or work or… I don't know, winter fashion or whatever," he finished lamely.

She laughed, dividing the scrambled eggs onto two plates and adding crispy bacon just as the toaster popped, shooting two pieces of cinnamon-raisin toast upwards. Olivia spread butter on the toast, put one slice on each plate. "I'll keep that in mind, Daddy. And really, I'm just fine. Actually… maybe better than fine."

Jack raised both eyebrows this time as she set a plate in front of him. "Well, you've got my attention. What do they say these days? 'Spill the tea?'"

She laughed, shaking her head as she took a seat across from him. "It's nothing, really. I mean, maybe it is. There's just this guy I've run into a couple of times. I've gotten to be friends with his sister and weirdly enough," she grinned and chuckled, "his grandma. They're great, and he's close to them." She shrugged. "It's nothing serious, just… he's someone I might want to get to know better."

"Now *that* sounds interesting," Jack said, he grinned and picked up his fork. "You'll have to tell me about this mystery man sometime."

They settled into their breakfast, catching up and talking over plans for Christmas Day, Jack hinting that without Stan to worry about, maybe she should spend the whole day at his place this year.

Olivia soaked up the warmth of another of these familiar mornings with her dad. She was tired from the long night, and aching for sleep, but she felt good. And as she looked across the table at Jack, she felt grateful—not just for this quiet, familiar breakfast tradition, or for her dad's unwavering support, or for her new friends who she was already coming to love, but everything that lay ahead.

She wasn't sure what that was, exactly, but she couldn't help being excited over the possibilities.

Chapter 14.

Stephen adjusted the weights on his bar and took a deep breath. That was what he always forgot when he was thinking about something else while trying to work out. He couldn't remember the exact science, but he did remember a lifetime of coaching—first back in middle school when he started with weights, right up to present day—but you needed to focus on your breathing, make sure the rhythm was correct, in order to get the best effect from lifting. Breathe in—one, two, three—breath out—one-two-three—he pressed the barbell up, feeling the familiar burn in his arms and chest. Around him, several of his Warriors teammates were scattered across Randy Roberts's home gym, grumbling through their own reps and exchanging banter about holiday plans and the chaos of last-minute gift buying.

Randy set down the huge kettlebell he'd been using and wiped his brow, catching Stephen's eye. For seemingly no reason, he smirked and asked, "So, Sloan—all set for the holidays? You get your gifts sorted, or are you one of those guys still running around on Christmas Eve? I'm sure you've got Grandma Flora all taken care of at least, right?"

Stephen laughed, gently replaced the bar on its rack and stood, rolling his shoulders out. "Honestly, I could use some ideas. Especially with, you know… the way things are now." He trailed off, hoping to keep the talk of gifts vague. It was never a problem with Liza; she always told him exactly what she wanted, complete with where he could buy the stuff. This year, that wasn't an issue—honestly, it was kind of a relief. It was easy shopping for Liza, but the last few years, it didn't feel like he was giving her gifts so much as he was just doing her shopping for her.

And now… now, there was someone else and he realized he wasn't sure anymore how to buy a gift for a woman. He also wasn't ready to tell the guys that he had someone new in mind this year, especially after the way Ken and Jake had talked back in the locker room, before the game this past weekend.

Besides that, he wasn't even sure if he really wanted to go through with it. He was still very much on the fence, unsure of his own mind—or heart. He'd only met Olivia twice, and she was really Kylie's friend, wasn't she? So why was he thinking about her so much?

Randy grinned, pretty much his default expression these days. Since Amy agreed to marry him, he'd been on cloud nine. Lucky guy. Stephen envied his happiness, but didn't begrudge it. Randy was a friend, a good teammate.

Randy stretched his arms above his head, then grabbed his elbows, locking his arms and rocked back and forth, stretching out his lats and delts. "Well, here's what I do: think about how you wanna go and what the person you're thinking about would like most. I know, I know." He released his arms and held his hands up, forestalling protest. "That sounds like a BS non-answer, but it isn't. Is this lady—oops." He grinned again. "If this *person* is into something specific, like a type of music or style of art or whatever. Or maybe, like, handmade stuff."

"That's the ticket, man," Mikey B chimed in from a bench a few feet off. "Girls love the handmade stuff. It makes 'em think you're artsy and sensitive and shit."

A couple of the other guys laughed. Mikey's head whipped around, throwing them a look, then he turned slowly back towards Stephen. "I'm serious though. Girls like the crafty shit and if you want that stuff, just look online. Search for—like, shit, I don't know. What did I use last time? 'Hippy jewelry' I think worked good. Oh, or 'handmade candles.' That's a good one, too. Anyway, search something like that and bam, you'll find all kinds of cool stuff any lady would like." He stood, shrugged and rolled out his shoulders as Stephen had earlier. "Remember Katie? The girl I was dating last year? Every gift I got her, that's how I found it and she loved it all."

Stephen nodded, appreciative of the tip. Like anyone else, he did a lot of shopping on Jungle dot com, but he wasn't actually very internet savvy. "That's pretty smart."

"Especially for Mikey," Jake teased, the first he'd spoken up in a while. Mike threw him another annoyed look.

Stephen ignored Jake, saying, "Thanks, man. There's still a few days before I gotta really worry, but you probably saved me from a last-minute mall run."

He was just about to shift the conversation back to their workout routine when Jake, leaning against the squat rack with a smirk, chimed in. "You know, fellas, while you're looking up Christmas traditions, get this—I heard Japanese girls go wild on Christmas. Like, I don't know why the hell they do, but I heard they think it's the best night of the year for, you know… 'romance' if you get my drift. Think we can import that tradition to Beantown?"

The other guys burst out laughing, exchanging grins and calling out risqué suggestions, but Stephen barely registered the comment or the shift in conversation, just grateful that he was no longer the focus.

As the guys chatted, he nodded along distractedly, tuning out their laughter and letting his mind wander. His thoughts drifted to Olivia, wondering what she'd think of a gift with a personal touch—something handmade, maybe unique. Something thoughtful, maybe even a little unusual—or at least unexpected. He pictured her surprise, the way her eyes might light up, that small, shy smile she showed him whenever she was feeling a bit caught off guard. Just picturing it made him smile.

Jake, seeing Stephen's smile, misinterpreted it, not realizing Stephen wasn't paying attention to their conversation. He slapped Stephen's shoulder. "This guy gets it."

Stephen was jolted from his thoughts, back to reality, but recovered quickly. "Oh, yeah. For sure, man."

The conversation shifted again, and Stephen's thoughts wandered back to where he'd been interrupted. He pictured Olivia's smiling face, the way her slightly plump cheeks dimpled. He wanted to see that again, and more, he wanted to be the one to make her smile.

With another jolt, a different kind this time, he realized that he wanted to make an impression on her. Sure, they'd only just started to get to know each other, but Olivia was different. He wasn't certain exactly why, but Stephen knew already that she wasn't just a casual acquaintance or his sister's friend—she was someone who made him feel at ease. Even with so many major changes going on in his life, the little time he'd spent with Olivia was relaxing, soothing, even healing.

He had to wonder though… did he even have a right to be thinking like that? The situation with Liza wasn't resolved yet. She was still living in his house after all. That wasn't a confrontation he was looking forward to in any way, shape, or form…

"All right, guys. Enough chitchat. Sloan, you're up," Randy called, snapping Stephen out of his thoughts once more.

Stephen stood, not remembering having sat back down on the bench, and grabbed his towel, shaking his head to rid himself of the mental haze. "Yeah, yeah, I'm here," he said, back to focusing on the workout. They were only half done and nobody wanted to spend all day at Randy's house, not when it was a rare day without a game or practice. But as he settled into his reps, a small smile crept onto his face. There were obstacles, sure… but maybe they only mattered if he let them. And he had a few more ideas now—and maybe even a bit of inspiration—to make this Christmas special, just in case he could find the right excuse—and the guts—to give Olivia a gift.

Chapter 15.

Olivia's phone vibrated, making it stutter an inch or two across the tabletop. She rinsed suds from her hands, dried them on the fluffy, Santa-patterned towel hanging next to the kitchen sink, and turned to retrieve the phone. A text from Kylie Sloan read *What's up, girl?*

It was after nine o'clock and Olivia was just cleaning up the dishes from breakfast with Jack. She hadn't meant to stay at her father's place as long as she had, but they'd gotten to chatting about so many things—first the funny full moon calls she'd received, then the hockey game, and her new friends, Kylie and Flora—and simply lost track of time. Even though she had breakfast with Jack at least once a month, it seemed like they hadn't caught up in ages.

N-M. At my dads. U? Olivia texted back, then replaced the phone on the counter. The dishes were almost done, and once she was finished, she'd go home and get some sleep. Jack had to leave for a doctor's appointment, and had told her to forget about the dishes, go home and get some sleep, but Olivia wasn't about to leave a kitchen she'd used without cleaning up after herself. Especially as she planned to come back later that night to have dinner with her dad before going to work. That wasn't part of their usual routine, but she'd suggested it on a whim and Jack had seemed very pleased with the idea.

She had just slipped the griddle into the soapy water when the phone buzzed a second time. Figuring it was Kylie, she almost let it go until she finished the dishes—nobody expected an instant response, right?—but was suddenly eager to know what her friend had in mind. Even if it was just wanting to chat, that was okay: Olivia loved talking with the younger girl.

Olivia rinsed soapy, grimy water from her hands and used the Santa towel—a legacy from her late mother, who loved Santa more than any other holiday icon—to dry them before retrieving her phone.

How you feel about games? Kyle's newest text read.

Olivia's brow creased. Was this a trick question? Did she mean, like, guy-girl games? Mind games? Scrabble? Monopoly? Hockey? She laughed, realizing she was overthinking it.

Olivia's fingers danced across the smartphone screen. *Depends what kind?*

Board. G-Ma wants to know if you wanna come over for games tonight. U choose.

Choose? The game? Except for Scrabble with Jack, she hadn't played a boardgame in years—not since middle school sleepovers, probably. And the last one she remembered playing was one of those boyband-themed guessing games where you tried to figure out which member of the group was supposed to be texting you, just from little clues. If you guessed correctly within a certain number of questions and answers, the musical hottie's voice played, confessing he had a crush on you.

She laughed at the memory. It seemed silly as a twenty-seven-year-old woman, but it was fun as a twelve-year-old girl. There was no age-limit on boardgames though, was there? Flora was, what? Eighty, and she'd apparently suggested it. It would probably be a lot of fun. There was one major obstacle though:

OLIVIA: *Got 2 work tonight. Graveyard shift :(*

That sux, Kylie responded almost instantly. *What time? Maybe before?*

OLIVIA: *Promised dinner w/ my dad first.*

Kylie: *G-ma says bring him along :)*

"Huh?" Olivia said out loud. She hadn't expected that response. They didn't know Jack Murray at all, and he was invited just like that? Well, she realized after a moment's thought, that actually was pretty in character for Grandma Flora. She seemed to make friends wherever she went. Pretty much the moment she met someone new, she was winning them over and welcoming them to her found family. The entire Back Bay Warriors team were part of that family, weren't they? Flora had certainly taken to Olivia and she was sure that the older woman would welcome Jack.

Olivia's phone dinged. *If you want* was displayed, Kylie's follow up message when Olivia hadn't responded.

Well, why not? Olivia decided. It would be up to Jack, of course—she wouldn't make her dad do anything he wasn't comfortable with. A game-night before work would make her night longer too, but it wouldn't be much more tiring than making dinner for herself and Jack before going off to work anyway, would it?

OLIVIA: *Sounds good, but let me check w/dad* Olivia wrote back.

K was the response.

Olivia texted her father *Invited for game-night at friends tonight. Both of us. Want to go?*

She wasn't sure if her father was with the doctor now or still waiting, so she put her phone down and went back to the breakfast dishes. She was just finishing when her phone rang—not a text, a call. There were only a couple of people who actually called her.

"Hi, Daddy," she answered.

"Hi, honey. What's this about games?"

"My friend Kylie invited me to a boardgame night tonight, with her and Flora. My new friends I told you about?"

"Yeah," Jack said. "Well, go on ahead if you want to, honey. We can have dinner any night."

"Kylie said Flora invited you too. I didn't want to

agree without asking you first. We don't have to if you don't want to."

Jack made a *hmm* sound, but Olivia could practically hear the gears turning in his head. That analytical cop mind was at work. The thought made her smile. Even if Jack wasn't a detective and never had any exciting "cases" like on TV police shows, she was always proud of her father and his work.

"Well," Jack said slowly. "I am curious. I admit it. Stan was the last friend of yours you introduced me to and you know how I felt about him."

It almost sounded like a joke, but Olivia knew it wasn't.

"You're sure they wouldn't mind having an old fart like me there? I mean, young girls—"

"Daddy, I'm almost thirty."

"You'll be my little girl when you're sixty—at least if I'm still around then. That's not the point." He sighed in frustration, though Olivia knew it was with himself and not with her. Jack wasn't exactly afraid to show his emotions like some guys of his generation, but he wasn't always the best at expressing them either.

"Look, what I'm trying to say, honey, is I want to go. I mean, if it's really okay with you," her father added, sounding almost embarrassed.

"Of course it is, Daddy." She smiled.

"You said your friend's grandma is going to be there?"

"Yup. It's Flora's house."

"At least I won't be the only senior citizen then."

Olivia laughed. "Daddy, to her, *you'll* be one of the kids."

Jack made a *harumph* noise in his throat and said, "Text me when to pick you up tonight, then get some sleep."

"Yes, Daddy," Olivia said, trying not to giggle at her father's attempt at gruffness. It was only to hide his embarrassment and she could forgive him for that. In fact, it was kind of cute. "Love you."

"Love you, too," Jack told her and hung up.

Olivia opened her texts and, fingers flying, wrote, *Daddy's in. See you at 7? We'll bring dinner.*

Yaaay! Kylie responded, following up with Flora's address.

It was just a night with friends, but Olivia felt herself growing giddy. She realized she was smiling like mad—if anyone saw her now, they might wonder what was wrong with her.

She laughed out loud. "Or right maybe?" she asked the empty kitchen, wondering if Kylie and Flora liked Indian food.

Chapter 16.

Olivia couldn't help but marvel at Flora's townhouse, a picture of old Boston elegance. It had either been gorgeously restored or well-maintained over the years. She wondered how old it actually was. Beacon Hill, in addition to being one of the wealthiest parts of the city, was one of the oldest. The house might well be two hundred or more years old. It was awe-inspiring just to imagine it, and she wouldn't have been able to even make a guess at its age. Small but perfectly trimmed boxwood hedges lined the walkway, and soft light spilled from the windows, giving the place a warm, inviting glow despite the chill in the air. Olivia didn't know much about architecture, but the house, with its brick façade, tall bay windows, and wrought-iron railings really could have existed just about any time. No, it was even more than that; the house seemed to her almost timeless—like something from a fairy tale book. She was beginning to get nervous just thinking about stepping inside.

"Wow," she murmured, glancing at her dad. "This place is… beautiful," she finished, unsure of how else to describe it.

She'd planned to bring a take-out dinner to the little party, but Kylie had told her not to—just bring themselves and be ready for some fun. She was glad Kylie had; she couldn't imagine how silly she'd look, or feel, carrying cartons of Indian takeout into such an elegant home.

Jack gave a low whistle, nodding in agreement. "Didn't know Stephen's grandma was living in a place like this," he muttered, taking in the details of the stately home, clearly very impressed—something Jack didn't often seem. "Beacon Hill, too. Must've done pretty well for herself."

"I wonder if Stephen bought it for her," Olivia said.

She could sense a touch of nervousness in her father, which ironically made her feel a little better about her own anxieties. Jack was a tough guy who had seen just about everything in his time as a police officer. As a little girl, she thought that he must never be scared or anxious or intimidated by anyone or anything. It was a little funny, but also kind of sweet to see him even a little at a loss.

Olivia took a step towards the brick stairs leading up to the house, putting herself in the glow from the faux gas-lamps that lit the walkway. As she did, she glanced down at herself, suddenly wondering if Kylie had undersold the whole "casual game night" dress code. Her jeans and old Taylor Swift tee were comfortable but far from fancy—they would seem as out of place in this lovely old home as they might have a hundred years ago. The pink jacket was her favorite, but it looked old and maybe a little worn beside the backdrop of the grand townhouse. She suddenly felt self-conscious. Only her handmade hat—something she crocheted herself and wore with pride—felt like maybe it was good enough to belong.

But before she could dwell on it too long, her dad gave her a reassuring nod. "You look perfect, Livvy," he said, reading her expression. "Besides, we're here to have fun, right? Don't worry about appearances so much. These ladies invited us, and if they're your friends they won't give a hoot if you show up in a bathrobe. So let's go see if these rich folks know how to play a decent game of Chutes'n'Ladders."

Olivia laughed, grateful as always for Jack's support. Giving his hand a quick squeeze, she moved towards the stairs and together they walked up the short flight of steps. Jack kept a steady hand on the railing as they reached the top, eyeing the patches of crusty ice warily, and Olivia reached to ring the doorbell. She heard the soft chime echo inside, followed by quick light steps approaching. *That must be Kylie,* she thought. For just a brief instant, she imagined the door being opened by a uniformed maid, maybe a snooty one who'd give her a quietly disapproving look before asking who she might possibly be here to see.

The door opened to reveal Kylie, her face breaking into a warm smile as she saw them. "Hey, you two! Come on in, it's freezing out there!"

Kylie moved aside, and they entered, stepping into a stunning foyer. The inside of the house was just as impressive as the exterior, with rich wood paneling, antique furnishings, and a grand staircase that curved up to the second floor. Holiday decorations were tastefully placed along the staircase and on the small tables around the room, adding a cozy warmth to the elegant space. To one side of the stairs was a small Christmas tree wrapped in twinkling white lights. Beyond a sunken, marble-floored niche immediately in front of the door was spread a huge Oriental rug of reds and greens and yellows, adding Christmas colors even to the floor.

"Wow, Kylie, this place is… amazing." Olivia chuckled, a little nervous, still very much in awe of her friend's home. "I don't know what else to call it. It's like something from a magazine."

Kylie grinned. "Yeah, it's clutch, right? I mean, you wouldn't think something so old could be so comfortable or classy. Anyway, Flora's lived here for a few years now—Stephen bought it for her after his first year with the Warriors. She's really proud of it. She's had a lot of restoration stuff done and she hired someone to research the history of the place, all the way back to like, the 1800s."

"Oh, really," Jack said, his eyes lighting with interest. He was a bit of a history buff himself and that sounded interesting.

The girl gave Jack a warm smile. "She'll probably tell you all about it if you give her a chance, sir."

"Oh, call me 'Jack,' please. A pretty young thing like you calling me 'sir' makes me feel like I'm back on the force."

"Daddy was a police officer," Olivia offered.

"Oh, cool," Kylie said, smiling and offering her hand to Jack. "It's nice to meet you, Jack." The old man took the young girl's hand, shaking gently.

Kylie said, "Let me take your coats," and once Olivia and Jack shed them, placed them on hangers in a nearby closet. Returning, she took the opportunity to give Olivia a brief hug, then and smiled. "Love the Taylor Swift shirt, by the way. You look perfectly comfy." Kylie herself was in a plain white t-shirt and soft, patterned flannel pants.

"Oh, I wondered actually..." Olivia said. "You know, the house being so fancy."

Kylie rolled her eyes theatrically. "This is game night, not a black-tie gala. What do you think we are—some kind of snobs?" She smiled to let her friend know she was joking.

Jack, still looking around, taking the surroundings in, said, "You know, I've been in some pretty nice places, but this one's got character. Real charm."

"Grandma can give you a tour later," Kylie told him. "C'mon! Let's go find her."

Just then, Flora appeared in the hallway, saving them the effort. "Is that them, Kylie?"

Her face lit up as she saw her guests and she rushed forward to greet them. "Olivia!" She took both of the younger woman's hands, squeezed and smiled warmly before turning to the man. "And you must be Jack. I'm Flora Deming, and you've met my granddaughter, Kylie." She nodded towards her granddaughter. "I'm so glad you could both make it. Come in, come in—make yourselves at home. Can I get you something to drink? Tea, coffee, a little wine?"

As they exchanged greetings, Olivia felt her nerves slowly easing, watching Flora warmly embrace her dad and pat him on the back, treating him like an old friend. The invitation was fun and unexpected, and she was eager to accept. Beacon Hill wasn't that far from Brookline on the map, but seeing how her friends lived made her realize there was a gap between them, and she was so nervous just to ring the bell.

She should have known better. Even if she'd only met these ladies less than a week earlier, she knew Kylie wasn't a snob—as she jokingly asked before—and Flora's warm, welcoming energy made her feel like family almost from the moment they met. Of course they'd welcome her to their home and of course, they'd treat Jack just as well as they did her.

"You can hang your shoes on the rack to dry," Flora said. "And then follow me."

A moment later, she was ushering them into a cozy sitting room, brightly lit and gaily decorated. There was a Christmas tree here too, a much larger one, and Olivia was amused to see a sprig of mistletoe hanging above the doorway. Flora stood to one side of the door, urging Kylie and Olivia into the room, where a low coffee table was set up with board games, a deck of cards, and some snacks. As Jack, bringing up the rear, stepped through the doorway, Flora placed a hand on his arm, giving him pause, then leaned up and kissed the big man on the cheek, making the old gray teddy bear flush pink.

"Tradition, don't you know," Flora told him with a wink. Kylie giggled and Olivia smiled to see her father's fluster.

Olivia settled onto the couch, a sense of gratitude replacing her worry. Was it really only a few days since she experienced the worst night of her life? A night that turned out not to be the worst at all but something wonderful instead. She knew even then that it was a start. She looked around the room, taking in the warm decor, and the sparkle of holiday lights.

"What d'you wanna play?" Kylie asked. "We got, like, a hundred and sixty-seven boardgames here, cards—there's even ping-pong in the basement." She turned to her friend. "You're the guest, you pick."

"Livvy plays a mean game of Scrabble," Jack told her.

"Oooh, an intellectual, huh?" Kylie grinned and rocked to the side, bumping into Olivia playfully.

Flora clapped her hands. "Perfect then. Scrabble it is."

"Sure, Scrabble's great," Olivia said, thinking it wasn't quite perfect. In her invitation, Kylie had only mentioned herself and Flora, but wasn't someone was missing?

"Is Stephen home tonight?" she asked.

"I'm right here," he said from the doorway.

As a body, everyone in the room turned. Stephen stood in the entryway of the living room. Backlit by the soft glow from the decorative lights in the foyer, he looked tall and slimly muscular, even wearing a ridiculously ugly sweater. The sweater was red, with a Christmas-lights-of-many-colors design winding around the body and sleeves, and reading SANTA'S LITTLE HO across the chest. It was so ugly and so ridiculous on such a gorgeous guy that Olivia started laughing. Suddenly, she didn't feel bad about her old jeans or Tay-tay shirt.

"What?" Stephen asked, entering the room. "You like my new sweater?" He gave the room at large a small smile. "An early gift from my sister."

Kylie giggled. "Oh, gawd. It's too perfect."

Now it is, Olivia thought, still smiling. Even if Stephen wasn't home, and the night was just the four of them—her, Jack, Kylie, and Flora—it would have been fun, but this was even better. Until she heard his voice, she hadn't admitted to herself how much she hoped he would join them.

Stephen settled into a chair situated kitty-corner to the end of the sofa where Olivia sat. "What're we playing?"

Flora told him, "Olivia chose Scrabble," and lifted the box from the middle of the pile of games on the table.

"Great. The one game where the dumb jock's at the biggest disadvantage." He chuckled and added, "Well, let's get the slaughter over with."

Soon, the Scrabble board was spread out on the coffee table, tiles scattered around as each player hunched over their racks, deep in concentration. Olivia, her eyes narrowed and lips pursed, played like a general moving her army into enemy territory. Flora and Kylie had a similar playstyle that seemed wild and carefree but, Jack thought, somehow managed a suspicious number of high-scoring words. Stephen mainly contented himself to modifying other players' words, deciding he had no chance of winning and happy to just go with the flow.

An hour later, the game ended: Olivia in first place, with a score of 413; Kylie and Flora somehow tied with 240; Jack with 220 and Stephen with 98.

"Ninety-eight?" Kylie giggled, trying not to snort at her brother. "How did you even manage that?"

"Oh, shush," Flora told her. "Don't tease your brother."

"Yeah," Jack added. "That sweater is humiliation enough." He grinned at the younger man. Olivia was glad to see her dad feeling comfortable, getting into the swing of things. It really did feel like a family atmosphere now.

Stephen stood, stretched. "Take five, huh?"

"Good idea," Jack said, climbing to his feet. "Where's, uh, the little boy's room?"

"My, that *is* a good idea," Flora said, standing as well. "Let's all take a little break. Come along, Jack. I'll give you the nickel tour on the way." Careful not to be obvious about it, she gave Kylie a signal and the girl, taking the hint, disappeared through a side door, leaving Olivia and Stephen alone.

There was a moment of silence. Olivia was painfully aware that she and Stephen had never been alone before. "Your house is so beautiful," she said, for lack of any other conversation topic.

"Well, it's Flora's," Stephen responded, scratching at the stubble on his neck. "I just paid for it." He realized that was a stupid thing to say as soon as the words left his mouth. "I mean—"

"No, it's okay. I get it," Olivia said. "I wish I could do something like that for my dad. Maybe someday. It's really sweet of you, the way you look after Flora and Kylie."

Stephen sat on the arm of the chair, towering over Olivia. She realized again just how tall he was, and she imagined his muscles beneath that hideous sweater—would she *ever* be rid of the image of Stephen as she first saw him, in his shorts on the side of a bus? *Not likely*, the intrusive little voice in the back of her head laughed. She honestly didn't mind that much.

"I want the best for them. They're the only family I have," he told her.

"Oh," Olivia answered. "I didn't realize… that's like me and Daddy—I mean, my dad. We've always been close, but after Mom died, it's just been us."

"Yeah?"

"Well," Olivia began. "I have a couple aunts—one lives in New York, and the other one's out in California. I haven't seen either of them or any of my cousins in years though. How about you?"

"Uh uh," Stephen shook his head. "Just the three of us. Mom and dad passed away in an accident when I was seven. Kylie was still in diapers." He smiled. "Don't tell her I mentioned that. She's one of those girls who likes to pretend she doesn't even pee."

Olivia laughed. "I won't."

"Anyway," Stephen continued. "Grandma Flora raised the two of us. I barely remember my folks, so she and Kylie are it."

"No aunts, uncles, cousins?" Olivia wondered.

"Uh uh. Just the three of us."

"Oh."

The conversation stalled. Sad as it was, Olivia liked learning more about Stephen. Frantically, her brain tried to come up with a new topic, something to keep this fragile new thing between them going before the others returned.

"I like your hat," Stephen said, saving her the effort.

"Oh!" She clapped her hands to her head. She'd forgotten about it when Kylie took her coat, and the younger girl hadn't mentioned it. She slipped the hat, pink with a white trim and a white snowflake design, from her head, holding it in both hands. "Thanks. I crocheted it myself. It was my first try, but it came out pretty all right."

"Looks good." Stephen held out his hand and silently, without hesitation, she handed him the hat. He examined it briefly before handing it back. "Honestly, I'd never be able to tell you didn't buy it. You're into that sort of stuff? Like, crafts, I guess you'd call it?"

"Oh! Yeah, I am," Olivia agreed. "I do some cross-stitching, and a little bit of knitting. I made a quilt once." She realized she was starting to ramble and forced herself to stop.

Stephen smiled. "Nice. Outside of the rink, I'm useless with my hands." He held them up before him—they were big, powerful-looking. Olivia wondered if they were rough or smooth, what they might feel like against her skin. She felt herself beginning to flush.

"Getting a little warm in here," Stephen said, standing again.

Had he noticed her blushing? *Oh God*, Olivia

mentally wailed.

"I'm gonna get some drinks," Stephen said, heading towards the hall.

"Oh!" Olivia said again, popping to her feet. "Let me help you—I always feel a little guilty being a guest." She laughed nervously, hurrying to catch Stephen and almost bumped into him as he abruptly stopped in the doorway. She stopped short to avoid a collision and was about to lose her balance but—

"Whoops," Stephen said, bracing her with hands on her shoulders, keeping her from tilting over sideways. "Careful now, the floors can be slippery in just your socks."

Those hands—so big, so powerful—were holding her so gently. Her heart fluttered and then began to race. Stephen's hands were actually on her body, touching her. Her face felt very hot and then before either of them realized what was happening, she kissed him—just once, but right on the lips.

Surprised, Stephen pulled back, releasing her. Olivia was instantly mortified. "I'm sorry, I just—I don't know what came over me. I—"

Myriad thoughts rushed through Stephen's mind—his situation with Liza, the loss against the Stallions, how pretty Olivia looked in the glow from the Christmas lights strung around the living room's doorframe.

He made a decision.

"It's tradition," Stephen said, lifting finger towards the mistletoe hanging just over his head. Slowly, a smile spread across his face. "Nobody can stand in the way of tradition." He leaned in and kissed her, and this time, with his full cooperation, it was soft and warm and delicious. Heat swirled throughout Olivia's body and she felt her knees getting weak.

As Stephen ended the kiss, he gave her a different kind of smile and said, "See? Tradition."

"Tradition," Olivia agreed, slightly breathlessly.

Chapter 17.

For a moment that lasted an eternity, Olivia stayed close to Stephen, relishing his nearness, his heat. The faint, warm scent of him wrapped around her, intoxicating her as much as the kiss. It was clean but rugged, with an earthy depth and a trace of something spicy. It wasn't overpowering or artificial; rather, it was understated and uniquely *him*. The scent seemed to suit his personality—strong, steady, quietly confident, with just a hint of something softer beneath the surface. Her pulse raced, and she couldn't help but be drawn closer, her senses lingering in the comfort and warmth of his presence. This was a moment she would remember for the rest of her life.

Flora's cheerful voice echoed through the house. "Round two, anyone?" she called, clearly in high spirits.

Olivia and Stephen jolted out of their shared moment, their heads snapping toward the far doorway on the opposite side of the living room. Jack, Flora, and Kylie had disappeared into the depths of the house only a few minutes ago, but to Olivia it seemed like a lifetime's worth of change had been crammed into the time they were gone. Now faint sounds of footsteps grew louder, signaling the others' return and panic sparked in both of them.

Stephen and Olivia pulled apart hastily, their cheeks flushed, their gazes darting everywhere and anywhere except at each other. Olivia realized she was still holding her hat, and quickly placed it on her head, adjusting the fit, using the action to cover her embarrassment. Stephen shoved his hands into his pockets, and moved back into the living room, returning to his chair. The drinks he had gotten up to retrieve were forgotten and he was suddenly very interested in the Scrabble board still sitting on the table.

When Flora, Kylie, and Jack entered the room, none of them seemed to notice anything out of the ordinary—at first. Flora threw Olivia a quick wink and the younger woman realized Flora's loudly announced return was for her and Stephen's benefit—she may not have known exactly what happened, but she obviously suspected *something*. Despite her embarrassment, and the new shyness she felt towards Stephen after that kiss, she smiled, thinking how amazing Flora was.

"You okay, Livvy?" Jack asked, looking from his daughter towards Stephen with a raised eyebrow.

Oh, my God, Olivia thought, resisting the urge to glance at Stephen. *Does he know?* Her father was a trained observer after all…

"You look like you've seen a ghost," he teased. "What'd we miss?"

"Nothing!" Olivia said too quickly, her voice high-pitched as she lost the battle with herself and shot Stephen a nervous glance.

"Just, uh, waiting for you guys," Stephen added. "Talking, you know."

Grandma Flora clapped her hands, saying, "Well, then!" and plopped down in her armchair with her characteristic energy, changing the topic in a less than subtle way. "Ready for another game?" She looked at Olivia. "Do you have time before you have to go to work, dear?"

Kylie looked towards Olivia for her answer and then she suddenly smiled. Maybe something on Olivia's face gave up her and Stephen's secret, or maybe the girl had whatever romantic sixth sense Flora possessed.

"Oh, yeah," Olivia said, slipping her phone from her pocket to check the time. It was only a little after nine. "I have about an hour or so."

Flora clapped her hands again. "Wonderful! Kylie, dear—will you set up the board again?" She looked at the faces gathered around the coffee table and asked, "Unless you'd all like to play something else?"

Kylie smirked. "Now that the gang's all here, maybe let's get serious?" She pulled a deck of cards from the pile of games on the floor to one side of the coffee table. "Olivia beat us all at Scrabble, but how are you at Go Fish?"

Olivia laughed, the tension broken, and within a few moments, the game was on. As the group played though, Olivia and Stephen carefully avoided each other's gazes. Her mind was racing with the unexpected intensity of the moment they shared beneath the mistletoe. She wondered exactly what was in his thoughts. She wished she could ask him—it almost hurt not being able to.

At the same time, she wasn't sure if she wanted to know the answer. She couldn't deny now that she liked Stephen and as long as she didn't know exactly how he felt, she could at least allow herself the hope that he returned her feelings. It *was* always possible that he was just trying to keep her from feeling too embarrassed by pretending it was all the mistletoe's fault.

Olivia, her hands fidgeting with the hem of her t-shirt, wondered how this sudden shift might change things between them. She'd come to Flora's tonight expecting nothing more than a cozy evening with friends, yet here she was, her lips still tingling from a kiss that was far too perfect to just be Stephen going with the flow. Yes, she'd kissed him first—it was probably, no *definitely*, the most impulsive thing she'd ever done in her entire life. It was the perfect moment, though. The two of them alone in a cozy room, standing beneath the mistletoe, Stephen backlit by the soft glow of the Christmas lights in the hallway. How could she resist? Even now, just thinking about it made her feel both weak and deliciously excited.

Kylie shouted, "Go fish, Jack!" strangely

triumphantly and while all eyes were on his sister, Stephen stole a glance at Olivia. Was she still blushing a little? Or was that his imagination? She usually seemed a little shy around him, but now he felt pretty sure he knew why, and he couldn't deny that he was at least starting to feel the same way about her. That realization somehow made her shyness more endearing. It was cute. He smiled; it coincided with some comment Flora made. He missed the comment, but Jack and Kylie were smiling, so it didn't seem weird, like he was grinning to himself for no reason. But the real reason he was smiling was the memory of that kiss. He couldn't believe how natural it felt to kiss Olivia, like it something that had been waiting to happen all along—maybe something fated. He had never believed in that fate and destiny stuff, but something about the moment they shared definitely seemed magical and he was certain she felt the same way.

A little after ten, Olivia shrugged into her coat as Jack adjusted his scarf, readying to head back out into the mid-December night. The Go Fish game ended with Kylie the winner—she had a weird talent for it like no one Olivia had ever seen, and the younger girl was still glowing with victory. Olivia was glad she and Jack came; it had been a long time since she'd had so much fun or spent an evening in this kind of family environment. She was grateful and told Flora so.

Flora clasped Olivia's hands in hers with a warm smile. "And *we're* grateful you came, Olivia dear. You're not just my hero, you're my friend."

"Hell, yeah!" Kylie chimed in. Olivia almost expected Flora to scold the younger girl, but instead she simply ignored Kylie.

Flora and Jack shook hands. Olivia's father smiled broadly and said, "It was great meeting you, Flora. And you kids, too." He waved to Stephen, lingering a short distance back in the foyer. "I'll probably see you on TV before I see you again, kiddo, so good luck on the ice, huh?"

"Oh, for heaven's sake!" Flora said suddenly, taking Jack by the arm. "Before you head out, I completely forgot to ask earlier—what are your plans for Christmas?"

Olivia and Jack exchanged a look, both hesitating for a moment before Olivia replied, "Oh, nothing big. Just a quiet day at Dad's place, I guess. You know, keeping it simple since it's just the two of us."

"Nonsense!" Flora declared, waving a hand dismissively. "You can't spend Christmas by yourselves. We have *plenty* of room, as you can see, and the more, the merrier! You *must* come over."

Jack held up his hands in protest, shaking his big, gray head. "No, no, Flora. That's kind, but I wouldn't want to impose. It's your family's day, and I'm sure you've got your traditions. We're fine, really. It's not our first Christmas without—"

Without Mom, Olivia thought as Jack cut himself short. She wondered why he almost let that slip. Jack wasn't exactly a closed-off person, but he also wasn't the kind of guy to suddenly start talking about emotional topics with people he'd just met.

"Jack Murray," Flora said, tiny fists on her skinny hips. "Imposing is what you do when you show up unexpectedly with a suitcase. This is me *inviting you*. I told you before: Olivia saved my life and that makes her important to me. You're important to her, so *you're* part of the family now, too—don't argue with me about it," she added firmly, giving him a don't-mess-with-Grandma look that Olivia suspected she'd used successfully for many years.

Kylie broke out laughing. "She's impossible when she gets like that, so it's best to just do what she tells you. But seriously. It would just be the three of us otherwise, so it'll be great to have you. If you wanna do your own thing, why not do Christmas morning then come over in the afternoon? We can have dinner and play games. I might even let you win once or twice—you know, my gift to you," she added with a smirk.

Jack hesitated, glancing at Olivia. She gave him a small shrug and a smile, silently agreeing. He sighed, clearly outnumbered, and nodded. "All right, all right. Far it be from me to argue with a lady this kind and gracious. I know when I'm beat." He smiled. "We'll come by in the afternoon, okay? But no fussing over us, Flora. Promise me that, at least."

"Oh, Jack, the fussing is half the fun," Flora said, patting his arm with a triumphant grin. "We'll have turkey and ham and green bean casserole and sweet potatoes and all the other trimmings. Stephen took us out for Thanksgiving this year, so I've got the itch to go hog wild in the kitchen. And my word! You'll think you've died and gone to heaven when you try my apple pie."

Olivia smiled, feeling warmth spread through her chest at the thought of spending Christmas surrounded by such a lively, welcoming group. And even though there was nothing official between her and Stephen—maybe nothing would ever even happen, she realized—she couldn't help being excited, thinking of how it would be their first Christmas together.

"Thanks, Flora," she said, genuinely grateful to this tiny, big-hearted woman who'd done so much for her in such a short time. "We'll see you then."

As Olivia and Jack stepped out into the chilly night air, Jack tucked his hands into his coat pockets, shaking his head. He gave a small laugh. "She doesn't take no for an answer, does she?"

"Not a chance," Olivia replied, grinning. "But don't you think it'll be nice? It's been a while since we had Christmas with so much company—well, I guess we'll be the company." She laughed once, lightly.

Jack gave her a sideways glance, his expression softening into a smile. "Yeah, kiddo. It'll be good."

"I really like them, Daddy. I'm so glad I met them all."

Jack patted her arm gently, feeling something welling up in his own heart that he hadn't realized he'd been missing these last few years. He loved his daughter so much, but he hadn't realized how empty things must have been for her. There was Stan, but the guy was a bum—a nogoodnik from the get-go—and he'd seen what being with him had done to Olivia, even if she hadn't. With him gone not even a week, she was opening back up, once again becoming the girl he'd always known: bright and cheerful and warm. He owed Flora Deming for a lot more than a game night and Christmas invitation.

"I know you do, honey. Me, too," Jack admitted.

With that, they made their way to the car, both feeling the warmth of Flora's invitation lingering even as the cold settled in around them.

Chapter 18.

"Here we go again," Olivia thought as she walked into the 911 dispatch center. "Full moon, round two."

Thirty minutes earlier, as Jack pulled the car into the parking lot of Olivia's building, he turned down the heat and glanced at her, half-illuminated by the glow from the car's dashboard. "So," he began, "Flora mentioned what you did for her that night at the restaurant."

Olivia, mid-reach for her bag, paused and gave him a sidelong look. "What about it? That's how all of us met," she said, trying to sound nonchalant.

Jack scoffed softly, shaking his head. He wanted to keep this casual, as if this was something he just thought of off the top of his head, but in truth, it bothered him a little. He almost didn't mention it, since Olivia hadn't, but it was a major event as far as he was concerned—preserving a life. It was something he took very seriously.

"You saved her from choking, Liv. That's not just 'what about it.' That's a big deal. She's alive today because of what you did. That's i*mportant* and Flora and those kids of hers obviously feel the same. I guess…" He faltered. "I guess I'm just wondering why you didn't tell me. It feels like something that should be shared."

Olivia shrugged, pulling her coat tighter around her. She really wasn't sure herself. Maybe it was because she didn't want anyone else treating her like something special. Or maybe it was because if she explained that, she would have had to explain about Stephen too, before she knew how she felt exactly. Was that it? She wasn't sure. It didn't seem quite right…

"I don't know, Daddy. Honestly, I don't. It didn't seem like a big thing. I just did what anyone would do."

"Seems like one to me," Jack said, his tone serious. "And to Flora, too. She told me you're part of the family now, remember? She was practically glowing when she said it."

Olivia felt a smile tug at her lips, but she tried to hide it, looking out the window instead. "It was sweet of her."

"I just wish you'd told me. I'm proud of you, you know," Jack said.

"Thanks, Daddy…"

Olivia couldn't see it, but Jack now wore a sly grin that would have reminded her of Flora, or even Kylie, when they were up to something. "So, anyway… that's the guy, huh?"

Her head snapped towards him, her cheeks heating up. "What guy?"

Jack chuckled knowingly, shifting in his seat, turning to more fully face his daughter. "You know who I mean. Stephen. The hockey player. Seems like a nice fellow."

Olivia hesitated, then let out a small, soft sigh, knowing there was no point in pretending. "Yeah," she admitted. "He's the guy."

Jack nodded thoughtfully, one hand resting on the steering wheel, the other on the center console. He wanted to say more—something encouraging, or maybe even protective—but he caught the way Olivia's gaze flickered, and he knew her well enough to know that she was becoming guarded. She wasn't ready to talk about it, not fully. He decided to let it go. No use in pushing if she wasn't ready; she'd only pull away. Just knowing who his daughter was interested, and having met Stephen for himself, was enough for now. Stan had given Jack a bad feeling right from the start, even when he was still on his best behavior. His cop's instincts gave him no such warning about Stephen Sloan.

"Well, he does seem like a decent guy," Jack said after a moment, keeping his tone light. "Just make sure he treats you right, okay?"

"We aren't dating or anything, Daddy. He's just a friend," Olivia replied, her voice steady.

She knew Jack was thinking of Stan. That was only natural—he'd never liked Stan and that relationship was barely over. Olivia was thinking about him too, if she was honest, and realizing just how wrong he'd been for her. It took distance for her realize that, but at least she got out relatively unscathed.

"But I'll be careful, Daddy. Promise."

As Olivia reached for the door handle, Jack's thoughts drifted to how she and Stephen had looked when they'd returned to the living room after Flora's house tour. Something had been… different. Not entirely subtle, but not obvious for either a dad or a cop to tell what that difference was. Maybe it was the way they'd avoided each other's gazes, or how Olivia had seemed unusually quiet while Stephen had busied himself shuffling cards in between rounds of Go Fish.

Jack exhaled quietly, resolving to keep an eye on things but to let his daughter figure it out on her own. She was an adult, after all, as Olivia kept reminding him. She'd have kids of her own one day and hopefully finally understand how he felt, regardless of how old she got.

"All right, kiddo," he said as she got out of the car. "Good luck with your shift tonight."

"Thanks for the ride, Daddy," Olivia said, smiling as she leaned down to look back in the window. "I'll see you later."

Olivia had then gone into her apartment, taken a five-minute shower to refresh herself and changed into a button-up blouse and slacks before climbing back into her coat and heading out the door for work. Now, she hummed softly to herself as she put away her coat and hat in the locker area—she wondered for an instant if it resembled the locker rooms Stephen spent so much of his life in--and went out onto the call floor. As she was settling herself into her workstation, Deann appeared, shrugging out of her coat, in a hurry to log into her own workstation so she would be on time for the start of their shift. The daytime supervisor wasn't overly picky, but the nighttime supe insisted that you weren't on time unless you were at your desk and *working* when the clock struck eleven.

"Hi, babe," Dee said, turning towards Olivia for an instant before flopping into her chair. She clicked on her computer monitor and moved to adjust her keyboard when suddenly she stopped, abandoning her work preparations, and looked back at Olivia, a big smile on her face. "Something nice happened, huh?"

Olivia paused mid-motion, her hand hovering over her headset. How could Dee know? Was she that transparent? She felt her cheeks heat up and knew that yes, to Deann, she must have been as transparent as glass. They'd worked together for so long, the older woman seemed to know her in and out

"What? No, nothing happened… I mean…" Olivia stammered, her voice faltering as she tried to come up with a reasonable explanation for her good mood without having to actually go into details. Like with Jack, she wasn't quite ready to talk to anyone about what happened and how she felt about Stephen.

Deann's grin widened, those sharp eyes of hers now sparkling with curiosity. She wheeled her chair closer to Olivia's desk, leaned on the edge of it, abandoning any pretense of getting logged into her own workstation on time. "Oh, come on, Liv. I've known you long enough to recognize that look. I used to see a lot, but not lately. Something nice *definitely* happened. Spill."

"You're gonna be late," Olivia warned her.

"Poop to that!" Dee waved a hand. "Who cares? I need deets, babe."

Olivia sighed, realizing there was no way out of this. Dee would pester her the entire shift if she didn't give in. She bit her lip, glancing around to make sure the room wasn't already buzzing with other dispatchers before leaning slightly closer. The room was about half-filled, but the workstations closest to hers and Dee's were still empty.

"Okay, fine. You win. Maybe something nice *did* happen," she admitted in a low voice, unable to keep the small, shy smile from sneaking onto her face.

Deann straightened, her grin practically splitting her face. "I *knew* it! Was it the guy? What's his name—Stan? No, wait, you said you were done with him." She tilted her head, squinting at Olivia. "It's someone new, isn't it? It's gotta be!" She leaned in closer. "Wee-llll?"

"Maybe," Olivia admitted, feeling the blush rise to her cheeks again. She fiddled with a pen on her desk, unable to meet Dee's gaze. "It's just… it's complicated. There's a guy I met recently that I like, but nothing's even really happened yet."

"Oh, 'nothing' never makes you smile like that," Dee teased, sitting back in her chair and crossing her arms. "Come on, give me *something*. Who is he?"

Olivia hesitated for a moment before deciding it couldn't hurt to share just a little. "His name's Stephen. Stephen Sloan."

Deann's eyes widened slightly, and then she let out a low whistle. "Wait, the hockey player? Didn't you go to a hockey game the other night?"

"Yeah," Olivia replied softly, brushing a strand of hair behind her ear. "He got me the tickets—I went with his sister and his grandma. We've gotten to be friends. And Stephen, well, we've only seen each other a few times, and it's not like we've actually talked about any of this, but… I don't know. He's just… different. I like him a lot." She grinned, unable to help it. It felt so good to say it out loud, to admit openly that she liked Stephen. She wished she could tell him directly, but baby steps.

Dee smiled knowingly. "Different as in 'I can't stop thinking about him' different? Or different as in 'we kissed under the mistletoe, and I haven't stopped blushing since' different?"

Olivia's eyes widened, and her silence betrayed her. Dee gasped, clapping her hands together and making a sound of delight. "Oh my God, you *did* kiss him, didn't you? Under mistletoe! That's so classic." She looked around. "Where are the cameras? This is a Hallmark movie, right?"

"Dee, keep your voice down!" Olivia cried, her eyes darting around to make sure no one was eavesdropping.

Dee waved her off, laughing softly. "Fine, fine. I'm sorry. I'll stop embarrassing you. I couldn't help it." She took Olivia's shoulder and shook the younger woman lightly. "But seriously, Liv, I'm happy for you. It's nice to see you smiling like this."

Olivia smiled despite herself, her thoughts briefly wandering back to Stephen and the warmth of that moment they'd shared. It kind of was like a Hallmark movie, wasn't it? Not even Dee knew this, but she secretly devoured those movies around this time of year. Sure, they were a little corny, but they were sweet and warm, and they made her feel good. Imagining herself as the star of one was sort of nice. Instantly, she saw herself and Stephen kissing beneath the mistletoe as it would appear on a TV screen, the camera zooming in close then maybe whirling around them to give the viewer an idea of how she felt, finally kissing the man she liked—might even fall in love with. Her cheeks started to heat up again.

"Thanks," she said. "But don't get too excited, okay? It's… still new. Really new."

Dee grinned. "New is the best part. Enjoy it, girl."

Finally, Dee went back to her workstation, leaving Olivia alone to shake her head with a quiet laugh and smile. More dispatchers were showing up and the familiar buzz of the center rose higher and then settled around her. Olivia put on her headset, feeling light and happy. Maybe Dee was right. Maybe "new" was something worth savoring. Who wanted to rush things when she already felt this good?

Chapter 19.

Stephen sat hunched over the small desk in Flora's guestroom, his fingers awkwardly tapping at the keys of his laptop. It wasn't a graceful process—he pecked away with two fingers, his brows furrowed as he squinted at the screen. Technology had never been his strong suit—he'd actually written his school papers longhand and paid or did favors for other kids to type them for him he disliked it so much—and every time he mistyped a word or clicked the wrong link, he let out a soft grunt of frustration. Still, he persisted—this was something he had to do, and he wanted to make sure it was done right. He felt he couldn't do that on a smartphone, no matter how handy it might be.

The room around him bore the signs of someone comfortably settled. His neatly folded clothes were stacked on a small chest of drawers. The bed, though made, had a casual lived-in feel, as if it had been his for years rather than weeks. A stray water bottle sat on the nightstand, along with his phone, its screen lighting up occasionally with notifications he ignored. There was a pair of well-worn sneakers by the door, and a hockey stick leaned against the wall beside his workout bag. It wasn't a stick he had played with in many years—in fact, it was a kids' stick, but Flora had kept it for sentimental purposes and when he began staying with her had slipped into his room one day while he was out. He half-suspected it was as much for her nostalgia's sake as his own.

Living here at Flora's house had been a strange adjustment at first—going from his sleek, modern penthouse to this Victorian guestroom felt like stepping into another era. But now, two months in, it felt like home. It reminded him of the smaller, simpler—and let's be honest, crummier—house Flora had owned when he was growing up. But Flora had always done her best to make that house a home for him and Kylie and the bedroom he had in that house, while a lot smaller, wasn't really that different when you got down to it. Both contained the rhythms of family life that he'd been sorely missing.

That sense of stability, of belonging, was something he hadn't realized he *had* been missing until he found it again. The chaos of his split with Liza, the tension of living in a place that had, despite his ownership, felt more hers than his, had left him adrift. But Flora's house—the warm meals, the laughter, the togetherness, even the quiet solitary moments like this—gave him an anchor and kept him steady when he might have drifted away and gotten lost on his own.

Stephen leaned back in the chair, stretching his arms overhead. His gaze wandered to the framed photo on the wall—a much younger Flora with her late husband, his Grandpa Joe, smiling warmly at the camera. Joe passed before Kylie was even born and Stephen barely remembered him, but looking at those smiling faces, it struck him how much Flora had always been the heart of their family, even when his parents were still alive. He knew how lucky he was to have her now, offering him a home when he was at his lowest.

Letting his memories wander, he thought back to earlier in the evening, the sound of Olivia's laugh as they joked around, played Scrabble, the way her face had lit up when she scored with a big word. And then the kiss under the mistletoe. It was unexpected but… perfect. A smile tugged at the corners of his lips as he stared at his screen, his focus on finding the perfect gift for lost for the moment.

Stephen let out a contented sigh, then stood and

stretched, pacing the room as he thought. Tonight had been great—more than that, even. Wonderful. Amazing? He thought of Olivia again, how pretty she looked smiling up at him, her face softly lit by the glow of the Christmas lights in the foyer. He remembered how warm and yielding her lips were and how the faint taste of her lip-gloss lingered on his own lips afterwards. He smiled and finally admitted to himself how attracted he was to her.

Olivia was so different than Liza—not just physically.

Liza was petite, about five-foot-one and maybe 110lbs, blonde and lushly curved. She looked like a pin-up girl from another generation, the ideal beauty as far as a lot of guys were concerned. She was a gorgeous, sexy as hell woman, that was true. But Liza the person…

Stephen shook his head. What the hell had happened there? He spent a lot of time the last few weeks thinking about it. Liza blamed his career, his being on the road so often, for her cheating.

"Cheating…" Stephen said out loud, then barked a bitter laugh, remembering the out and out orgy Liza was hosting in his penthouse. *His* penthouse, and she dared—

He caught himself. Getting angry wouldn't serve any purpose. It was done and that was over. Liza had once been a loving partner, but something changed and not for the better. He didn't realize how bad things had gotten until he had that distance from her, from the situation, and from their relationship, but now he knew. It wasn't that they weren't once good together, it was that they no longer fit. Liza wanted something different than Stephen could give her and that was fine—he wanted something different too.

Is that Olivia? he thought. It was. He knew that now, after that kiss. He smiled again and without realizing what he was doing, touched his lips in remembering.

A sudden cloud darkened his mood. He liked Olivia and he was certain she liked him too—she'd kissed *him* that first time, after all—but did he have any right to get involved with her? With anyone? The situation with Liza wasn't yet resolved. She was still living his penthouse. He'd had no contact with her at all since that afternoon in October. She'd tried calling and texting and even Insta-messaging him dozens of times the first week or so, but he ignored her and eventually blocked her on all social media apps. She apparently got the message because she stopped trying after that. He would have to talk to her soon though, one way or another. He glanced at the calendar hanging on the wall. Less than a week until Christmas, less than two weeks until the deadline he'd given Liza for vacating the penthouse. He wasn't looking forward to that, but it needed to happen, he realized. Until Liza was gone from the penthouse, and he could move back in, they were still connected, their relationship ended but not really severed. He wanted it to be done with once and for all.

Stephen blew out a breath and sat back down at his computer. He wanted to get Olivia the perfect gift and between what Mike B had told him about shopping online for handmade stuff and what he'd seen of Olivia tonight—that hat she made herself and her love of Scrabble—he had a great idea, he just needed to find the right outlet to make it happen. He knew it was out there somewhere; you could find just about anything on the internet, couldn't you? And once he did find it, he certainly had the money to make what he was thinking of happen. There wasn't much time left before Christmas, and he couldn't waste any of it… maybe Kylie would be able to help.

He leapt from his chair and, biting the bullet, went to go ask his sister. She would want to know why he was asking, but seeing that it was Kylie, he suspected she already knew and would just want to hear him say it out loud before agreeing to help.

Stepping out into the townhouse's second-floor hallway, he chuckled to himself, realizing that when it came to his own feelings, somehow he was probably the last one to know…

Chapter 20.

When Olivia finally pulled into Jack's driveway Christmas morning, it was later than she'd intended, the clock already creeping past nine. The days (and graveyard shift nights) had flown by so quickly, she hardly knew where the time went. It was almost difficult to believe it was already Christmas and that the new year was only another week away. This had been such a weird year—really, most of the weirdness was just crammed into the last couple of weeks, which made it seem like a lot more—but not necessarily in a bad way, and she was genuinely looking forward to the future for the first time in a while.

Grabbing the bag with the gift she'd picked for Jack in one hand and the bag of groceries she'd bought the night before with the other, she hurried to the door of Jack's little house, bracing against the chilly air. Before she could knock, Jack opened the door, wearing his favorite worn-out old sweatshirt and a good-natured grin.

"Merry Christmas, kiddo," he said, stepping aside to let her in. "Get lost on the way here?"

Olivia rolled her eyes, smiling as she brushed past him into the warmth of the house. "Merry Christmas, Daddy. Sorry, I overslept. My sleep schedule is always wonky for a few days after graveyard shifts. I guess that and some holiday stress caught up with me."

Jack closed the door behind her, shaking his head, as he took the grocery bag from her and set it on the floor. "You ask me, it's a good thing. I'm sure you needed the rest. You've been pretty busy lately. Don't want you running yourself ragged." He took her coat and hung it in the closet in the entryway. His tone softening, he added, "Glad you got a little extra shuteye." He leaned in and gave her a quick kiss on the cheek.

"Daddy, I'm fine," Olivia told him, setting her gift bag on the small table in the entryway, and picking up the groceries again. "I promise. Being busy isn't so bad, especially this time of year."

"Yeah, yeah," Jack replied, waving her off as he headed for the kitchen. "But worrying about you is my job. So tough luck."

Olivia smiled despite herself, knowing this was just who her father was—and she wouldn't change him for the world. "All right, fine. Be that way. I'll graciously accept your concern, but only because it's Christmas."

"Generous of you," Jack said from the kitchen.

The smell of cinnamon and sugar filled Jack's cozy kitchen as Olivia followed him, still shaking off the morning chill. She stopped mid-step, her eyes widening a little in surprise as she spotted the tray of homemade cinnamon buns cooling on the counter, so fresh that steam still swirled off of the pastries, dancing through the shafts of morning sun spilling through the kitchen windows.

"Daddy?" she asked, her tone laced with disbelief and delight. "Did you… make those?"

Jack, standing at the sink and rinsing off a sticky spatula, turned and gave her a sheepish grin. "Yeah, well… I might've watched a few YouTube videos." He gestured toward the tray with a shrug. "Figured it was about time I started pulling my weight when it comes to these breakfasts of ours."

Olivia stepped closer to inspect his handiwork. "They look pretty good for an amateur." She laughed. "Honestly, I'm impressed."

"Don't get used to it," he warned with a smirk, though the slight blush creeping up his neck betrayed his embarrassment. "I'm not about to become some kind of professional baker."

Olivia grabbed a plate and helped herself to one of the buns, still warm and gooey. "You should be proud of yourself," she said after taking a bite. "These are *so* good. And it's kind of adorable. Maybe I should buy you a cute little apron," she teased.

Jack rolled his eyes but smiled as he joined her at the table, bringing Olivia a cup of coffee. "Well, I figured you're always the one doing the cooking. I wanted to try returning the favor for once."

"I love it," Olivia said, beaming at him. "You're full of surprises today."

After they each ate a bun, Olivia unpacked the grocery bag, putting away some of the things she'd bought away for another day. She never could have expected Jack to make cinnamon buns, but it was a wonderful surprise—kind of a Christmas miracle, really. She mentally laughed. Jack knew his way around a barbeque grill, and he could handle some basic things in the kitchen, but she couldn't remember him ever having baked anything in her life. Her mom, Francine, was the baker. Growing up, not a Sunday morning went by that Olivia didn't wake up to fresh-baked muffins or scones or coffee cake. Thinking about those long-ago mornings, she felt a pang—she missed her mom. She knew Jack did too, though they'd never really talked about it. Maybe the cinnamon buns were partially a way for him to connect with his wife, even if from afar.

Olivia whipped up quick omelets, fried bacon, and then they sat down and ate the rest of their breakfast, including another cinnamon bun apiece. Conversation flowed as easily as it always did between them, though it was flavored more by reminiscence of past Christmases, including some stories from Olivia's childhood she'd forgotten about. Afterward, they tackled the dishes, working side by side—Olivia washed, Jack dried.

"So," Jack said, breaking the comfortable domestic rhythm, "what do you think we're in for this afternoon? Flora kinda worried me when she said that fussing was the 'fun' part."

Olivia chuckled, rinsing a plate before handing it to Jack. "I'm sure she'll do something crazy, but it's Christmas and it is her house after all. We'll be the guests so we just have to go with the flow, right?"

"I suppose," Jack said slowly.

"Oh, whatever it is, just let her enjoy it, Daddy. Besides, it was sweet how excited she was getting just talking about it the other night."

Jack sighed, nodding. "Yeah, I know. It was pretty cute at that. I just don't like being fussed over. But I guess I can survive one afternoon."

Olivia smiled, bumping his shoulder playfully. "You'll be fine and it'll be great. We just met them but it's like… we've known them for years."

"Funny how that works with some people, isn't it?" Jack smiled.

"Yeah," she agreed. "Plus, you've got me there to back you up if it gets overwhelming. I'll just tell everybody you're having a heart-attack or something and rush you right out of there."

Jack smirked. "All right, kiddo. I'll hold you to that. Better brush up on my acting before we get over there."

A few minutes later, the kitchen was clean and they moved into Jack's living room, modestly decorated, mostly with things that were older than Olivia and as familiar to her as anything of her own. Maybe more so, since they'd been around longer. On the faux mantel, Olivia's childhood Christmas stocking hung, making her smile, and small sprigs of holly and pinecones were arranged along its top.

In the corner by the window stood a small artificial Christmas tree, its branches a little sparse but decorated with a mix of old, sentimental ornaments and newer ones Olivia had bought Jack over the last few years. Francine bought a new ornament—or two, or three even—every Christmas season and Olivia had taken over the tradition in her mother's place. Topping the tree was a star, slightly crooked but shining brightly, and a strand of multicolored lights blinked gently, spiraling down the tree from top to bottom, casting a warm, cozy glow.

Beneath the tree, there were a small number of wrapped gifts. Two were things Jack had bought and the others were Olivia's gifts to her father. Jack's were easily identified by their simple paper and neat ribbon, suggesting his practical approach to everything, even Christmas. Olivia's were more ornate, the wrapping paper glittery and festive.

Jack collapsed onto the sagging couch, letting out a sound like he was exhausted. "Livvy, I gotta tell you: after all that good food, I'm not sure I'm up to presents. Maybe a nap is in order."

"Don't go all old man on me yet, Daddy. The day's just starting." Olivia whacked her father's arm playfully then moved to the Christmas tree to retrieve the carefully wrapped packages she'd brought. She brought both—one medium, one smaller—back to the couch and handed them to Jack. "Merry Christmas, Daddy."

Jack's expression softened into a contented smile, remembering an Olivia from twenty years earlier, a plump, redheaded little girl, saying those exact same words.

"Go ahead, open them," Olivia told him.

"Let me savor the moment, okay?" he said, but he was still smiling and began peeling back the paper on the larger of the two packages.

"*Midnight Blues!*" Jack exclaimed, his eyes lighting up. "This is perfect, Livvy. I've been meaning to rewatch this."

"I know. Since about 1990, right?" She smirked. "Well, now you can binge it anytime."

Jack leaned over and gave her a quick hug before shooing her off the couch. "All right, your turn. Go pick a gift."

"What am I? Eight?" Olivia laughed, moving to the tree and picking up both gifts from Jack. He wanted to tell her that he wished she was—at least for a little while—but held his tongue, knowing she wouldn't appreciate it.

The larger gift was weightier than Olivia expected as she carried the packages back to the sofa.

"Go on," Jack told her. She opened the larger package to find a limited-edition Taylor Swift collector's album, complete with glossy artwork, bonus tracks, and an honest to God trading card. Her face lit up in delight as she held it, already imagining where it would go in her collection.

"Oh my God, Dad! I looked for this everywhere over the summer!" she said, her excitement genuine. "Where did you find it?"

"YouTube isn't the only thing on the internet. Open the other one," he added.

Inside the smaller package was an envelope and inside of *that* was a generous gift card to her favorite craft store.

"Now you can stock up on all that yarn and stuff for your projects," Jack said with a grin.

"Dad, this is perfect," Olivia said, her voice soft with gratitude. "Thank you."

They hugged again, sharing a quiet moment of appreciation for one another before Olivia glanced at the clock. "Oh wow, it's already almost noon! We should get moving if we don't want to keep Flora waiting."

"All right," Jack said, lumbering to his feet. "Let's go get fussed over."

Olivia laughed with delight, both because she was pretty sure Jack hit the nail right on the head with that one, and because she couldn't wait to see her new friends—and of course, Stephen.

Chapter 21.

Kylie opened the door almost the instant Olivia hit the doorbell, squealing, "Hiiii! Merry Christmas!" and throwing her arms around Olivia. "Come in! Come in! It's freezing out here!" Kylie said, wrapping her arms around herself and doing a little jig against the cold.

Olivia laughed at her friend's antics as she and Jack stepped into Flora's house, greeted by a wave of warmth and the scent of pine. Flora popped out of the living room and bustled towards them with open arms, her face lighting up with the same enthusiasm that had made them feel like family from the very start.

"Merry Christmas, dears!" she cried, pulling Olivia into a warm hug and then patting Jack's arm fondly. "I'm so glad you could make it!"

"Merry Christmas, Flora," Olivia said, her smile brightening as Flora's festive energy seemed to fill the entirety of the huge foyer. She retrieved the tote bag she'd brought, once again feeling immensely grateful to whatever power led her to meet Flora and her family.

Stephen appeared in the hallway leading deeper into the house, offering the newcomers a relaxed smile as he crossed the space between them. "Hi. Merry Christmas. Here, let me take those for you," he said, holding out his hands for their coats.

"Thanks, Stephen," Olivia said, her heart fluttering and cheeks flushing slightly as their hands briefly brushed.

Before Stephen had even stowed their coats in the closet, Flora was ushering them into the living room.

"Come, come! You have to see how we've transformed the place since you were last here."

"What do you mean?" Olivia asked. "It looked pretty good last time—"

"Pshaw!" Flora said with a wave of the hand. "I'm always redecorating, especially during the holidays. An old lady needs a hobby and I've just got so many ideas all the time I can't help myself."

Jack followed the ladies, his hands tucked in his pockets, but in the doorway to the living room, he stopped short as Olivia gasped softly, her eyes wide with delight.

The living room had been transformed into a Christmas wonderland. Every surface seemed to sparkle; rich garlands draped the mantel and twinkling lights circled the room, high up near the ceiling. Flora's Christmas tree, which had been beautifully decorated on game night, now stood even grander with extra strands of ribbon and shimmering ornaments catching the light from the strings on the walls. Beneath it, a pile of neatly wrapped presents spilled out, each one bearing a ribbon tied with care and precision.

The room smelled heavenly—like fresh pine, spiced cider, and something warm and sweet was baking in the oven, the scent wafting in from the entryway on the opposite side of the room, towards where the dining room and kitchen were. On the coffee table, a platter of cookies and treats had been laid out, along with a pair of elegant crystal bowls filled with candied nuts and chocolates. A fire crackled in the hearth, casting a golden glow over the room and completing the scene.

Jack let out a low whistle, shaking his head with a wry grin. "Well, Flora, I've got to hand it to you. You sure as hell know how to deck the halls."

"Daddy, language," Olivia chided.

Flora beamed, clearly pleased with the reaction. "Oh, I've heard worse in my day, Olivia, dear. Think nothing of it. And you, Jack, you haven't even seen the dining room yet," she added with a wink. "But all in good time. First, come and sit! Make yourselves comfortable."

Olivia stepped further into the room, taking it all in with a delighted laugh. "This is amazing, Flora. It's like a Christmas card come to life."

"Well, if we're going to celebrate, we might as well do it properly," Flora said, waving them toward the couch. "Stephen, dear, bring everyone some cider, will you?"

Anticipating Flora, Stephen appeared from the direction of the kitchen with a tray of steaming mugs. Olivia couldn't help but glance at him with a smile, feeling the warmth of the house—and the moment—settle over her. Flora's over-the-top decorating wasn't just festive; it was a reflection of her love for bringing people together. She realized that now. She'd thought Flora lived for her grandchildren, and that was certainly part of it, but all of a sudden, she knew that Flora wanted everyone—not just her family—to enjoy their lives to the fullest. And it was working; already Olivia felt like this was the perfect way to spend Christmas afternoon. Better than going to the movies like she and Jack had last year.

Kylie breezed into the room with a big grin, carrying a shining-white set of portable speakers in one hand and her phone in the other. "All righty, folks," she announced, setting the speakers down on the side table and quickly connecting her phone. "Everyone's here, so the party can start! I've got the *best* Christmas playlist all picked out. Seriously, I spent like two hours on this, so no complaints allowed—it's the scientifically perfect holiday mix of classics new and old. And yes, Mariah Carey *is* on here. Twice." Her grin widened.

Flora chuckled, settling into her favorite armchair with her mug of cider. "Oh, Kylie, you've always been my little mood-setter."

"Who do you think she gets that from?" Stephen asked.

Ignoring him, Flora continued, "Go ahead, dear,

let's hear it."

With a very Kylie-esque theatrical flourish, the girl hit play, and the room was instantly filled with the cheerful opening notes of *It's the Most Wonderful Time of the Year.* Olivia smiled as she took a seat beside her dad on the couch, her fingers wrapped around her warm mug, absorbing the heat and relishing the feeling. They hadn't been outdoors long, but long enough for her to appreciate a little warming up.

Everyone was comfortably settled, and Flora leaned forward, her eyes twinkling as she turned her attention to Olivia and Jack. "So, tell me, dears," she began, her voice full of curiosity, "how have you been? How's work treating you, Olivia? And Jack, I don't think we discussed it before, but you're retired, yes? Tell me all about how your fill your time."

Jack smirked, leaning back and holding his mug in one hand. "Retirement's just fine, Flora," he replied. "I read, I putter. Livvy got me a set of DVDs of one of my favorite shows. That'll keep me out of trouble for a while." He leaned forward, lowering his voice just a shade though not low enough that the rest of the gathering couldn't hear him. "As for this one," he jerked a thumb towards Olivia. "You know, here it is, Christmas morning, I'm waiting for her on pins and needles—my one and only daughter, the light of my life—she walks in late. Overslept she says. I had to be the one making breakfast this time."

"Daddy!" Olivia protested, laughing. "He was happy I slept in. Tell them! I just gave him time to show off his cinnamon bun skills."

"Cinnamon buns?" Flora repeated, her eyebrows lifting. "Oh, Jack, I love a good cinnamon bun. Smell that?" She sniffed the air. "I load my apple pie up with the stuff. You should have brought your masterpiece over."

"It's no big deal," Jack said. "I just watched some YouTube stuff," he said.

Olivia teased, nudging him gently. "They were

really good."

Flora smiled warmly, her gaze shifting to Olivia. "And how about you, dear? How's the graveyard shift treating you? I hope it's not wearing you out too much."

Olivia took a sip of her cider before answering. "Oh, I'm back on days. We only do graveyard a week a month. But, yeah, it was busy. Nightshift plus full moon?" She laughed. "We had a few wild calls."

"Wild calls, huh?" Stephen chimed in from his spot near the fireplace, his voice curious but light. "Can't just leave it at that, you know."

"Let's just say aliens might have been involved," Olivia told him with a grin, earning a laugh from everyone.

Flora clapped her hands together, her smile widening. "Oh, you must tell us that story later. But first—how was your Christmas morning? Was Santa good to you?" She gave both father and daughter a playful wink.

Olivia chuckled, her cheeks warming. "Santa was great, Flora. Dad—I mean Santa—really knocked it out of the park this year."

Jack gave a modest shrug but couldn't hide his pride. "What can I say? She deserves it."

"Well, it sounds like you two had a wonderful morning," Flora said warmly. "And now we get to make your Christmas even better."

The music swelled into *Rockin' Around the Christmas Tree* as Olivia asked, "Except for dinner, I don't see how you could." She smiled at the older woman. "We really appreciate the invite."

Flora smiled back. "Well now, I know we talked about no gifts, but I see you've got that bag." She nodded towards the canvas tote at Olivia's feet.

Flushing slightly, Olivia said, "Well… I know, but—I mean, you've been so good to us." She looked towards her father for help, but he just smiled and shook his head.

Flora laughed as Kylie sprung around the side of

the couch, holding out a small giftbag to each of them. "Ta-da!" She grinned and added, "We figured you were the kind of girl who'd bring gifts anyway."

Olivia didn't know what to say; she was touched, and both surprised and happy that Kylie and Flora already understood her so well. She threw a glance towards Stephen, who smiled.

"Open them, open them!" Kylie urged.

Inside Olivia's bag was a necklace of two small, silver Scrabble tiles bearing the letters O and M, her initials. "Oh, it's so cute!" She looked up. "Who picked this out?"

Smirking, Kylie pointed towards Stephen, causing Olivia to instantly flush with pleasure and shyness. She wouldn't have expected Stephen to come up with such a perfect gift—she was glad she'd decided to bring gifts. She was so happy she thought she might burst. "Thank you, Stephen," she said, trying to put every ounce of gratitude she had into those three words.

Stephen was glad she was happy with the gift. It wasn't something flashy like he would have given Liza—correction, that Liza would have more or less *told* him to give her—but he had the idea after seeing how much Olivia seemed to enjoy the game last week. Kylie had helped him find the perfect crafter online to make it a reality and a sizeable rush fee got the necklace made and in Stephen's hands in plenty of time for the holiday. The look on Olivia's face was worth it. He hoped he could make her smile even more in the future.

Chapter 22.

Stephen sat on the edge of the bed in the guestroom—less a guestroom at this point than his room in Grandma Flora's house—staring at the open suitcase on the floor. His clothes, neatly folded, were stacked in small piles nearby, ready to be packed. The room that had become his sanctuary for the past two months was slowly being stripped of the signs of his presence. The magazines that had been on the nightstand, his laptop, the battered sneakers by the door—all now tucked away, ready for the next chapter, a chapter he wasn't looking forward to facing. He stood and looked around the room; other than the furniture, the only things that would remain were the pictures on the wall and the hockey stick propped in one corner. That was more Flora's than his really, a reminder for her of his childhood.

He rubbed the back of his neck, trying to ease the tension building there. Two days. That was all the time left before he had to walk back into the penthouse. He hadn't set foot in his own home since he abandoned it, fleeing here, to Flora's, and handing his place over to Liza. Remembering the scene in his apartment, built in his memory until it was now like something of out a Medieval portrayal of Hell, made his stomach churn. He couldn't believe Liza was keeping that side of herself from him and to have the nerve to tell him it didn't mean anything… he clenched his fist bitterly.

For weeks, he'd been able to avoid thinking about what might be waiting for him back home. But now, as January 1st loomed, his mind churned, knowing he couldn't avoid it much longer. When he considered what he might find, he was honestly afraid of the possibilities. Had Liza taken him seriously when he'd told her to leave? She must have—he made himself pretty damned clear. But what if she hadn't? Worse, what if she'd trashed the place out of anger—or let someone else move in? Maybe the apartment had become a nonstop orgy since he left. The idea of strangers occupying his space, defiling his home, made his jaw clench and his stomach faintly ache.

But there was another possibility, one that made his chest tighten in a different way. What if she *had* left? Quietly, without argument, accepting that their relationship was over? Stephen didn't know what he wanted more—for her to be gone, proving she'd finally let go and that he was free to move on with his life, or for her to be there, forcing them to have one last, painful confrontation to end things completely. They were together so long, and for nearly a third of his life, she'd been the most important person in it. The way she betrayed him… was it better for her to simply fade away, to disappear, and leave him to try to forget the bad parts and remember the good? Or did he *need* that confrontation, that chance to battle it out and prove to himself that he was really through with her?

He exhaled sharply, running a hand through his hair. The truth was, if he was being brutally honest with himself, he was afraid of facing Liza again. Not because he doubted his decision—he knew the breakup had been the right move; he could never forgive the vile way she'd betrayed him—but because it meant stepping back into the wreckage of what their relationship had become. He wasn't sure how he'd feel seeing her, or the penthouse they had shared, or all the pieces of their life together that would inevitably still be there.

But regardless of how it worked out, he knew this was a step he had to take. There was no getting around it.

Grandma Flora letting him move into the guestroom had been a blessing—the kindest thing she could have done for him. Being around Flora and Kylie almost every day was the best healing he could have asked for. It was a chance to regain some sense of stability and reconnect with the parts of himself that made him Stephen Sloan. He knew he would miss seeing his family as often, but he couldn't hide forever, no matter how comfortable it was here in Flora's house. He needed a chance to heal, to lick the wounds Liza had inflicted on him, but if he didn't go back and face that situation, it wasn't healing anymore, it really was just hiding. Moving back into his penthouse wasn't only about reclaiming his space and his home; it was about moving forward, about proving to himself that he could rebuild his life on his own terms.

Stephen moved to the other side of the room, reaching for another stack of clothes to pack, and caught his reflection in the mirror over the dresser. For a moment, he stared at himself. He was a muscular, heavily tattooed guy with short, vaguely spiky hair and gray-blue eyes. That was the surface, what anyone would see. He knew himself well enough to also see the uncertainty behind those eyes.

He grunted, squared his shoulders and moved closer to the mirror, looking himself straight in the eye—literally confronting himself. "This is just another game, Sloan," he told his reflection, his voice low and steady. "You're gonna face it, you're gonna play through it, and you—are—going—to—win."

He turned back to his packing, forcing himself to focus on the task at hand. There wasn't much left, and he had already stalled enough, making the job take several times longer than it should have. He picked up the sweater Kylie had given him as an early Christmas present. Ugly as hell, and that slogan: SANTA'S LITTLE HO. He smiled. His sister was such a little weirdo, but he loved that. She kept him on his toes, and she was always able to make him smile.

Shrugging into the sweater—because why not?—

he realized another gift had been beneath it: the hat Olivia had crocheted for him. He took the hat in both hands, feeling the softness. It was just like the hat she made herself, except instead of pink and white, it was royal blue and gold—the Back Bay Warriors' colors—and it said SLOAN across the front. Stephen had no idea how much work might go into making something like this, but the fact that she'd made something for him, and in less than a week between his first seeing her own hat and Christmas… She'd made customized ornaments for Flora and Kylie too.

"Damn, she must have worked her fingers off," he said aloud.

Warmth and gratitude welled up inside of him. Nobody had ever given him something handmade like this—it was easily the most thoughtful gift he'd ever received, for Christmas or birthdays or anything else. He felt the material of the hat again and smiled. Remembering the way Olivia's face lit up when she opened her gift, he was glad he'd gone to the effort and expense of having that necklace made. He was glad that he'd asked for Kylie's help, and glad he'd told her why too. He was sure his sister would tease him when he did, but she just smiled—not her happy-go-lucky smile or her mischievous one. He realized, looking back now, that it was a knowing smile, as if she had a feeling this would happen all along. Well, it was nice being able to tell someone either way.

Gently, he folded the hat and placed it back on the dresser. It was getting colder as the month wore on and the year ran out. No reason not to wear it when he went out.

With a deep sigh, Stephen plunked himself back down on the edge of the bed. There were still two days before the New Year. Two days left with Flora and Kylie. Two days to relax and prepare himself. Two days before he had to fight that battle. He wasn't looking forward to it, but he going to fight it—there was no doubt about that.

Not anymore. Maybe there never was. Maybe he just needed to psych himself up for it. He knew now that whatever waited for him in the penthouse, whatever Liza had done or had left waiting for him, he'd deal with it. That was all there was to it.

And when everything with Liza was over and done with, he'd finally be free to start fresh, get a handle on whatever his life was going to become and decide what to do next—and with whom.

Chapter 23.

The End Zone sports bar buzzed with the sound of conversations, clinking glasses, and a dozen TVs all tuned to different channels, showing games, news or highlights of as many different sports. Olivia, Jenny, and Barb lounged at a small table, unwinding after another long day at the dispatch center. The pitcher of beer in front of them was already half-empty, their glasses filled as they relaxed and chatted about the day's calls. Jenny was officially done with training as of that shift, and it called for a little celebration. Olivia had invited Deann as well, but with the "party" being impromptu, she wasn't able to get someone to pick up her kids from daycare.

"So, did you hear about Kim?" Barb asked, lowering her voice slightly but still loud enough to carry over the bar's background noise. It wasn't likely that anyone in the bar knew their coworker, but she was a discreet gossip, if there is such a thing. "She's taken so much time off lately—like random afternoons or mornings. A friend of mine saw her going into a lawyer's office the other day and then I heard a rumor that she and her husband are splitting up."

Jenny shook her head, her expression sympathetic. "That's awful. I mean, I know she keeps to herself, but still… she must need some kind of support if that's true. Poor thing."

Olivia nodded, though her attention was caught by the TV nearest their table. It had just switched to hockey highlights and the familiar sight of Stephen Sloan filled the screen—his determined face, his jersey, and the way he moved on the ice. The clip showed him scoring a goal at a game in a Midwestern team's home arena, his stick rising and then quickly slashing down and forward, sending the puck rocketing past a helpless goalie and into the opposition's net.

"Oh, look at that," Barb said, her tone brightening as she abruptly changed the subject. "My husband's a huge Warriors fan. That Sloan guy is always on the highlights—Chris wanted one of his jerseys for Christmas a couple years ago. I tried to get him an autographed one, but—" she made a *whoo* noise, "ex-*pen*-sive!"

Jenny squinted at the screen. "I don't know much about hockey, but… yeah, he's got a cute little butt, doesn't he?" She laughed, grinning at the other ladies, making Barb cackle with delight.

Without thinking, the words slipping out in her excitement, Olivia jumped in, telling the girls, "The TV doesn't do him justice—he's so much hotter in person. And he's the sweetest guy. He's kind of shy, even, and it's just so cute." A slightly dopy grin spread across her face.

Barb and Jenny turned to her, their eyes widening, and Olivia realized too late what she'd said. Jenny was the first to recover, her mouth curling into a mischievous grin that reminded Olivia of Kylie. "Wait a second… *you* know Stephen Sloan? Like—" she pointed to the TV, "*that* guy. The one who was just on TV?"

Olivia hesitated, her face flushing as she glanced at the TV and then back at her friends. But there was no taking it back now; she'd have to trust them. *Then again,* she thought. *Why should it be a secret?* It wasn't like Stephen ever said not to brag about knowing him or anything—not that she was usually that kind of person, but the cat was out of the bag now anyway.

Thinking of what Jenny had just said and remembering the times she'd seen that cute little butt in the flesh, she smiled, maybe a little sheepishly. "Yeah… I do." Quickly, she told her friends the story of how she'd met Flora, Kylie, and Stephen and how they'd become friends, leaving out only the parts concerning why she was at Enclave and how she was coming to feel about Stephen.

There didn't seem to be any point though—not when she saw the way Barb's eyes lit up as she leaned across the table, playful energy practically pouring off of her in waves. "And we don't have to guess how you feel about him, do we, sweetie?" she teased, giving Olivia's arm a light slap. "You're over here talking about his sweet personality and how cute his shyness is. Oh, you've *got it bad*."

Olivia laughed, trying to brush off the heat rising to her cheeks. She didn't realize Barb was like this—she was usually pretty reserved in the dispatch center, and they didn't often see one another outside of work. "Okay, okay, fine. Maybe I like him a little," she admitted.

"A *little?*" Jenny teased, raising an eyebrow and grinning like mad. "My girl, you're practically glowing just talking about him. So, spill! You're dating him, aren't you?"

Olivia took a sip of her beer, trying to compose herself. "Oh, no. It's not that. We've just been… spending some time together. Nothing serious," she added quickly, though the look on her face said otherwise.

"*Yet*," Barb chimed in, winking. "Nothing serious *yet*."

Olivia could only laugh, knowing there was no escaping their teasing now. But deep down, she didn't mind. Stephen *was* someone special, and maybe she liked the idea of sharing a little bit of her happiness with her friends.

"Call him," Jenny said suddenly.

"Facetime him!" Barb blurted. "Let's see that sexy jawline up close." She laughed.

"Oh, I couldn't," Olivia protested, embarrassed now. Sharing a story was one thing, but—

"Here," Barb said, reaching across the table to pluck Olivia's phone from where it rested at her elbow.

"Lean in, ladies!" she told them and pulled Jenny and Olivia in, the three of their heads close together. "And smiiilllee!" The camera went off and Barb handed the phone back to Olivia. "Send that to him! Tell him, I don't know, that we just saw him on TV and we congratulate him on that score or something."

"But why?" Olivia asked, confused by her friend's enthusiasm over this.

"So he'll send us a pic back, *duh*!" She laughed. "If you're friends, it's not a big deal, right?"

"I guess not," Olivia said, still unsure. It wasn't though, was it? Friends sent each other selfies all the time—she and Kylie had exchanged at least half a dozen silly pictures—and she didn't have a picture of Stephen.

Before she could second-guess herself, she opened up her contacts, scrolled down to Stephen's entry and typed out *Saw you on TV! Girls say nice shot!,* attached the picture, and hit send.

A minute went by, during which Olivia drank more of her beer, hoping the alcohol would calm the hammering in her chest a little. *It's not a big deal,* she told herself. *Just a selfie with friends.*

Then her phone buzzed and before she could pick it up, Barb snatched it away, thumbed open the text and squealed with pleasure. "Look! Look! Oh, my gaaawd!" She waved the phone at Jenny then handed it back to Olivia, squeezing the younger woman's arm excitedly. "It's really him! Chris is gonna die when I tell him!"

Olivia ignored her for the moment and stared at the photo displayed on her screen. A slow smile spread across her face and a warm, tingly feeling grew inside her belly. Stephen had responded not just with words—a simple "Thanks, ladies!"—but included a selfie, giving the camera a thumbs up and a big smile.

Barb and Jenny were talking, chattering away excitedly, but Olivia couldn't hear any of it over the racing of her heart and the thoughts swirling around inside her head. Looking up, making sure the other ladies' attention was focused away from her for the moment, she set the photo Stephen sent as both his contact icon and her phone's background. She smiled to herself, then turned back to her friends, changing the subject by asking, "So—New Year's plans?"

Chapter 24.

The elevator came to its customary nearly silent stop on the top floor, Winning Towers' penthouse suite. The doors opened without a sound. A well-maintained machine. For once, Stephen Sloan couldn't appreciate it.

He crossed the small foyer, his shoes sinking into the thick, rich carpeting, but hesitated in front of the door to his penthouse. The cool metal of his housekey felt almost foreign in his hand. He'd taken it off his keyring the afternoon he last saw Liza, afraid that it would be a constant reminder of what he'd seen in the place—in his own home. For an instant, tendrils of anger crawled through him as he remembered those scenes, but he tamped them down. He needed to do this calmly. That was the only way. If this really did turn out to be the confrontation he feared, getting upset would just make it worse.

What was there to be upset about now anyway? he asked himself. He had two months to get used to the idea of Liza being gone from his life—it was his decision, and he knew it was the right one. He couldn't have lived with her after what he learned that day and if he'd somehow forced himself to, he wouldn't have been able to live with himself. That part of his life was over, but not yet done. This was the real end, and he'd avoided it, unsure of what he'd find when he finally stepped back inside his home, far too long already. He recognized that a part of him wanted to keep it this way, to remain in the safety of not knowing, but he couldn't let fear hold him back. He'd never lived life that way on or off the ice and he wasn't going to start now.

"Don't be a wuss, Sloan," he muttered under his breath. "You've got this."

Even so, he stood a moment longer, staring at the door, wondering if he could somehow hear movement on the other side, get an idea of whether Liza really was in the apartment or not. That was impossible, he reminded himself—Winning Towers prided itself on each apartment's total soundproofing. The only way to find out whether she was in there or not was to go in.

Stephen took a deep breath, slid the key into the lock and turned it. There was satisfying click, providing the first relief he'd felt all morning. The last time he'd used this key, the lock had been left undone, and strangers wandered his home, signs of how little Liza had respected him and his space. Now, at least, it seemed like at least one boundary had been restored.

He pushed the door open, scanning the entryway, his heart pounding in his chest. The low, leather-covered bench was right where it was supposed be against one wall; the small table that Liza used to keep flowers on stood across from it, holding no flowers, but no wine bottles either as it had when he'd last been here. She'd done—or hired done—a little bit of cleaning at least. Another good sign.

He stepped inside and closed the door behind him. The apartment was quiet. Not the quiet of someone hiding just out of sight, but the deep, complete silence of emptiness. He wondered why he'd thought of that—hiding. He listened a moment longer and heard nothing so he shrugged it off. He stood in the living room, noticing how clean it was, almost sterile even. The wine bottles and the abandoned food were gone, and the furniture had been placed back in its rightful spots. The chaos from that last afternoon he'd been here—when he'd walked in on Liza and her friends treating his home like their personal playground, acting like deranged, oversexed teenagers—

was gone.

Stephen's chest loosened as he moved from room to room, his footsteps echoing faintly against the hardwood floors. Like the restored living room, the dining table was perfectly set as though ready for a photo shoot. He moved through the kitchen, where the counters gleamed under the soft overhead lighting. No dishes in the sink, no stray bottles of wine or empty glasses or rotting food dried to dirty dishes. The detritus of Liza's orgy was gone, and not a single thing was out of place.

He began to let himself believe it as he walked through each room. The guest bedrooms, his gaming room, the master suite—everything was just as he'd left it, or cleaner. Even his closet had been organized, his belongings tidied and put away. Liza had been busy. Or someone had at any rate; this really wasn't Liza's style. He threw open her closet and found it empty. He laughed in disbelief, even though he was seeing it with his own eyes. Empty. Empty. Empty!

The master bedroom was the last place to look, the far country of his penthouse, and seeing no sign of Liza, the tension he'd carried for months finally began to ebb. He sat on the foot of the king-sized bed and exhaled deeply, his shoulders sagging as relief washed over him.

"She's gone," he said aloud, just to make it real. The words felt foreign, but they were *so* freeing. Liza had actually listened to him, had believed him when he said he'd have to call the cops on her if she was here when he returned on January 1st. It didn't seem real that she wouldn't put up a fight, lay some kind of ambush for him to throw him off guard and then either try to win her way back into his life or punish him for removing her from it. He laughed again, softly, faintly stunned that Liza had really left, and that it was over.

The last lingering weight of their relationship—so toxic that he couldn't even see it until it was over—lifted as he sat at the end of the bed, taking in the emptiness around him. For the first time in months, he felt like he could breathe—really breathe and be free.

It was just him now. His space, his life. And finally, he could start again. He thought of Olivia and smiled.

"Hi, honey-bear."

Stephen froze, every muscle in his body tensing at the sound of that voice he hadn't heard in months, and never wanted to hear again. Slowly, he looked towards the bedroom door, his pulse quickening and saw the source of his dread: Liza, standing casually in the doorway, her arms crossed over her breasts and a sly smile playing on her lips.

"Liza," he said, his voice sharper, not hiding the anger building rapidly inside of him. "What are you doing here? You were supposed to be gone."

She tilted her blonde head, feigning innocence. "Oh, come on, honey-bear. Did you really think I'd just pack up and leave? I've been waiting around downstairs all morning for you. I just wanted to give you a chance to see how nicely I had the place done up. It's as much mine as it is yours, so of course I want it to look good." Her tone was light, but there was a hard edge beneath it that made his jaw tighten. "I've been at the Plaza the last couple nights while the company I hired worked on the place, but my stuff's still in the basement lock up. I'll get Mr. Belding to bring it back up."

"It's *not* yours," Stephen said firmly, standing and stepping forward to tower over her. Somehow, he'd forgotten how tiny she was. But he hadn't forgotten that habit of hers, of simply stating what she wanted to happen and expecting that it was just going to be so. He let her get away with it for years, telling himself he loved her and wanted her to be happy. Neither was the case anymore.

"I bought the damned place. It's *mine*. You lived here because we were—" he almost choked on the word, surprised at how it affected him, "together, but that's over and you damned well know it. We're done. You gave me a song and dance when I had every right to kick you out onto the street, so I let you have the two months—plenty of time to figure things out."

He pulled his cellphone from his back pocket. "I told you what I'd do if I found you here. Well, I'm doing it."

Liza sighed dramatically, pushing off the doorframe and strolling into the room like she owned it—as she clearly thought she did. She was dressed impeccably, as always, in a sleek black dress that looked more suited to a night out than it did wearing around the house. Was that for his benefit?

"Oh, Stevie, you're so extra." She sighed again, turning bright blue eyes on him, widening them in mock wonder. "I've been gone, haven't I? For two whole nights. And I got your precious penthouse cleaned up. I even let you have your space while you ran off home to Grammy Flora." She smiled, and right before his eyes, it turned cold, as if she'd dialed down a thermostat. "And now I'm back. You know, I thought we'd just pick back up where we left off, but if you want, we can talk for a bit first. You owe me that much, don't you?"

"I don't owe you one God-damned thing," Stephen shot back, his voice rising. "I made it clear, Liza. We're over. Through. You walking in here pretending you didn't understand or whatever isn't going to change that."

Her eyes narrowed, and whatever vestiges of fake charm she reserved for him melted away, replaced by something hard and deadly. "You think you can just walk away from me? From *us*? After everything we've been through? I've wasted almost my entire twenties on you, you big, stupid bastard.

"There *is* no us, Liza," Stephen said, his tone resolute. "You made that clear when I walked in on your little Sodom and Gomorrah you made out of my home. I let you stay here as long as I did because it seemed like the right thing to do, but this has gone on plenty long enough."

For a moment, neither of them spoke, the silence stretching uncomfortably. Stephen's heart pounded, and something inside him was screaming that he could turn, run away, go back to Flora's house and live in peace and comfort and security with his grandmother and sister. But he held his ground. He wasn't going to let her manipulate him. He'd spent a third of his life letting her twist him around her little finger, but she no longer had any power over him. It didn't matter how beautiful she was or how perfect her body—all he saw now when he looked at her was something vile.

Finally, Liza's expression shifted again, the corners of her mouth lifting in a tight, humorless smile. "You've changed," she said, almost wistfully. "I used to be able to talk you out of anything. But now… look at you. All strong and self-righteous." She sneered, but her eyes flicked over him, scanning him as if she were assessing his value at an auction, deciding how much worth he really had and how much she would have to spend to claim it for herself.

"Is there someone else, Stephen?" She looked up at him, her eyes narrowed. "Is that what this is about? Trading me in for a newer model?"

The question caught him off guard. He wasn't sure if it showed on his face—he hoped not; she'd use any opportunity to attack. "This isn't about anyone else," he said, his voice steady. "It's about me taking back my life. I didn't realize what you really were until…" He didn't want to say it. "You know as well as I do what happened, so why bother going into? All that matters is that I'm doing this for me."

She let out a laugh sharp as broken glass. "Oh, spare me, Stevie. Taking back your life? Please. Aside from hockey, I *am* your life. What have you ever had that you didn't get from me? You don't even have any friends who aren't on your precious hockey team."

Stephen took a deep breath, forcing himself to stay calm. "That's not true," he said, realizing that in a way it actually *was*. Aside from the guys on the team, all of his and Liza's friends had really been *her* friends—he'd just been her plus-one. He thought of Olivia again, and of her dad, Jack, whom he met at Christmas. Even if at one time he'd just been Liza's plus-one, it wasn't true any longer.

He shook free of his momentary confusion, realizing he still held his cellphone. "Why am I even humoring you discussing it? I'm giving you to the count of ten. Give me your key and then get out or I'm calling the cops."

She looked at him, her expression turning unreadable. Then, with a small shrug, she moved towards the door. "Fine," she said, her tone flippant. She threw a key, identical to the one in Stephen's pocket, to the floor. "You win. I'm gone. I hope you enjoy your precious freedom—while you can." The look she gave him before she turned and walked down the hall was absolutely vicious. Stephen couldn't remember seeing anyone ever look like that outside of a TV show or movie. He didn't think that kind of… evil actually existed.

Tension still thrumming through his veins, Stephen stood in the middle of the bedroom, listening to Liza's heels clicking down the hardwood floor of the hallway. The sound disappeared and he realized she was in the living room, moving across the plush carpet, then faintly he heard her footsteps again before, finally, the opening and slamming of the apartment door.

He exhaled, his body sagging with relief. It was over—for real this time. He resisted an urge to run around the apartment checking all the nooks and crannies for places Liza might be hiding. He had no idea how she'd gotten into the apartment to surprise him the way she did—key or no key—but she wasn't magical. She was vicious, but she wasn't an actual witch. She couldn't wave a wand and reappear inside the penthouse.

Just the same, he moved quickly to the front door and made sure it was locked before allowing himself to really believe that she was gone. Only then did he realize what she'd said just before she gave him that withering look and left. What did she mean "while you can?"

Chapter 25.

The Rogers Roasters Arena in Mobile was packed with fans, their cheers and chants echoing through the building as the puck dropped for the first period. The Mobile Manatees, energized by their home crowd, skated with fierce intensity from the start, determined to give the Back Bay Warriors a run for their money. Stephen Sloan, "The Warriors' star center," the announcer called him—and it was true—leaned forward in the faceoff circle, his stick poised and his expression sharp. He locked eyes with the Manatees' captain, Brendan Hayes, across from him. If all you saw was the fierceness in their eyes, the sharp focus and dedication to winning, they could almost have been mirror-images.

The puck hit the ice with a faint *crack* and the crowds began getting amped—the game was on. Stephen snapped his stick forward, winning the faceoff cleanly and sending the puck back to Ken Johns, his most reliable defenseman and linemate. Ken fainted to the left, catching one of the Manatees' attention, but then immediately sent the puck shooting to the right across the ice, straight to Jake Archer. The crowd of Warriors fans, definitely the minority here, fifteen hundred miles from home, roared. As a winger, Jake was known for his speed and aggressive forechecking; getting the puck into his hands was a solid opening play. Jake dashed down the left boards, deftly ducking around a Manatees defender before firing the puck deep into the offensive zone.

Stephen chased after it, his skates carving the ice like he was made simply to shred. He closed in on the

Manatee player who had retrieved the puck, a defenseman he recognized but whose name he couldn't remember. It didn't matter. Anticipating the other's play, Stephen angled his body to cut off the pass the Manatee was setting up, and before the other player realized it, Stephen was stealing the puck with a lightning swipe of his stick. Without even an instant's hesitation, he sent a sharp backhand pass to Jake, now waiting near the slot.

Jake's window of opportunity was tiny. He took a quick shot, but the Manatees' goalie, a solid wall of muscle and padding named Marcus "Tank" Tyler—long the Manatees' star goalie and for good reason—snagged the puck with a glove save that seemed so effortless, the home team crowd exploded into frenzied cheers.

The Manatees pushed back—hard. Brendan Hayes led their charge, leading his team by example as he barreled into the Warriors' zone, pushing the puck before him. With scarcely any warning, he passed to his winger, who pivoted and let loose a blistering slap shot from the blue line. The Warriors' goalie, Cam Dexter, tracked it perfectly, expertly dropping to his knees and trapping the puck against his chest. The Manatees' fans groaned, but Dexter was pleased, especially as one of his teammates swung by, giving him nod of confidence.

For the next ten minutes, the teams traded possession back and forth, back and forth, in a fiercely contested battle. The Manatees were known for relying on heavy physical play, and they didn't disappoint their fans, delivering heavy hits and pinning Warriors along the boards at every opportunity. Jake Archer took an especially rough check behind the net, jarring him to the bone, but he popped back up, giving the defenseman a hard glare before skating back into position. The Warriors fans in the crowd loved him for it.

Late in the first period, the Warriors got their first real break. Stephen won another faceoff in the neutral zone, tapping the puck back to Ken, who quickly advanced it to Mikey B. Mike carried the puck into the Manatees' zone, faking a pass to Stephen before shooting the puck to Jake. Jake circled behind the net and, as Stephen darted into the slot, shaking off his defender, Jake sent a blisteringly fast pass to him. Stephen snapped a wrist shot high on the blocker side, the puck sailing past Tank Tyler and into the net. The red light flared, and the Warriors' bench erupted in cheers. The end of period score was 1-0 Warriors.

The Manatees upped their tempo, desperate to at least equalize the score in the second period. Their pressure paid off just under five minutes in when Brendan Hayes capitalized on a defensive turnover by Ken. Hayes stole the puck near the Warriors' blue line and rifled a shot through heavy traffic, beating Dexter's defense and scooting over his shoulder. The crowd roared as the scoreboard read 1-1.

The Warriors regrouped; it was only a tie and still anyone's game. Stephen and Jake led the charge, creating several dangerous chances to make the most of the time left in the period. Stephen used his strength and agility to win several puck battles along the boards, finally managing to feed Jake in the slot for a pair of shots, both narrowly deflected by Tyler. Ken and the others anchored the defense, breaking up rushes and transitioning the puck smoothly up the ice.

Twelve minutes into the period, the Warriors retook the lead. Jake intercepted a clearing attempt in the neutral zone and rushed back into the offensive zone, Stephen trailing, pushing past Manatee defenders. Jake pulled two more defenders toward him before slipping the puck behind his back to Stephen, wide open with Jake distracting the Manatees. Stephen wound up, putting everything he had into a rocketing slap shot that ricocheted off the crossbar and into the net. The goal light flashed, the airhorn blared and the scoreboard ticked up to 2-1. The Warriors fans cheered and even the Manatee fans in the stands agreed that it was masterful teamwork. Grinning like a madman, Stephen headed back to the Warriors side, only to be mobbed by his teammates with congratulations and celebratory head, shoulder, and butt pats.

The Manatees were getting desperate. They'd lost their last away game; they couldn't lose a home game back-to-back with that loss. They put on extra speed as they crashed around the ice, extra power into their shots and checks, but the Warriors' defense held strong. Ken was a wall in front of Cam Dexter, blocking multiple shots and dishing out punishing retaliatory hits that kept the Manatees' forwards at bay and on the defense themselves. Dexter, in-net, made several highlight-reel saves, including a diving glove save on a breakaway just before the second period buzzer went off.

The third period was make or break for the Manatees, but the Back Bay Warriors were energized by their success and determined to make the final round a showcase of their skill, discipline, and teamwork. They played smart, defensive hockey, forcing the Manatees to take low-percentage shots while waiting for opportunities to counterattack. Already demoralized, the Manatees' game began to slip—maybe not enough that a casual observer would notice, but both the fans who knew the team well, and more importantly, their coach saw it. There'd be some difficult discussions after the game if they didn't turn it around.

With just over five minutes remaining in the period, the Warriors delivered the killing blow. Jake, in his element and feeling like no one on Earth could beat him, carried the puck into the zone, faking a shot before sliding a perfect pass to Stephen, nestled over in the corner away from the Manatee defenders. Stephen sent a no-look pass across the ice to Ken, who had crept in from the blue line. Ken one-timed the puck into the back of the net, sealing the game at a final score of 3-1.

The remaining minutes ticked down. The Manatees went into a frenzy, wild to recover if it was at possible, throwing everything they had at the Warriors defense, and especially Cam Dexter. One of the younger members of the team, he was battered almost brutally by the Manatee attackers, but he stood firm. Finally, the buzzer sounded, ending the assault. The Warriors fans who'd traveled to see the team erupted into crazed cheers as the Warriors gathered at the center of the ice. They lined up to shake hands with the Manatees, doing their best to remain respectful. There'd be time to celebrate later, without adding insult to the Manatees' injury.

Chapter 26.

It was almost midnight; Stephen was wiped, but happy. The victory against the Manatees was by no means a lock when the puck first dropped. Something rattled them, but that wasn't the Warriors' problem. They played their best and won—the points, and the right to celebrate, were theirs.

In celebration of the win, Stephen, Ken, Mikey B, Jake and half a dozen other guys had spent almost three hours club-hopping, drinking and dancing, mostly on other people's dimes. A winning sports team in a strange city can always find people willing to celebrate with them, and that included a lot of women. Both Jake and Ken had left that last club at some point without saying goodbye.

Stripping off his sweaty shirt and slacks, looking forward to a shower before bed, Stephen smirked, imagining what Ken and Jake were probably up to right now. It wasn't hard to guess—they'd both left the locker room bragging about their options for the evening and both talked to a lot of girls at the clubs. Stephen wondered which of the guys had ended up with which of the girls. Stephen had gotten just as much attention, and tomorrow, they'd tease him mercilessly for turning down all the girls that had crowded him, flashing smiles and cleavage and batting eyelashes. Everyone loves a winner, and they were all eager for a chance to cozy up to the star center of the Warriors. Part of him enjoyed it, but he wouldn't let it go beyond the flirting stage. The other guys didn't understand, and he didn't expect them to. They called him Saint Stephen or teased him about being too picky.

But it wasn't pickiness. He simply wasn't wired like Ken or Jake—or a lot of other guys for that matter. Sure, he absolutely had his "manly needs," as Jake would probably call them with a wink and a nudge, but just satisfying the physical wasn't enough for Stephen. As long as he could remember, sex and love were so deeply intertwined that they were nearly inseparable. The idea of spending the night with someone who didn't truly know him, someone he couldn't see himself sharing more than a fleeting moment with, didn't appeal to him. He might enjoy it in that moment, but he'd hate himself for it the next day.

He exhaled, his mind drifting to Liza, as it often did when he was alone. Their relationship had been so full of highs and lows, of passion and chaos, that it had taken him far too long to realize just how destructive it had become. He could never have imagined the filthy things she was doing behind his back. How could he? He thought he knew her and realizing he hadn't at all—maybe not for years—was an almost crippling blow.

That final confrontation at the penthouse, as stressful as it was, brought so much relief in its wake that he almost couldn't believe it. And when she finally walked out the door, he was more glad to hear her go than he'd ever been to see her arrive. He hated that, but it was the truth. And in the days since then, he'd replayed the years of their relationship over and over in his head, picking up now on cues that should have been obvious at the time but that he'd completely missed. He wondered why it had taken him so long to see his relationship with Liza for the dumpster fire it had become. Maybe because he hadn't been ready to admit how bad things were, even to himself. Maybe he secretly hoped things would get better, though he couldn't imagine now how that might have been possible. Or maybe it was simply a matter of being too wrapped up in the illusion of what they'd once had to recognize that it was gone.

Now, though, his thoughts had shifted. He still thought about Liza when his mind wandered, but just as often his mind turned to Olivia.

Stephen let out a soft laugh, scrubbing a hand down his face. He wasn't sure when it started, but Olivia had been on his mind a lot lately. She wasn't flashy like Liza, and she didn't try to command the room with charm or drama. She was… real. Down to earth. And the way she'd lit up during their game night, the sound of her laughter echoing in Flora's living room—it stuck with him.

He thought back to the mistletoe kiss, how unexpected and perfect it had been. In that brief moment, he'd felt something he hadn't realized he was missing. Warmth. Ease. Connection.

He reached for his phone on the nightstand, unlocked it, then hesitated as he considered. Was it too late? If it was, would it be weird for Olivia to wake up to a text from him? It wasn't like he was going to confess his undying love over a text, but waking up to a text from a guy might be weird. They had a few moments together, but maybe he was reading too much into them. Was he? He didn't think so… he was pretty sure she at least kind of liked him. Either way, he could at least reach out, see how she was doing. That wouldn't be weird; they were at least friends, and friends texted to say hi, right?

His phone buzzed, vibrating in his hand.

OLIVIA: *Saw your game. Good job! :)*

Stephen laughed. If that wasn't a sign, he didn't know what was.

STEPHEN: *Thanks! Weird, just thinking about you.*

Was that too much? His heart skittered inside his chest like a frightened animal. All the confidence he felt after winning the game against the Manatees suddenly evaporated.

Wondering how you been he added in a second text, hoping he wasn't digging himself a hole.

For a moment, nothing happened. Then three little dancing dots appeared next to her name.

Fifteen hundred miles away, Olivia leaned back against her couch, the dim glow of her phone screen the only light in the room as she smiled at Stephen's message. She took a sip from her wine glass, thinking how silly it was that a little text message made her this happy. She started typing a response to Stephen when her phone vibrated. A text from Dee.

DEE: *Just got the baby down finally. Sick, cranky mess all night! Too hyped to sleep now. Whatcha up to?*

OLIVIA: *Drinking a little wine… and texting with Stephen!* She included a squealing face emoji for emphasis.

She switched back to the convo with Stephen, quickly typing out a response.

OLIVIA: *I'm good! Glad to hear from you. Figured you'd be out celebrating with some cute little puck bunny tonight. :P*

The response was nearly instant.

STEPHEN: *Some of the guys are still celebrating, but I'm in my hotel room. About to grab a shower and hit the sack.*

Olivia's stomach did a little flip. He wasn't out partying; he'd chosen a quiet night in—or at least an early night, comparatively. And either way, he'd taken the time to text her. That meant he was thinking of her. That *had* to mean something, right? Her heart beat faster.

OLIVIA: *Hope you get some rest! You earned it. :)*

Switching back to Dee's chat, she saw her friend's follow-up message waiting.

DEE: *Get it girl! Show him those tig bitties of yours lol*

Olivia laughed so hard she dribbled wine down her chin and over the front of her shirt—fortunately not one she cared much about. But the spill made her look down at her chest and laugh again. She put down her phone, hopped up and grabbed a paper towel to clean herself and the couch with. That done, she flopped back onto the couch, picked up her phone and quickly tapped out—

OLIVIA: *Show him my boobs? Lol*

She poured more wine into her glass, replacing what she'd spilled, realizing she was getting tipsy. She didn't usually drink during the week, but she felt like she had to celebrate Stephen's win just a little bit—maybe too much? She laughed at the thought as her phone vibrated. She opened the screen and read:

STEPHEN: *That came out of left field… lol?*

"Oh, my God!" Olivia squealed out loud, burying her face in a throw pillow and squirming around on the couch in an agony of embarrassment.

In a hotel room in Mobile, Alabama, Stephen lifted an eyebrow and half-smiled. He was sure that text wasn't for him, and maybe the polite thing to do would have been to ignore it. He fully admitted to himself that he was starting to like Olivia, and it wasn't as if he hadn't noticed her body… she was a little on the plump side, but nobody—not even a confirmed lech like Jake Archer—could have complained about her breasts. He imagined them and felt the first stirrings of arousal.

DEE: *Still there?*

OLIVIA: *No. I'm dead. U killed me.*

DEE: *What lol*

Olivia grabbed a screenshot of the conversation with Stephen and sent it to Dee.

DEE: *OMG! STOP TOO FUNNY!!!*

OLIVIA: *It's not! I'm seriously about to die! What do I do?*

DEE: *Do it! Do it! This is your chance, girl*

"No," Olivia said to the empty room. "Oh, my God, I couldn't…" Her face felt like it was on fire and she knew the wine was only part of it.

Her phone buzzed repeatedly.

DEE: *Do it!*

DEE: *Do it!*

DEE: *Do it! Who could resist those knockers? ;)*

"Urrrggghh," Olivia groaned, rolling over onto her side. She looked down the length of her body, eyes lingering on her breasts. If there was one part of her body she could be proud of…

OLIVIA: *Should I?*

DEE: *YES I've been saying lol*

For the millionth time, the moment she first saw Stephen Sloan sprang to mind—a guy so sizzling hot he could melt the panties off any girl he met, mostly nude on the side of a bus. Over the last couple of weeks, the more she remembered that image, the less the memory became of the ad and the more it became intermingled with her own firsthand memories of Stephen until it wasn't an ad at all she was seeing in her mind, but Stephen Sloan in the flesh—and he wasn't always wearing the underwear.

Olivia realized her breathing had gotten heavier and it wasn't just her face that felt hot now—her whole body was warm and tingly. Unconsciously, she rubbed her thighs together, fidgeting. She grabbed the wine glass, drank off its contents in a single gulp, and before she could talk herself out of it, stripped off her shirt, thrust out her impressive chest and snapped a picture. She switched back to Stephen's chat and sent him the photo. Her heart was hammering so hard it very nearly hurt, and she could actually feel her pussy getting wet now.

Stephen's phone vibrated. He was seated on the edge of the mattress in his room, nude, his journey to the shower interrupted by that last text from Olivia. He wondered if she was going to respond at all. It had been several minutes since he answered what was obviously a mistaken text and he was worried—maybe he should have ignored it after all. The poor girl was probably too embarrassed to say anything. He unlocked his phone, opened her text and felt not just stirrings… his penis started growing, quickly standing to attention.

"Holy shit," he whispered. "Holy shit."

His pulse started to race, and he was painfully aware of his swollen member, but what the hell was he supposed to do? He was just thinking a few minutes ago about how down to Earth and wholesome Olivia was and here was this… amazing picture. Maybe she'd been drinking, maybe this wasn't meant for him either—maybe, maybe, maybe!

"Oh, shit," Stephen said.

He peeled back his foreskin, exposing the head of his cock for maximum effect, snapped a picture and sent it back to Olivia then began stroking himself to the photo of her huge, perfect breasts. It had been months since he was last with Liza, and he had been too depressed for weeks after their initial break up to even consider sex of any sort. Now he rubbed his cock furiously, as if making up for lost time, feeling the pressure at the base of his shaft building rapidly. He dropped the phone onto the bed, stood and turned, staring down at Olivia's gorgeous, lush breasts, stroking his cock even faster with his right hand while cupping and squeezing his balls with his left. Right as the pressure began to feel intense, he turned, moving quickly into the bathroom. Never missing a beat in stroking himself, he stepped into the shower, pinched his left nipple hard and blew a load so huge all over the shower stall's wall that it actually splashed back and splattered against his legs and feet.

Olivia was fully nude now, pressed back against the cushions of the couch as far as she could to give herself room, her legs spread wide, her phone propped against the wine bottle on the side table, displaying Stephen's cock. She'd seen bigger in porn, but never in real life and never once anywhere saw a penis as perfect as his. It was long, faintly curved, with thick veins running up the shaft. His foreskin, bunched around the base of the head of his cock fascinated her—she'd never seen one before and she wondered what it would feel like inside her. Would it be different than a circumcised cock?

With her right hand, she rubbed the hood of her clit, relishing the delicious feeling of her stubby, faintly reddish pubic hair between her fingers and her clit hood. Her other hand probed lightly at her slit, rubbing her lips, running her fingertips up and down her labia, sometimes ducking inside to tickle her vaginal wall. She let out a gasp and arched her back, rubbing her clit faster with her palm, pushing two fingers inside of herself now from the top while her other hand probed from the bottom.

She couldn't believe this was happening—she'd sent nude pictures to guys before, but she and Stephen weren't even dating. She forced those thoughts aside and focused on the photo—that gorgeous, perfectly sexy cock—and her own pleasure. She felt the heat inside of her building towards a climax and rubbed herself faster, faster, faster. At the exact moment she felt herself tipping over the edge, she pulled the hood of her clit back and pinched it directly—totally unaware that Stephen was doing some pinching of his own at nearly the same moment.

With first a gasp and then a whimper, Olivia finished. It was stronger than she could ever remember orgasming. She was out of breath, hot and sweaty, her entire body felt like mush—and it was delicious. She hadn't felt this good in years.

She lay in the semi-darkness of her living room, still only lit by the glow from her phone—still showing Stephen's erect cock. It was like she couldn't take her eyes from it. The phone vibrated with an incoming text, knocking itself from its precarious perch against the wine bottle. It tilted to the table with a *clunk* and Olivia sat up to reach it, aware now of a hot stickiness between her legs. The reality of what she'd just done was catching up with her and she wasn't sure how to feel.

"The wine…" she said out loud, navigating to her texts. One new message.

STEPHEN: *Can I see you some time real soon?*

Olivia squealed and let herself fall backwards onto the plush couch, kicking her legs in the air with excitement.

Chapter 27.

Olivia's car crunched to a stop on the blacktop-paved driveway of the Mountain View Hotel as her breath caught at the sight laid out before her. The four-hour drive from Boston to the Catskills was tiring, and the drive up the mountain was pretty if a little harrowing in places—it was the middle of winter after all, and this place was pretty deep in the hills. But sitting here now, it was worth it just for this view alone.

The hotel was magnificent, a sprawling structure of stone and glass that seemed to rise organically from the snow-covered ground, rising up to four stories but still dwarfed by the mountains beyond it. The building's architecture blended seamlessly with the winter landscape, every detail thoughtfully crafted, ensuring that it perfectly complemented the area's natural beauty. And more impressive than the hotel was the towering mountain itself, its peaks wrapped in a blanket of pure white snow so pristine it almost didn't look real. Sunlight danced off the surface, scattering in shimmering crystals, and Olivia had to remind herself to breathe it was so gorgeous.

This is going to be so much fun, she thought, angling her car deeper into the parking lot, looking for a space. She found one and then climbed out of the car, hugging her coat tighter around her as a sudden gust of icy air swept past her, gazing up at the distant mountain. She shivered, but she was smiling, happy to be there. She had been looking forward to Randy's wedding ever since Flora and Kylie convinced her to come, and she knew it would be somewhere fancy—Randy *was* a millionaire, celebrity athlete after all—but she hadn't expected it to take place somewhere so breathtakingly beautiful. If you'd asked Olivia to describe her idea of luxury, she still wouldn't have been able to come up with anything as grand as this place. And the setting! It was a perfect winter wonderland that felt like something out of a storybook—or maybe a Hallmark movie. Olivia chuckled at that idea. She did enjoy those movies after all.

She took her small overnight bag from the back of her car and made her way toward the grand entrance, pausing for a moment to take it all in. The hotel's doors were large, welcoming, flanked by artfully arranged icicles—no way that was natural, but it was very pretty—that glistened in the afternoon sun, while warm light spilled from the windows, promising comfort within. The entry area was bustling, and Olivia recognized a few members of the Back Bay Warriors. She wondered how many people were on the guestlist all told. It occurred to her at that moment that she was actually invited to an honest to God celebrity's wedding and that the event would probably be swarming with other famous people. It was a little dizzying.

But then she thought of Stephen and smiled. Stephen was a celebrity too and he was a regular guy—more than just regular, she reminded herself, flushing with memories.

Stephen. Just thinking of him made her feel warm and tingly. They hadn't seen each other in person since Christmas. Between his game schedule and her work, it seemed like the world was conspiring against them. They'd been texting a lot though—almost constantly—and even had a few video-chats late at night. Nothing naughty, though she'd "used" the photo Stephen sent her plenty of times. She hoped Stephen was enjoying the one she'd sent him. She blushed deeply, remembering that special night, and hoping nobody would notice how red her face was.

The fact was, they hadn't talked about that night,

but they were definitely growing closer. Reading his words, hearing his voice through them, seeing his smiling face on her phone was enough to slowly close the gap between them. She was really falling for Stephen Sloan.

She wondered what Stephen was up to now; he must have been at the hotel somewhere. The Warriors had a game Tuesday night and then the entire crew, plus some outside friends of Randy's, had gone down to Atlantic City for a three-day bachelor party. Olivia wanted so badly to hear from him over the last few days, but she didn't want to interrupt his guy time—it was an important event for Randy and the guys were pretty much all good friends. Interrupting that just because she missed a guy she wasn't even actually dating would have been selfish. Besides, she didn't want to seem clingy. Still, she missed him.

Maybe I should text him, she thought. She'd definitely see him this weekend, but she wanted it to be sooner than later.

She stopped in the hotel's huge lobby, decorated with garlands and an enormous Christmas tree that had yet to be taken down. There was also a giant banner strung from the ceiling reading CONGRATULATIONS, RANDY & AMY! and decorated with wedding bells and soaring doves.

Olivia smiled, saying a little prayer for the couple's happiness. She'd only met Randy once, and hadn't met his fiancée at all, but he seemed like a good guy—and Flora certainly thought a lot of him. That was the best recommendation she could ask for. She chuckled, thinking of what Kylie had told her about Randy being the eternal ladies' man. Not anymore, she hoped. She hoped his match with Amy was a good one and that they would both be very happy.

Weddings had always held a special place in her heart—there was something so hopeful, so joyful about them and, still smiling, she moved to the front desk to check in.

"Hi," she told the young male clerk. "Olivia Murray, checking in? There should be a block for the Roberts-Becker wedding."

"Yes, of course." He smiled, showing a flash of white teeth. "Welcome to the Mountain Crest, Miss Murray." He turned to his computer, hit a few keys. "Let's see—oh, here you are." He stooped, came up with a plastic keycard, ran it through a reader, then looked up and offered it to Olivia. "You're in 313, with Miss Sloan."

Accepting the card, Olivia asked, "Miss Sloan? Kylie Sloan?"

"That's her." His smile turned slightly uncertain. "Is that a problem, Miss Murray?"

"Oh, no, no," Olivia answered hurriedly. "I love Kylie to death. I just didn't realize we'd be sharing rooms."

"Ah," the clerk said, understanding on his face. "I'm sorry if that wasn't communicated. As you probably saw, we are a relatively small establishment and the wedding's guestlist is quite long. A number of guests are sharing doubles."

"Oh, okay. Thanks!" She gave the young man a bright smile and strode towards the elevators. It was a surprise, but it was fine. She wasn't paying for the room so she couldn't be picky. Besides, sharing with Kylie would be like having a sleepover.

With a soft chime, the elevator doors opened to reveal a plush hallway with deep carpeting and tasteful artwork. She found her room easily and stepped inside, letting out a sigh of delight as she moved to the big picture window on the opposite side of the room and took in the view. The room was small, but luxurious, and the large windows offered an uninterrupted view of the snowy mountain beyond.

She turned to place her bag on the foot of the king-sized bed and realized the shower was running. She had been so entranced by the view that she hadn't noticed either the sound of the water coming from the bathroom or the duffel bag laying on the floor between the bed and the door to the bathroom. It was a weird thing for a girl to carry her things in, even just for a weekend trip, Olivia thought, but her brother was a professional athlete, so maybe it was a family thing or maybe it was a hand-me-down of Stephen's that had sentimental value.

She shrugged and moved back to the window. From this vantage point, the mountain was even more breathtaking that it had been from the parking lot, its snowy expanse seeming to stretch endlessly up towards the sky, now turning pink and purple with the early winter sunset. The scene was so perfect, so serene, it felt like stepping into a postcard.

Thinking of the setting—the beautiful hotel in such a gorgeous location and how wonderful the wedding would be—her thoughts wandered to the wedding she'd once dreamed of with Stan. She could picture it so clearly—the flowers, the music, the vows they would exchange. It was bittersweet to think about how much she'd wanted that future at one time. She was lucky she found out what a skunk Stan was before it was too late.

Olivia turned from the window and began unpacking, laying out the dress she'd brought for the wedding. It was a deep emerald green, a color she'd chosen because Kylie had insisted it would look amazing on her. She couldn't wait to show the younger girl how it looked. She smoothed her hands over the fabric, picturing the celebration ahead. The idea of the vows, the dancing, the laughter, and even the toasts, which would definitely contain more than a few terrible jokes—all of it filled her with a kind of quiet joy. Weddings weren't just about romance; they were about family, friendship, and the hope that something beautiful could be built between two people.

And who knows, she thought, a smile playing on her lips as she hung up the dress in the closet to allow the wrinkles to fall out. *Maybe someday I'll have the perfect wedding of my own...*

She realized that the sound of the shower had stopped, and she turned to see Stephen, freshly showered and very much *naked*, stroll out of the bathroom, a towel slung over his shoulder as he rubbed his damp hair with another.

For a split second, Olivia couldn't move or speak. Her brain stuttered to process what she was seeing—Stephen, his toned, athletic, heavily tattooed body on full display, muscles glistening slightly from the steam of the shower, completely unaware that he was not alone. Her heart stopped in her chest and the fantasy image she'd nurtured in her imagination—a combination of that underwear ad and her own experiences with Stephen—flashed into her mind and she realized that it didn't even come close to the real thing.

"Oh, my God…" she whispered, feeling her body tingle all over.

Stephen looked up and froze. His eyes widened, and for the span of a heartbeat, they simply stared at each other, time stretching impossibly long. Then, realizing his state of undress, he scrambled to cover himself with the towel, fumbling as he tried to keep it in place around his hips.

"Olivia?!" he exclaimed, his voice breaking slightly in his surprise. "What… what are you doing in my room?"

"I—" Olivia began, her face flaming as she spun around to give him some semblance of privacy. Her voice came out high-pitched and rushed. "What am *I* doing in *your* room? This is *my* room!"

Stephen blinked, gripping the towel tightly as his own blush deepened. "Wait, what? No, this is my room—well, mine and Kylie's. She isn't here yet, won't be 'til later, but I when checked in earlier they told me there wasn't enough space so —"

He paused, his brow furrowing as realization began to dawn. "Oh, no. Jesus Christ, don't tell me…"

Olivia groaned, still facing the window, her hands covering her burning face. "Oh my God, Kylie. She *switched the room assignments,* didn't she?"

Stephen sighed, exasperation mixing with embarrassment as he grabbed another towel and draped it over his shoulders for extra coverage. "That sounds like something she'd do. I can just imagine it—'Oops! Must have been a mix-up!'" he said, mimicking Kylie's cheerful tone.

Olivia turned her head slightly, just enough to glance at him out of the corner of her eye. He was now more or less decently covered, wrapped in a towel, though the sight of him had already been seared into her memory. "I'm going to *kill* her," she muttered, but her voice lacked any real venom.

Stephen chuckled nervously, running a hand through his damp hair. "Well, I guess this explains why there's only one bed."

At that, Olivia's eyes darted to the king-sized bed between them, neatly made and clearly meant for two people. She expected a fun night of girl-talk and laughter, but the situation was so much more awkward now.

"So… what now?" she asked, her voice hesitant, biting her lip, unaware of how coy it made her look.

It didn't escape Stephen though. He looked down at the floor, rubbing the back of his neck, his embarrassment giving way to a sheepish grin. "Well, I'm not exactly thrilled about Kylie tricking us," he said, his voice light and teasing, "but it's not like you saw anything you haven't already, right?"

He gave Olivia a wink, making her blush deepen. It was true though—she'd looked at that photo so many times she could effortlessly conjure it from memory.

"I'm fine with sharing the room if you are, Olivia," he told her. "I mean—the hotel's pretty full and I don't think we have many options at this point. I can just sleep on the floor or something."

Olivia's blush lingered, but her composure was slowly returning. She wanted to spend time with Stephen, didn't she? Was she really going to turn down this opportunity? If she looked at it from a certain angle, it was a great opportunity to get to know him better. It might be a little awkward since they'd never really spent any time alone… and maybe it was unorthodox but… you had to start somewhere.

"You don't have to do that. It's a big bed—we can just… split it. Pillows down the middle, no funny business."

Stephen raised an eyebrow, his grin widening slightly. "No funny business, huh?"

"None," Olivia said firmly, though the corner of her mouth twitched upward and she wondered how far she'd be able to trust herself if Stephen actually made a move.

"Deal," Stephen said. "But just so we're clear, Kylie's not getting away with this one. I'm gonna have to find some way to get her back."

Olivia laughed, the tension in the room finally beginning to ease. "Agreed. She's gonna regret this little stunt."

As Stephen grabbed his clothes and retreated back to the bathroom to finish getting dressed, Olivia sank onto the edge of the bed, letting out a deep breath. Sharing a room with Stephen was going to be… interesting.

"To say the least," she said out loud and chuckled.

"Had anything to eat?" Stephen called from the bathroom.

"Nope!" she answered.

"There are two restaurants—casual and gourmet. Think about which one you wanna try. My treat," Stephen said, his voice faintly echoing off the bathroom's tiled walls.

"Okay," she said, but her thoughts were firmly fixed on the image of Stephen Sloan, star hockey player, fresh out of the shower, fully nude and glistening. She was a little embarrassed, but the excitement far outweighed it.

Thanks, Kylie, she thought, her lips curving into a private smile.

Chapter 28.

"I'm really glad to see you, Olivia," Stephen said.

The hotel's casual-style restaurant was warm and inviting, the lighting low but not dim, making it seem cozy rather than dark. There was a small fire-pit in the center of the room, its crackling flames providing a contrast to the snowy mountain landscape just outside the large picture windows.

Olivia and Stephen sat at a corner table, menus propped up before them. After ordering drinks, they had largely ignored the menus, but until Stephen spoke there had been a sort of awkward silence between them. Until the encounter in the room twenty minutes earlier, they'd never spent any time alone together after all—except those few minutes beneath the mistletoe on Christmas.

Stephen speaking up and breaking the comfortable silence made Olivia happier than she would have liked to admit. After getting over the initial shock in the room, she was so glad to see him that it was almost painful.

"I'm glad to see you too," Olivia said finally, her voice soft and sincere. She folded her menu and set it aside. "It feels like forever since Christmas."

Stephen smiled, his cheeks crinkling, showing those tiny laugh-lines that Olivia first noticed that night in Enclave. His smile made her feel a warmth that had nothing to do with the merry little fire-pit. "I'm sorry it's been so long. We've been on the road so much this month—

"My schedule hasn't been much better," she cut

in. She smiled. "But we're here now, right?"

Stephen nodded, smiled. The smile disappeared as he leaned slightly forward and lowered his voice. "And, uh, about the room thing… I'm sorry for Kylie's little prank. I had no idea she was planning something like that. I swear."

Olivia laughed softly. "It's not your fault. And honestly… it's not the worst thing that could've happened."

He smiled slowly. "Still, I should've guessed she'd try something like this. She's been teasing me about… well…" He trailed off, glancing away, unsure if he should finish the thought.

Kylie knew how he felt—she'd helped him find Olivia's Christmas gift, but she wouldn't help until he told her what it was all about. He loved his sister and ultimately, he did trust her more than almost anyone else on the planet—only Flora rated higher and that was mainly because she'd tease but never pull pranks the way Kylie did—but sometimes he wanted to wring her neck. Honestly, switching rooms to get him and Olivia together was just like her, but it had never even occurred to him she'd do such a thing.

Olivia's heart fluttered. *About what? About us?* She wondered, but she didn't press him. She knew how she felt, and she was pretty sure she knew how Stephen felt. She desperately wanted to hear him say it, to confirm it with his own words so there wouldn't be any doubt. She didn't want to pressure him though—she couldn't do that to either of them. She had realized a lot about herself in the weeks since breaking up with Stan, and one of those things was how much pressure she'd put on Stan to make what they had "official" in the early days of their relationship. She knew what happened between them wasn't entirely her fault, of course, but she knew now that their relationship had started on a wrong note and she wasn't going to repeat those mistakes ever again.

Olivia smiled across the table at Stephen. "I really

like Kylie, even if she is a little punk."

Stephen laughed. "Well, she keeps things interesting anyway."

The conversation drifted into more casual territory. Their waitress arrived to take their orders: Olivia chose a light pasta dish and Stephen opted for a steak sandwich. The food arrived faster than expected and was excellent—as Olivia *had* expected based on everything else the Mountain Crest had offered so far. As they ate, the pair chatted about everything from the hotel's incredible location to the Warriors' last game, and to Randy's wedding the next day. Olivia asked about the bachelor party, but Stephen laughed and said, "What happens in AC, stays in AC."

"I think that's Vegas," she told him with a grin.

It was a good meal and a better conversation, but beneath the surface, both were keenly aware of the other's presence—and conscious of how the other felt, even if it still hadn't been put into words.

They were so engrossed in conversation, and each other, that they didn't notice the two familiar figures approaching their table until Flora's bright voice cut through the hum of the restaurant.

"Well, don't you two look cozy!" the old woman teased, her eyes twinkling as she and Kylie joined them.

"Grandma," Stephen began as he put down a French fry that hadn't yet made it to his mouth. "And we were having a perfectly nice dinner too," he teased back, standing to give his grandmother a hug.

Flora patted Stephen on the back and then released him, saying, "Don't mind us. Just keep talking about whatever you were so interested in." She smirked and slid into one of the two empty chairs at the table.

"Don't we always add to the fun?" Kylie asked, grinning unapologetically and giving Stephen one of her patented mischievous looks. She took the other empty chair, next to Olivia, and said, "I was just telling Grandma how nice it is to see you two getting along so well. You're welcome, by the way."

Stephen's eyes narrowed, a look Olivia had seen him give opposing players on the ice a time or two when the TV cameras zoomed in on him. "Don't think I'm letting you off the hook for the room stunt. That was *not* funny."

Kylie shrugged, her grin only widening. "Seemed funny to me." She looked at Olivia. "What do *you* think, Olivia?"

"Oh, it's not so bad," Olivia said, hiding a smile. Her cheeks flushed slightly with a mixture of embarrassment and amusement and sheer pleasure thinking of how she was going to spend the night with Stephen. Even if nothing happened, just being near him was like a gift from heaven—in the form of Kylie. She laughed mentally, imagining the younger girl with wings and a halo. Beneath the table, she gently squeezed Kylie's leg, silently thanking her for the meddling. Kylie glanced at her, her grin softening into a knowing smile and a wink only the other woman could see.

Flora sat back in her chair, fingers laced across her little belly, observing the scene with a delighted expression, clearly approving of every moment. "Now, Stephen," she said, interrupting his chewing Kylie out with a wave of her hand, "it's done, and everyone's here, and we're all going to have a lovely time. Let it go."

Stephen sighed and poked at his food sulkily, not entirely convinced. He never could go against Grandma Flora. "Fine." He looked up at Kylie from beneath lowered brows. "But you owe me."

"I don't owe you a thing, big bro," Kylie said cheerfully and picked a menu from the wire rack in the middle of the table.

Stephen signaled for the waitress and Flora and Kylie ordered. The two newcomers' drinks arrived and the four of them settled into conversation. Just after their food arrived, Randy Roberts appeared from the opposite side of the restaurant, his booming voice drawing attention even before he reached their table. "Hey, is that Stephen Sloan over there? He's the star of my favorite team!"

Randy marched up to their table, his fiancée, Amy, trailing behind him with a shy smile. "Mind if we crash the party?" he asked.

Flora, ever gracious, waved them over. "Of course, Randy, dear. Pull up chairs."

Kylie laughed. "You're asking us? You're footing the bill, man!"

Randy laughed and tugged over two chairs from a nearby table, offering one to Amy. He leaned down and gave Flora a quick kiss on the cheek, ruffled Kylie's hair like she was a little kid, and slapped Stephen on the shoulder before sitting down.

"Glad to see you guys," he beamed. "Olivia, I'm glad you came."

"Thanks for inviting me, Randy," Olivia said. "It's so nice here. It's like a dream."

"Oh, it's sweet as hell, but it ain't perfect. Listen to this shit—"

Randy launched into a story about a wedding planning mishap, something involving floral arrangements, but Olivia's attention was on Amy. She had expected someone larger-than-life to match Randy's bold personality—the kind of movie star beauty that you usually saw professional athletes with, or at least so it always seemed. But Amy wasn't flashy in anyway—her clothes were simple and comfortable-looking, a blouse and slacks, and she wore barely any makeup. She was almost plain-looking, but her laughter was easy and genuine as she listened to Randy's story and she seemed very… wholesome, Olivia finally decided. She looked like a nice girl.

"It's nice to meet you," Amy said warmly when Randy finally paused long enough to introduce her to

Olivia. She stood and leaned across the table to shake Olivia's hand. "I've met Flora and Stephen before, and Randy's told me all about Kylie, but he just said you were a friend of Stephen's."

"Oh, well—" Olivia glanced quickly at Stephen, then back at Amy. "That's true, I am. Kylie and Flora, too. A friend of theirs, I mean."

Amy smiled. "I'm glad you could come."

"Me too," Olivia said, smiling. "Thanks again for having me."

Before anyone else could take the conversation back up, Randy launched into another story, but Olivia barely heard it. She was watching Amy, obviously very much in love with Randy from the way she looked at the big goofball. It gave Olivia an unexpectedly hopeful feeling. Amy wasn't some unattainable, picture-perfect ideal woman, the kind Olivia always figured every guy wanted, but who were mostly reserved for the rich and famous. She was a regular girl, just like Olivia. And Randy, for all his outgoing loudness and his constant flirting with every woman around him—even the waitress, right in front of his fiancée, the jerk—was clearly as head-over-heels for her as she was for him.

Maybe, Olivia thought, stealing a peek at Stephen as he laughed at one of Randy's jokes, *being with Stephen isn't just a dream after all...*

Stephen looked over at that very moment, catching Olivia looking at him, and giving her a small, private smile. She grinned back, and leaned over, secretly squeezing Kylie's leg again and whispering to the other girl, "Thanks."

Chapter 29.

After dinner, Stephen excused himself to join Randy for the final wedding rehearsal. The big man had jumped from his seat and said, "Oh, shit. I forgot about the run-through tonight." Amy had laughed, patted his hip and told him, "I didn't. We still have a few minutes." She smiled gently at her future husband then stood and excused herself and Randy, telling the other ladies how glad she was to see all of them.

Before Stephen followed, he gave Olivia a soft smile as he left. "I'll catch you later," he told her, then disappeared into the hotel's grand hall, trailing after Randy and Amy. Olivia's gaze lingered for a moment before Kylie nudged her with an elbow, snapping her out of her thoughts.

"So," Kylie said brightly, turning to include Flora. "You guys wanna explore the hotel? They've got a game room, and like four bars—and I hear they've got some uh-*may*-zing boutiques on the promenade. Like, one of a kind designer clothing stuff."

Flora gave her granddaughter a small, tired smile and shook her head. "Not tonight, Kylie, dear. The drive up was enough excitement for one day. These old bones are still sore from that car ride. It's no fun getting old." She chuckled and rose to leave. "I think I'll turn in early."

"That's fair," Olivia said, smiling at her. "Get some rest. We'll see you in the morning."

Pausing by Olivia's chair, she patted the young woman on the shoulder and said, "Enjoy your evening, dear." To Kylie she said, "I'll see you in our room. Try not to be too noisy when you come in, hmm?"

"Wait," Olivia said slowly, turning towards Kylie. "You're sharing with Flora?"

"Oh, yes," Flora said breezily, waving a hand. "I can't seem to recall who I was supposed to stay with, but Kylie insisted on switching to be with me. She's such a good girl and she takes such good care of me, don't you, dear?" Flora's eyes twinkled as she smiled at the younger women.

Kylie grinned mischievously. "Of course—that's me all over. I'm just a thoughtful, selfless person."

Olivia couldn't help but laugh at the show these two were putting on. They all knew why Kylie had switched room assignments at the last minute. She should have been embarrassed, but she felt so close to these two already that she couldn't. She was just grateful for the push Kylie had given her.

Olivia and Kylie saw Flora to the elevator. Kylie offered to help Flora upstairs, but she declined, insisting the two girls go off and enjoy themselves. They wandered the hotel, sticking their heads into the bars, spending a few minutes in the game room checking out antiquated videogames. Then they made their way to the hotel's promenade, where the inviting glow of numerous small shops beckoned. They browsed through a high-end dress boutique first, marveling at the designer clothing and sparkling jewelry, before Kylie dragged Olivia into a lingerie store, her eyes lighting up at the rows of delicate lace and silk.

"Oh, I love dress-up!" Kylie declared, twirling like a little girl and grabbing a fiery red bra at random. She held it up against herself and asked, "Whatcha think? Too much?"

Olivia laughed, shaking her head. "Not for you. You're so cute, you could pull off pretty much anything, I think."

Kylie struck a mock pose, tossing the bra aside

before diving into another rack. "How about this one?" she asked, holding up a lacy black teddy with dramatic and strategic cutouts, designed to show off the wearer's most intimate assets.

"That's… something," Olivia said, giggling as Kylie twirled it playfully. "Is it even legal?" she asked laughingly.

"You should try something on," Kylie teased, rummaging until she found an even skimpier piece—a sheer, wine-colored teddy with a plunging neckline and slits cut all the way up the sides, only loosely held together with crisscrossed lace. She held it up against Olivia. "Oh-em-gee, Liv. You know, this would look sexy *AF* on you."

"Oh no," Olivia said quickly, her face flushing, pushing the lingerie away. "I could never pull that off. I'm too thick in the middle for something like that." It was a little embarrassing to say out loud, but she was aware of her body, and she knew Kylie wouldn't tease her about something like that. Kylie was a little twisty, but not malicious.

Kylie raised an eyebrow, her grin growing wider. "Well, I'm pretty sure Stephen wouldn't think so." She paused, humming a little song as she tilted her head in mock contemplation and held the teddy up in front of Olivia again. "Yeah, actually, I just so happen to *know* he wouldn't. You'd have him drooling."

Olivia's face turned beet red as Kylie burst out laughing, giving her friend a quick squeeze. "Relax, Liv. I'm just saying you'd look great. Think about it. Every girl deserves a chance to be her sexiest self once in a while—and I think you know how my brother feels, right?" She smiled at Olivia, and it wasn't teasing or mischievous for once—there was real warmth in it.

Chapter 30.

The soft hum of the bathroom fan filled the room as Olivia finished drying her hair. The damp warmth of her shower lingered in the air and her body felt deliciously relaxed, every muscle at ease from the hot water, and the nightcap she and Kylie had in one of the hotel bars before splitting up. The sports bar, naturally. Olivia smiled at herself in the mirror. The long drive from Boston to the Catskills was worth it just for this evening she'd already had. Dinner with Stephen, shopping and hanging out with Kylie—it was about the best Friday night she could have asked for.

Wrapped in a towel, she exited the bathroom, her eyes drawn to the single huge bed that dominated the room. She realized that wonderful as the night had been it wasn't yet over, and she wasn't sure what to expect. She felt her cheeks flush for what felt like—and probably was—the hundredth time that evening. She forgave herself. After all, she was going to be sharing a bed with Stephen Sloan, of all people—how was she supposed to keep her cool?

She whispered to herself, "It's not a big deal. It's just a bed. Two people—two mature, adult people—can share a bed and it's totally fine. Nothing *has* to happen. We're just two tired people who need rest, one of whose sister is a manipulative little—"

She cut herself off, laughing, shaking her head. *Kylie*, she thought and smiled. Olivia knew her friend intended it as a favor as much as a prank. For her and for Stephen too, for that matter.

Pushing aside all potentially embarrassing thoughts for the moment, she rummaged through her bag and pulled out her favorite set of pajamas: a soft, loose-fitting pair with a design depicting Snoopy as the World War I Flying Ace, zipping across the sky-blue fabric. They were practical, worn out just enough be comfy, and completely un-sexy. *Perfect,* she told herself as she slipped them on. She hoped they'd make her feel a little less self-conscious. "Better than sleeping in the buff at least," she said out loud with a laugh.

She pulled back the covers from the big bed and climbed in on the side she'd chosen, feeling like she was boarding some massive ocean-going craft. Her bed at home was just a full-sized, perfect for one person, but big enough for two should the need—or opportunity?—arise. She'd never slept in a bed this big. "Guess we'll have plenty of room…" she said, her thoughts wandering to Stephen.

Stephen. Her brain repeated his name like a mantra, and she couldn't stop seeing his face, his body… especially a certain part of it… in her mind's eye. It wasn't exactly a new thing: he was a stunningly handsome, incredibly sweet guy and he had been occupying her thoughts for weeks. And now, thanks to Kylie's meddling, they were sharing this room—and soon they'd be sharing this bed.

Olivia let out a small, muffled squeal, burying her face in the pillow, giddy excitement and nervousness rushing through her. She liked him. "I like him," she said to the ceiling, relishing the way it sounded. She let out another little squeal of excitement, kicking her legs like a small kid too excited to sleep.

Olivia liked Stephen. That much was obvious at this point to pretty much everyone, she realized. But she was also pretty sure he liked her too, and the thought was almost too much to process.

For another moment or two, she let herself enjoy the deliciousness of the excitement before taking a deep breath and forcing herself to calm down. She rolled onto her hip, staring at the curtained picture window, wondering how late Stephen would be. The wedding rehearsal should have started already when she and Kylie went off to explore the hotel. Was it still going on? She wasn't really sure how long something like that lasted. For that matter, she wasn't entirely sure what it even entailed. Would they go through every step of tomorrow or just certain parts? She picked up her phone and saw that it was after eleven. It had to be done by now, right?

She rolled onto her other side, facing the door. Stephen might walk through that door at any minute. Or maybe he and Randy were having drinks with the other groomsmen now, one last guys-only send-off before Randy's big day tomorrow. Maybe he ran into old friends and was busy catching up. Maybe, maybe, maybe. She could think of a hundred things Stephen might be doing if she tried, but she knew she was just torturing herself. As nervous as she was about the situation, she wanted to see him. She wanted him to walk through that door right this minute, smile at her and—

She sat up, the thought striking her suddenly. *The night-latch!* What if she'd latched the door and he couldn't get in? Climbing out of bed, she padded over to the door to check. The latch was open, she saw, but just as she turned from the door, headed back to bed, she heard a soft beep from the hallway, followed by the sound of the door unlocking.

She froze as the door swung open, revealing Stephen. He stepped in, his hair slightly mussed and his suit jacket slung casually over his arm. He looked tired, but his smile when he saw her was warm, lighting up both the room and Olivia's heart.

"Hey," he said, his voice soft. "You're still up."

Olivia smiled nervously, stepping back to let him into the room. "Yeah, I wasn't sure how late you'd be. How'd the rehearsal go?"

Stephen shrugged, dropping his jacket onto the chair near the door. "As well as could be expected. Randy's great—he's one of my best buds—but I think you know how he is by now. He couldn't shut up for five minutes. Every time we tried to go over something, he'd start telling some story or cracking a joke."

Olivia laughed, picturing the scene, Randy obliviously chattering on as his friends and teammates grew more frustrated with him. "Sounds like Randy."

"Yeah," Stephen said, chuckling. He glanced at her pajamas and tilted his head slightly. A teasing smile crept onto his face. "Nice pajamas, by the way. Very stylish. I didn't know you were a Snoopy fan."

Olivia felt her cheeks heat up, and she folded her arms self-consciously across her breasts. "Oh, come on, they're comfy. And who doesn't like Snoopy?"

"True. It's hard to hate a beagle." His grin widened. "But, no, really. I mean it. They're cute."

"Thanks," she mumbled, trying not to grin herself as she walked back toward the bed.

Stephen grabbed a bottle of water from the minibar and leaned against the long dresser that covered most of the wall opposite the bed. He unscrewed the cap, took a hefty gulp, then asked, "So, did you and Kylie get into any trouble exploring the hotel?"

"What kind of trouble could we get into?" Olivia asked laughingly.

"You know my sister. She's bound to find it if it's out there somewhere." Stephen raised an eyebrow, sensing something from her. "Wait—what did she do?"

"Oh, nothing too bad," Olivia said, settling onto the bed and tucking her legs under the covers. "She just got a little too excited in a lingerie shop. It was kind of embarrassing," she admitted.

Stephen choked on a sip of water, picturing his sister prancing through a lingerie shop in her underwear. Coughing, he set the bottle down, raised a hand to his mouth and wiped away some water he'd spilled. After a moment, shaking his head, he said, "That sounds about right. Did she rope you into it?"

"Of course," Olivia answered, laughing. "She even picked out a piece she wanted me to model for her."

Stephen tilted his head, curious. "Did you?"

"Stephen!" Olivia cried, her face burning as she threw a pillow at him.

He laughed, dodging the pillow effortlessly. "Hey, I'm just asking! You're the one who brought it up."

She rolled her eyes, though she couldn't help but smile. "You're impossible."

Stephen grabbed the pillow and tossed it back onto the bed. "Maybe," he said, smirking. "But you're stuck with me—at least for tonight."

He disappeared into the bathroom to get ready for bed. Olivia leaned back against the pillows, a little smile curling her lips. She had been so nervous waiting for Stephen and then there he was, and the conversation flowed so naturally, she forgot all about her nerves. Before a few hours ago, she and Stephen had never really spent any time together, just the two of them, and now it was like they'd known each other for years. She wasn't sure if it was Stephen or something unique between the two of them, something that couldn't exist for either of them with anyone else, but she liked it. She liked how relaxed he made her feel without even seeming to try, even in a situation that could've been unbearably awkward.

Stephen reappeared a few minutes later, dressed in a plain t-shirt and sweatpants. Olivia remembered his exit from the bathroom that afternoon and felt heat suffuse her entire body. The room was dimmed, only one of the bedside lamps lit now, and she hoped he couldn't see her cheeks reddening. Stephen climbed into the bed, an uncharacteristically shy smile on his face. Careful to keep to his side, he let out a sigh of relaxation then propped himself on one elbow to face her.

"You know," he said, his voice quiet, "I wasn't sure how this was going to go. Sharing a room, I mean. But… I'm glad it's you, Olivia. Earlier, I mean when you first got here, I was surprised," he chuckled remembering that scene, then continued, "but I really was glad to see you."

Olivia's heart fluttered and her breath caught in her throat. Her eyes found his, her cheeks warming under the intensity of his expression. "Me too," she said softly.

The space between them felt charged, the air heavy. Olivia, still gazing into Stephen's eyes, bit her lower lip. "Stephen?"

"Yeah?"

She hesitated. What was she going to tell him? Was she going to confess how she felt to him? Now, lying in bed together? That didn't feel right…

"Nothing… just, goodnight, Stephen," she said, as she reached over to switch off the lamp.

"Goodnight, Olivia," he said, his voice gentle.

Darkness fell over the room. Olivia settled under the covers, her heart still racing. Stephen lay back against the pillows propped behind his head. The springs of the mattress made small sounds as they shifted their weight. Olivia could hear Stephen's soft breathing, and faintly smell his cologne. The scent drifted through the darkness, combining with it, the warmth of the room, the gentle sounds of Stephen's breathe. All of it seemed to surround her, to wrap her in its embrace.

Slowly, Olivia became aware of other sounds: the faint hum of the heater, wind brushing against the window. She lay on her side, staring into the void. Her body had relaxed, but left to its own devices, her mind was racing, too restless for any hope of sleep. The warmth of Stephen's presence beside her, only a couple of feet away on the other side of the bed, was both comforting and maddening. She adjusted her pillow and began counting backward from one hundred in her head. It didn't help.

Being this close to Stephen, lying in the same bed, made sleep impossible.

She wasn't sure how much time had passed. Minutes? Hours? In her haze of restless thoughts and racing emotions, time had no meaning. It felt like her heart was thudding louder with every passing second—so loud Stephen must have heard it. She turned onto her back, staring at the faint outline of the ceiling, before finally giving in.

"Stephen," she whispered, her voice barely audible in the stillness. "Are you awake?"

For a moment, there was no response, and she wondered if he'd actually managed to fall asleep. The thought annoyed her vaguely, but she couldn't have said why. Then there was a soft, gentle laugh from his side of the bed. Her heart skipped a beat.

"How am I supposed to sleep?" he murmured, his voice warm and laced with quiet humor.

Even knowing he couldn't see her, Olivia smiled. There was something so endearing about the way he said it, as if they were sharing a secret—as if only the two of them could possibly answer that question. Her nerves retreated a little, just enough to gather her courage and say what she hadn't been able to earlier.

"You know," she began, the words coming slowly, as if finding their way from someplace deep inside of her, "we never talked about what happened that night..."

Her voice trailed off, and she turned onto her side, propping herself up slightly on one elbow as she faced him. She couldn't make out his features in the darkness, but she hoped he was facing her too. It wouldn't feel right to talk about this to his back.

"When we… shared those pictures with each other," she finished, her voice quieter now, hesitant. She'd come this far; she couldn't stop now.

The memory sent a rush of heat through her body, as if her blood had turned to molten lava. Her heart pounded so hard that now she was absolutely certain he could hear it. She pressed her lips together, trying to steady her breath. Admitting out loud what they shared felt like baring a part of herself—even more so than when she literally bared herself in taking the photo she sent Stephen. It took so much courage to even say that much, and now the silence stretching between them, the wait for Stephen's response, was unbearable.

What would he say?

Would he brush it off, act like it didn't matter? Girls probably sent him nude pictures all the time. Those signs the puck bunnies carried—with the eggplant emojis? They would send him anything he asked for.

Or maybe he regretted what they did? The thought sent a pang of anxiety through her, and she almost wished she could take it all back, pretend she hadn't said anything at all and leave those memories as they were, to stand alone, divorced from anything else.

Stephen shifted, the rustling of the sheets seeming loud in the quiet room. When he finally spoke, his voice was steady but soft. He understood the weight of what she'd said.

"Olivia," he began, "that night… I don't think I've stopped thinking about it for longer than the length of a game."

Her breathe caught. She hadn't expected him to be so direct, and hearing it sent a new wave of heat surging through her. Without realizing she was doing it, she rubbed her thighs together slightly.

"I wasn't sure how to bring it up," Stephen continued, his voice lower now, becoming intimate. "I didn't want to make things awkward, but… it meant something to me. I don't know if you'll think I'm, like, old-fashioned or whatever… but love and sex aren't two different things for me. They're so wound up together, and I can't have one without the other. Does that make sense?"

Olivia's fingers curled around the edge of the

blanket, her nerves buzzing like an angry beehive inside of her. But there was something else growing now too—hope. She swallowed hard, forcing herself to speak.

"It meant something to me too," she admitted, her voice trembling slightly. "I didn't know how to say it, and I didn't want to… I don't know. I really like you, Stephen, and I didn't want to scare you off or anything."

"You could never scare me off," Stephen said quickly, his sincerity apparent even if she couldn't see his face. "I've been going through a lot the last few months, and honestly, I've wanted to tell you how I felt for a while, but I wasn't sure if I had the right."

"What do you mean?"

He let out a heavy sigh. "I was with someone for a long time—basically, since we were kids. I found out something really terrible she'd done to me, and I broke it off, but it was messy, and it was still happening when we met and then—I don't know. It's over with now."

She could feel the mattress move, shifting with Stephen's weight as he inched a little closer to her. "That's over. It's done. And I realized how I felt about you, but I guess I didn't know if you felt the same way."

"I do," Olivia said softly, the words tumbling out before she could second-guess herself. "I really, really do."

There was a beat of silence. Olivia could feel the shift between them, an understanding that bridged the space that had kept them separate since she first knew how she felt about him. Stephen changed positions again, and Olivia imagined him lying there, facing her fully now, his expression as open and vulnerable as his voice.

"I've been thinking about you a lot," he admitted. "Not just about that night, but… everything. When we first met, you were just some girl who saved my grandma. I didn't expect her to make you part of the family." He chuckled. "Maybe she knew something we didn't right from the start."

Olivia's chest tightened. She was so filled with

emotions that she felt like she might explode. She reached out slowly, hesitantly, her hand brushing against the blanket near where she thought his arm might be. She felt the faintest movement, and then his hand met hers. His fingers were warm as they intertwined with hers.

"I don't know where this is going," Stephen said quietly, his thumb brushing against the back of her hand, "but I want to find out. If you do too, I mean."

Her heart swelled and her head felt light. "Of course I do," she whispered, her voice steadier now, finally knowing where they stood.

For the first time that night, Olivia felt her nerves begin to ease. The tension she'd been holding onto melted away, replaced by the quiet comfort of knowing they were on the same page.

Stephen squeezed Olivia's hand gently, but he couldn't hold back anymore—the feelings that had been building inside of him for weeks demanded expression. Slowly, he reached out, his hand finding her cheek, his fingers brushing softly against her skin.

"Olivia," he murmured, his voice low and warm, filled with everything he didn't know how to put into words.

She barely had time to respond before he pulled her toward him, his lips meeting hers in a kiss that was both tender and urgent. Olivia gasped softly against his mouth, her body responding instinctively as she melted into him. The kiss deepened, their lips moving together as though they'd been waiting for this moment forever. She opened her mouth, flicked her tongue against his lips until they opened for her, and then her tongue was inside his mouth, exploring it as her hands explored the firm contours of his body.

Stephen's hand slid from her cheek to the small of her back, pulling her closer. The warmth of her body against his made his heart pound, and he let himself sink fully into the kiss, pouring every unspoken feeling into it—

his affection, his longing, and the quiet, growing love he hadn't known how to express until now.

Olivia's hands found their way to his shoulders, clutching at him like she was afraid this moment might slip away—maybe this was just another one of those dreams she woke from gasping, her pussy wet, and her heart slightly broken.

But this couldn't be a dream—she could feel the smoothness of his skin, the hardness of his muscles, the stiffened penis pressing against her thigh. Her heart raced faster, hard enough that it hurt, as her body pressed more tightly against his. Breaking the kiss, not wanting to be separate from his lips for even an instant, she pulled back slightly, her breath mingling with his as she looked into his eyes. This close, even in the darkness, she could see an intensity that sent shivers through her.

Without a word, she reached for the hem of her pajama top, tugging it up and over her head in one swift motion even as Stephen was wriggling out of his t-shirt. Both of their chests were bare now, and she leaned forward to let the full, soft curves of her huge breasts press against Stephen's bare skin. She heard his sharp intake of breath and felt his hands tremble slightly as they slid down her back, caressing her ribs for a moment before moving up and tracing along the outside curve of her breasts.

"Olivia…" he whispered, his voice thick with emotion, as his hands roamed gently over her skin.

She silenced him with another kiss that lasted long enough they were both gasping for breath when it broke. Their bodies came together again, Stephen pulled himself higher on the bed then rolled onto his back, pulling her on top of him. She felt his engorged cock pressing between her thighs and the liquid heat inside of her began flowing, making her pussy so wet she could actually feel it soaking her panties. A little awkwardly, laughing in sheer joy, she tilted onto one knee and freed herself from her pajama bottoms, stripped off her panties, balled them up together and flung them aside.

The balled clothing struck the curtain and somehow knocked a fold of it aside and pinned it back, preventing it from falling back into place. Just a crack of window was revealed, but enough for a shaft of moonlight to pierce the room, landing on the middle of the bed like a cool, bluish-yellow spotlight. Olivia wouldn't have been able to manage that in a million years if she tried, but it was perfect—another sign that she and Stephen were meant to be.

Olivia leaned forward, pressing her breasts against Stephen's chest and kissing him again, her tongue flicking against his before she moved her head and trailed her tongue down his chin, his throat, to his neck, to his chest. Playfully, she nibbled one of his nipples, making him yelp.

He grinned up at her in the moonlight. "Your turn," he told her, gently pushing her to one side, wriggling from beneath her and then pressing her back against the mattress. He slid off his sweatpants, freeing his cock. Olivia thought he looked like some sort of god, lit by the moon, his perfectly muscled body and big cock the envy of all of Olympus.

She smiled up at him as he leaned down to kiss her, gently at first, then harder, more fiercely, making her gasp. He trailed kisses down her throat to her breasts, cupping one lovingly while he gently sucked on the bud of the other before switching. He covered her breasts in gentle kisses before moving on to her belly. His palm brushed against her pubes, sending electric jolts through her entire body. Still gentle, he cupped his hand to her pussy, feeling and relishing the heat and the wetness.

"You like that?" he asked her.

"Yes," she gasped, adding, "Oh, God, yes..." the last moaned as he rubbed his palm against the lips of her pussy.

Stephen lifted his hand to his lips and licked his palm, tasting her. He made a noise in his throat and held his hand out towards Olivia. Without hesitating, she tilted her head forward and licked his palm too, tasting herself on his skin.

He leaned up and kissed her. "I'm sorry it took me so long to tell you—everything, I guess. But I'm going to make up for lost time."

He trailed his lips over her breasts lightly and then moved down to her pussy, running his tongue up and down it several times before lazily circling her clitoris, making her cry out in pleasure. She reached down and stroked his head while he lapped at her sex, each brush of his tongue sending fire surging upwards throughout her body and into her brain. It was so good she could already feel herself welling towards explosive orgasm.

Stephen sat back on his haunches, resting between her legs. He gently massaged her thighs with both hands. Backlit by the thin stream of moonlight, Olivia thought he was the most beautiful being she'd ever seen.

"You like that?" he asked.

"Uh huh," she told him, her brain too sodden with pleasure to come up with anything else. "I want you inside me," she managed after a moment.

"I don't have a condom," Stephen told her.

"I don't care," she answered. "It'll be okay. Just don't—you know—when you're inside."

The moonlight fell across his chest as he leaned down to kiss her again, then shifted his hips to reposition himself.

Even before Stephen's throbbing erection penetrated Olivia, she let out a gasp in anticipation. When his penis did enter her, she shivered full-length, her entire body quivering in absolute ecstasy. "Stephen…" she said against his ear.

He began rocking, thrusting forward and up inside her with a slow, steady rhythm as gentle but as insistent as his tongue had been against her clit. "You're a good girl, taking this big cock, aren't you, Olivia?"

"Stephen… oh, oh, God, Stephen," she moaned, wrapping her arms around his shoulders and swinging her legs up to wrap around his thighs, pulling him closer, pulling him deeper inside of her. She wanted his entire length inside of her body. She thrilled at the feeling of his hard, muscular body on top of her, his weight shifting and pressing her back against the mattress and the pillows as his cock explored her most secret places.

"Olivia," he gasped, just once, before starting to move faster. The rhythm remained steady but picked up pace. She moved her hips, trying to match that rhythm, to meet him as he thrust inside her. She wanted him deeper, as deep as possible. She knew in that instant that she loved him and wanted this, wanted him, for the rest of her life.

"Stephen, Stephen, Stephen!" she cried. "I'm—I'm going to cum," she told him.

"Me—too," he gasped.

Heat washed over her as she felt her pussy tighten, gripping his cock like a fist before she exploded. Delicious agony flooded through her brain and her body for an instant before dissolving into a euphoria both physical and emotional that she'd never known before.

And then Stephen was right there with her, pulling his cock from her still-quivering pussy, stroking himself hard and fast before his own climax exploded, sending thick, ropey streams of cum blasting all over her, covering her belly and her breasts and her pubes.

Breathing heavily, like a winded racehorse, Stephen collapsed next to her on the bed, his chest visibly rising and falling, making his tattoos writhe in the moonlight. Olivia leaned down, took his face in both hands and kissed him, softly. The fierceness was gone from their need and only love was left.

Stephen rolled over, climbed from the bed, and a moment later returned with a damp washcloth. Gently, lovingly, he cleaned her up, then tossed the cloth towards the bathroom and once again took her in his arms.

"Olivia…" Stephen whispered.

"Oh, Stephen," she answered before nestling her head against his shoulder and dropping off to sleep.

Chapter 31.

The sunlight filtered through the partially open curtain, casting golden streaks across the hotel room. One fell directly across Olivia's face and she stirred, blinking groggily as the warmth of the light teased her awake. For a moment, she was disoriented, unsure of where she was. The plush bedding beneath her was unfamiliar, softer than she was used to, and the air carried the faint scent of pine and hotel linens. Her brain sluggishly pieced together her memories, and everything came back—the long car-trip from Boston, the "dinner date" with Stephen, the fun she had window-shopping with Kylie… and the rest of the night.

Then she felt it—the solid, comforting weight of Stephen's body next to hers, his lean but muscular arm draped loosely around her waist. His warmth radiated against her skin, making her tingle wherever they were in contact. She turned, looking over at him, reliving every moment of their first night together the night in an instant. A soft smile spread across her face as a feeling of profound love and contentment filled every cell of her body.

Stephen was still asleep. His face was serene, utterly relaxed and without a hint of tension, even his breathing slow and even. Asleep, he looked so very different from the confident, larger-than-life hockey player the world knew. Awake or asleep, his features were always handsome, with that chiseled jawline and those perfect cheekbones, but they were softer now, his brow relaxed, his lips parted, moving slightly as he dreamed. Relaxed and defenseless like this he looked younger, even boyish. It gave him a kind of vulnerability that made her heart swell. She wanted to wrap her arms around him and provide him with all the comforts she could.

But then her gaze drifted downward, moving over the tattooed expanse of his well-muscled chest as it rose and fell with each breath he took, and there was no mistaking that he was a man. She reached out slowly, careful not to wake him up, and let her fingers brush lightly against the inked designs that decorated his skin, tracing the edge of a line before pulling back.

She thought again about everything that happened between them the night before, how they'd finally let go of their fears and hesitation, admitting their feelings to one another and giving in to what they had both wanted for so long. She savored the memory of his touch, how he whispered her name, how he unleashed all of that passion to show her how he really felt about her—all of it made her cheeks flush and her chest tighten with affection.

She remembered too, what Stephen told her, about how sex and love weren't separate things—how he couldn't have one without the other.

This is real, she thought, her smile widening. She touched his chest again, light as a feather, and whispered so quietly only she could hear it, "This is us—Olivia and Stephen. Me and you."

For weeks, Olivia wouldn't allow herself to believe that she could have something like this. The years with Stan took something from her that she didn't realize was gone until it was over—even realizing that she wasn't sure what exactly that thing was, only that she was different than before. But now, lying here with Stephen Sloan, with the man she'd fallen for so deeply, she felt none of those old doubts. This wasn't a dream, and it wasn't some fleeting, too-good-to-be-true moment. It was real, and it was theirs.

Stephen began to stir, his hand flexing against her

waist before he relaxed again, his face nuzzling into the pillow. The movement tickled a little, making her laugh softly, and she covered her mouth, not wanting to wake him just yet. She wanted to savor this just a while longer—this quiet, golden morning with him beside her, the world outside the room forgotten. She couldn't imagine anything more perfect.

He stirred again, rolling partially onto his back. Stephen was so beautiful that it almost hurt to look at him, but still she took the chance to study him, trying to memorize every detail of his face. There was heavy stubble on his jaw, and his dark lashes cast shadows against his cheeks. There was a small, dimpled scar near his temple that she hadn't noticed before. She wanted to ask him about it some time, but for now, all she really wanted was to watch him, to experience this unguarded version of him.

Stephen was beautiful, yes, but it wasn't just his looks that left her breathless. It was *him*. The man. The person. He was thoughtful, kind in ways she hadn't realized she needed until she met him. He could be shy and vulnerable, but he was also strong, and she knew that he could be fiercely protective—she'd seen how much he cared for Flora, and for Kylie, and even for his teammates.

And more than that, last night at dinner, and again, later, when they were alone—the way he looked at her, the way he touched her, she knew he was focused entirely on her. In those moments, he gave her everything he had, and she was the only person in the world who mattered.

Olivia sighed gently, letting her head sink back against the pillow. She wished this moment could last forever. At the very least, she wished she knew what the future held—what would happen when they left the safe, warm cocoon of this hotel room and went back to their busy lives. Relationships take work—she knew that—but it was even harder when someone was on the road as much as Stephen. But the hockey season doesn't last forever, she reminded herself, and for now, she couldn't worry about things that hadn't happened yet. Right now, she was exactly where she wanted to be.

A low groan interrupted her thoughts. She looked just in time to see Stephen stretch lazily, his muscles rippling beneath his skin. He blinked, his eyes unfocused as he woke, then reached up to rub the sleep from them. As he lowered his hand, he turned to her with a slow, sleepy smile that made her heart dance inside her chest.

"Morning," he murmured, his voice still rough with sleep.

"Hi," she replied, her voice soft and warm.

Stephen reached up, rubbing a hand over his face before propping himself up on one elbow to look at her. "You been awake long? What time is it?" He fumbled towards the nightstand for his watch.

"Not really," Olivia lied, not wanting to admit she'd been watching him sleep like some love-struck teenager. "The sun woke me up."

Stephen glanced at his watch, saw that it was after ten, then followed her gaze to the curtain. His smile became a playful smirk, and he teased, "That, or I was snoring."

She laughed, batting his shoulder lightly. "You weren't snoring. At least, not loud enough to wake me."

"Good to know," he said, his eyes warm as they searched hers. He reached out, brushing a strand of hair from her face, his touch lingering against her cheek. "You look beautiful."

Olivia's breath caught, and she felt her cheeks flush again. "Please. You're just saying that because you're still half-asleep."

"No," he protested, his voice sincere. "I'm saying it because it's true."

For a long moment, they simply looked at each other, the world outside the room falling away. Stephen's hand moved to hers, their fingers intertwining as he gave her a gentle squeeze.

"I don't think I've ever felt this way before," he admitted, his voice barely above a whisper. "I'm not gonna make up stories and say I've never been in love before or anything. But, like… everything just seems to make sense when I'm with you."

Warmth spread through Olivia's body that had nothing to do with the glow of the sunlight. She leaned in, pressing a soft kiss to his lips. "Me too," she said against his mouth. "You make me feel safe. And loved."

Stephen's smile widened, and he pulled her closer, their foreheads touching as they lay tangled together. For the first time in a long time, Olivia was completely at peace. This was all she needed, all she'd ever hoped for. She said a silent prayer, asking that it could remain this way between her and Stephen forever.

Chapter 32.

The wedding reception was in full swing, the Mountain Crest Hotel's huge reception hall filled with people, celebrating the new couple's life together with joyful chatter and laughter. The room was bathed in warm, golden light from massive, ornate crystal chandeliers hanging overhead, and closer to Earth, their sparkle was mirrored by glasses of champagne carried on silver trays by busily circulating waiters and waitresses dressed in formal attire. Except for the giant TV screens scattered across the room, mounted high on the walls, showing slideshows of photos from throughout the couple's relationship, it could have been a scene out of almost any time period. It was almost like the modern version of a fairytale ball, Olivia thought with a smile.

Nearly two hundred guests milled about the giant room, everyone dressed to the nines. They chatted in clusters, laughed at shared jokes, gave impromptu speeches to the bride or groom or both, and repeatedly raised their glasses in toasts to Randy and Amy Roberts. On the far side of the hall, a band on a raised dais played both new and classic songs and the dance floor was packed with couples letting loose, allowing their bodies to express their happiness for their friends' union.

Stephen and Olivia had sat with Flora and Kylie during the ceremony, but at the reception, Flora had chosen to chat with Randy's parents and older relatives while Kylie was circulating like the social butterfly she was.

Now, Stephen stood at one of the tall cocktail tables with Olivia, an arm on the edge of the table, drink in hand. His other hand rested lightly, casually, on Olivia's hip. On the other side of table were Stephen's fellow Warrior Ken Johns and his date, Veronica, a pretty and petite Latina girl of about twenty with dark, glossy hair. Olivia was initially surprised seeing Ken, who was about thirty, with a girl so young, but after talking to them both for several minutes she decided that Veronica was a surprisingly good match for him.

The four of them had been swapping stories for the better part of twenty minutes, trading jokes and stories about Randy mostly, before the conversation moved on to tales from Ken and Stephen's respective college days. Stephen was in the middle of a story about a particularly wild hockey game from his sophomore year, gesturing animatedly as he described a last-second goal that had turned the tide of the match—not his shot, sadly, but at least the team won.

"And then," Stephen said, grinning as he leaned forward, "This guy, Dave—great wing, but a total doofus off the ice—he completely wipes out during the celebration. I mean, full-on faceplant. The guy didn't even score the goal, but he was just so hyped the second the skates were off—BOOM!" He clapped his hands. "Trips over his own feet."

Ken laughed. "I got a story like that. Details don't matter, but I used to play with a guy—this was before I was on the Warriors—he was like a little kid he'd get so excited. This one time we were lining up post-game, and I don't know how the hell he managed it, but down he goes. His helmet flew off, and he tried to play it cool like it didn't happen. Meanwhile, he's got ice burn on his forehead for a week."

Veronica giggled, picturing it. "I just got into hockey recently, but it sounds like you guys have a good time at least." She turned to Olivia and smiled. "I bet you hear all kinds of crazy stories, being around these guys."

Olivia laughed softly. "Oh, yeah." She nudged

Stephen with her elbow. "With this guy, it's like being in the audience of a sitcom or something. Just comedy twenty-four-seven."

Veronica smiled, her eyes flicking over Olivia's outfit. "I love your dress, by the way. That color looks amazing on you. And your hair—it has so much volume! I wish mine was like that. No matter what I do, it's just kinda there." She brushed a strand from her shoulder.

Olivia felt a blush creeping into her cheeks but smiled graciously. "Thank you. You look incredible too—that dress is gorgeous, and I think your hair is lovely. It's so shiny and looks silky."

Veronica grinned, twirling slightly to show off the fitted sapphire-blue gown she wore. "Thanks! You're sweet. I spent half the morning agonizing and finally just picked the most expensive thing in my closet." She laughed, then gestured towards Ken with a tilt of her head. "And this guy never even said a word when he saw it."

"Hey, I noticed," Ken protested. "You look amazing, babe. I'm not that oblivious—I just like, I'm not good with words, okay?"

Veronica rolled her eyes playfully before turning back to Olivia. "So, how did you two meet?" she asked, jutting her chin slightly towards Olivia and Stephen.

A smile came to Olivia's lips as she thought of how best to summarize the whirlwind of events that had brought her and Stephen together. But before she could get a word out, Stephen stiffened beside her, his hand gripping the edge of the table.

"Are you kidding me?" he muttered, his voice low and sharp. "Shit."

Olivia turned to him, her brow furrowed in concern. "Stephen? What is it?"

He didn't answer right away. His jaw was tight as his eyes locked onto something—or someone—across the room. Following his line of sight, Olivia's heart sank when she spotted her: Liza Gardner.

Liza stood near the bar, her sleek, platinum-blonde hair catching the light as she leaned in close to a man who looked vaguely familiar, likely one of Randy's extended family members. She was dressed in a form-fitting black cocktail dress that stood out starkly against the pastel colors and jewel tones worn by most of the other guests.

"What is *she* doing here?" Stephen muttered, his tone a mix of anger and disbelief.

Ken frowned, following Stephen's gaze. "Liza? Seriously? I thought she was history."

"She is," Stephen said tersely. "At least, she's supposed to be."

Olivia felt a wave of unease roll through her, but she took a breath and steadied herself. She reached out, resting a hand lightly on Stephen's arm. "Hey," she said softly, trying to calm him. "It's okay. She's probably just here with someone. We can just avoid her."

"No," Stephen said, shaking his head. "This is some kind of game or trick—she knows she isn't welcome here."

Ken moved around the table and clapped Stephen on the shoulder, a hint of concern on his face. "Don't let her ruin your night, man. This is a party, not a drama fest. Just ignore her."

Stephen let out a slow breath, glancing down at Olivia's hand, still on his arm. The touch of her hand was reassuring and seemed to ease some of his tension. "Yeah," he said quietly. "Maybe you're right."

"Sure, I am," Ken said. "Hey, come on. Let me get us some real drinks." He set his champagne flute down and headed towards the far end of the bar, avoiding the area Liza was in.

Veronica, spoke up. "That's awkward. I'm sorry," she said, directing it at both Olivia and Stephen.

Olivia smiled, grateful for the support, even as her stomach churned. Stephen nodded, forcing a tight smile.

"Thanks."

Randy and Amy appeared out of the crowd. They had already stopped by earlier while making their rounds, thanking everyone for coming and accepting people's well-wishes, but this was different—it was clear from their expressions that something was wrong, a cloud fallen over their special day.

"Hey, guys," Randy said, his voice uncharacteristically crestfallen. He rubbed a fist against his cheek awkwardly. "Uh, listen, I gotta apologize. I completely forgot to update the guest list after, well… everything that happened, and I forgot to uninvite Liza."

Amy added, "I honestly didn't even think she'd come, since you guys split up." She put a hand on Stephen's arm and looked towards Olivia. "I'm so sorry if this makes things difficult for you both."

Stephen shook his head, offering them a reassuring smile. "It's okay. I get it—you've had a million things on your plate with the wedding." He forced a laugh. "And we're adults, right? This isn't middle school."

"I feel like an idiot," Randy said. "This was supposed to be fun for everyone, and she's stirring up drama. I hate it."

"Randy, man—it's fine. Really. This is your day—yours and Amy's. Don't worry about me." He glanced Olivia. "Us. I'll steer clear of her."

Amy smiled, visibly relieved, and Randy gripped Stephen's shoulder. "Brother, you're a class act, you know that?"

They lingered for a moment longer, but it was obvious that the couple wanted to move on, to distance themselves from the discomfort they knew Stephen must still be feeling. As they left to greet more guests, Olivia watched them go, proud of how much Stephen cared about easing their minds, even when he was clearly tense about Liza's being at the wedding. She reached out and squeezed his arm, reassuring him.

Ken returned to the table, carrying a small tray of cocktails. There was tightness around his mouth and anger in his eyes. He set the drinks down harder than necessary, making the tall glasses wobble before settling down.

"Everything okay?" Olivia asked.

Ken glanced at her, then turned to Stephen. "Can I talk to you for a second?"

Stephen frowned but nodded, following Ken to a quieter corner of the hall.

"I don't wanna cause trouble, but you should know," Ken began, his voice low but firm. "I just heard Liza talking some shit. I'm pretty sure wanted to make sure I heard her, cuz she's telling people you two are getting back together soon. That you're just, like, going through a phase or something and she's giving you your space."

Stephen's jaw clenched, his eyes narrowing as he remembered that Liza had said something similar to him when he confronted her in the penthouse. "Are you serious? For real? She's telling people that?"

"Dead serious," Ken replied. "She was saying some nasty shit about Olivia too." He looked embarrassed for a moment, adding, "I don't wanna repeat it, man, but it's not good. Like, nasty stuff about her looks, but she's also saying Olivia is just some rebound you're playing around with to make her jealous."

Stephen clenched his fists. "Unbelievable. She's just—damn it. She's got no right to say anything about Olivia. None. They've never even met."

"I just thought you should know," Ken said, his voice softening. "I'm sorry, Stephen. I don't wanna cause trouble, but she's stirring up shit and I didn't want it to blindside you."

Stephen shook his head, his expression hard but resolute. "Thanks. I appreciate it and I'll handle it. I'm not going to let her ruin tonight. Not for me or for Olivia."

Ken nodded, patting him on the shoulder. "That's what I figured, but I've got your back if you need me. The whole team does, man."

"Thanks. I know you do," Stephen told him.

Stephen's mind raced as they went back to the table. He knew Liza's manipulative streak all too well, but dragging Olivia into her little drama parade very much crossed the line.

Retaking his place beside Olivia, Stephen met her questioning gaze with a small, reassuring smile. He reached for her hand under the table, giving it a gentle squeeze.

"Everything okay?" she asked softly, searching his eyes.

"Yeah," Stephen told her, voice steadier than he felt. "Everything's fine. But listen, there's something I gotta take care of. I'll be back in a few minutes, okay?"

Olivia took his wrist, as if to keep him where he was. "If it's about her, it's fine. I'm okay. Really. She doesn't bother me."

He looked into her eyes, holding her gaze the way she held his wrist. "I'm just gonna talk to her. I don't want to, but—"

Olivia saw Stephen's turmoil. She wished he could just let this go—Liza hadn't bothered them so far, after all—but she was afraid if he didn't get it out of his system, he wouldn't be able to relax.

"Just hurry, okay?" She smiled and released his wrist.

"I will," he told her, nodded to Ken and moved off into the crowd.

Stephen spotted Liza almost immediately. She wasn't exactly trying to blend in—in fact, he was certain everything she did, from her loud chatter to the way she was playing up to members of Randy's family, was intended to draw attention. She tilted her head back as she laughed at something one of Randy's cousins was saying. Once he'd loved her laughter, but now the sound grated on his nerves.

He crossed the room, stepped between Liza and

the man she was talking to, and lightly but firmly took her by the arm. "We need to talk."

Liza turned to him, bright red lips curving into a syrupy-sweet smile. "Stephen," she said, her voice practically dripping mock surprise. "So nice of you to make time for little old me."

He kept silent, already guiding her toward the door. She resisted for a moment, her smile tightening, but finally allowed herself to be led from the reception hall, out into one of the rear hallways used by the hotel staff. As the door closed behind them, muffling the sounds of music and laughter, Liza's demeanor shifted.

"What the hell do you think you're doing?" she snapped.

"I should be asking you that," Stephen shot back, keeping his voice low but letting some of his anger seep out. "What are you doing here, Liza?"

"I was invited," she retorted, crossing her arms.

Stephen's jaw tightened. "That was before—"

"Before what?" she cut in, her eyes narrowing. "Before you lost your puny little mind?"

Stephen's anger flared, burning so hot it threatened to spill out, but he held it back, tamped it down. "Before we split up. You don't even like Randy, and you've met Amy—what? Once or twice. I seem to remember you calling her 'the mouse girl' or something like that. They don't want you here and neither do I—and you know that."

Liza's expression darkened, her perfectly painted lips pressed into a thin line.

"I really think you should just leave," he said.

Her laugh was sharp and brittle, like splinters of glass. "Or what, Stephen? You going to have me dragged out? Call hotel security?" She smirked, fully aware he wouldn't do anything to upset his friend Randy or Randy's new wife.

He took a deep breath. "Please. Just go. Don't

make a scene. This isn't about you or me. This is Randy and Amy's day. You know that, right?"

Liza tilted her head, her eyes gleaming with malice. "No," she said, her voice cold. "It's not. This is about *you*—and what you've done to me—and about that cow on your arm."

Stephen's face colored. He knew Liza was meanspirited, but attacking Olivia was low—Liza had never even met her.

He clenched his fists at his sides. "Keep her out of this," he said, his voice low and dangerous, tight with his anger. "This is between us—and there *is* no us. Do you understand that? It's done. I've told you before, this isn't some 'phase' or any of the other bullshit you keep telling yourself. I just finally realized who you are, and you're not someone I want anything to do with."

Liza's eyes flared with pure fury. She stepped closer, her voice rising, taking on a slight edge of hysteria. "I was willing to give you another chance," she spat. "But that's it. You've blown it, Stephen, and now you're going to regret it."

He stepped back, putting distance between them, shaking his head. "I don't regret walking away, and I never will. But I'm asking you one more time, one last favor if I ever meant anything at all to you: just go. Please."

For a moment, Liza hesitated, her expression flickering between hatred and something less definable. Then she straightened, her smile returning, but now it was cold and vindictive.

"You'll regret it, Stephen," she said again, her voice quieter this time, but more menacing.

She turned on her heel and went back into the reception hall, leaving Stephen standing in the hallway, his chest heaving with the strain of the confrontation.

He ran a hand through his hair. That went about as badly as it could have, but at least he tried.

Stephen found his way to the men's room,

splashed cold water on his face, then relieved himself. He was just buying a few minutes to put himself back together, afraid of what he might find when he went back into the wedding reception. Liza was capable of almost anything, but he hoped she still had enough composure to keep from doing anything to ruin the reception for Randy and Amy.

He stepped back into the hallway, calmer, but still uneasy. He told himself that at the very least, he had said what he needed to say to Liza and all he could do now was go back to Olivia and try to salvage what was left of the evening.

Stephen noticed immediately on entering the reception hall that the atmosphere had changed. The warm, friendly buzz of wedding celebration and laughter was gone. In its place was a darker, charged murmur of whispers that rippled through the crowd. Something unexpected, and unpleasant, had clearly happened.

Sloan frowned, scanning the room as he made his way back to their table. People glanced at him, some quickly averting their eyes, while others glared or whispered to one another. He quickened his pace, feeling an uncomfortable pit forming in his stomach. *What the hell did Liza do?* he wondered.

When he reached the table, his heart dropped.

Veronica was next to Olivia, her arm draped around the older woman's shoulders in a protective gesture. Olivia's head was down, her hands covering her face as her shoulders shook with barely contained sobs. Ken stood nearby, his arms crossed tightly over his chest, his expression dark. He glared angrily at Stephen.

"What the hell is going on?" Stephen demanded.

Ken's jaw clenched, and he pointed to the nearest of the large TV screens mounted on the walls of the hall. "Jesus Christ, man," he said, disgusted and angry. "What the fuck is *that?*"

Stephen turned, his eyes locking onto the screen.

The cheerful slideshow of Randy and Amy's happiest moments during their relationship was gone and in its place was a sharply defined video, the kind taken by a high-end smartphone.

Ice flooded Stephen's veins. The video showed scenes from Liza's party, the one that finally opened his eyes about her and drove him to remove her from his life. He watched, shaking with fury and disbelief as a fully clothed Stephen Sloan moved through the groups of strangers having sex in every imaginable position in his own home. In his mind, he relived those moments as the Stephen on the screen experienced them. He remembered his shock and how his disgust and anger grew as he realized the extent of Liza's betrayal and what kind of filth she was up to behind his back.

But you couldn't tell that from watching this video. Whoever had been filming got plenty of shots of Stephen's face, but somehow the shock and anger and sense of betrayal he'd been feeling wasn't captured at all. He realized that the video must have been edited, because it seemed to tell a very different story than what actually happened that afternoon.

The faces of everyone in the video were blurred, except Stephen's—his was crystal clear, and the way the footage had been cut made it seem as though he was actively participating in the sordid behavior.

"What the hell…" Stephen whispered, his voice trailing off as the reality of the situation hit him.

The whispers in the room grew louder, and Stephen's ears burned as he felt the weight of hundreds of eyes on him. He turned back to Ken, his expression frantic. "This isn't what it looks like. You know that, right?"

"I don't know what to think, man."

"It was Liza!" Stephen cried. "I just saw her—out in the hall—and she said—I don't know how she did it, who she bribed to—"

"It doesn't matter," Ken cut in. "Whatever happened, now Olivia's in the middle of it."

Stephen's gaze snapped to Olivia, who trembled under Veronica's arm. His chest tightened painfully at the sight of her tears, and he crouched down beside her, his voice gentle but desperate. "Olivia," he said softly. "Olivia, look at me. Please."

She lowered her hands slowly, her eyes red and glistening. Her expression was hurt and confused. It was like a knife to his chest.

"Is it true?" she asked, her voice trembling. "Were you… were you part of that? After what you said about love and…"

"No," Stephen said firmly, shaking his head. "Absolutely not. Olivia, you have to believe me. That video—whatever it looks like—it's not what happened."

"But your face…" she started, her voice breaking. "Why would someone even have a video like that of you?"

Stephen ground his teeth together, his thoughts churning. Even knowing Liza well, he couldn't believe she was spiteful enough to not only make such a video but play it in the middle of Randy and Amy's wedding reception, simultaneously destroying their special night and Stephen's reputation.

"Liza," he said, his voice low and filled with venom. "She did this. She's trying to ruin me—and us," he said, his voice rising slightly before he caught himself.

"I can't—" Olivia said, the tears coming again. She stood and hurried towards the exit, the skirts of her dress swirling and trailing after her.

"Olivia!" Stephen called, not caring who heard him, reaching out as if he could take her by the hand and pull her back into his arms. The image of her tear-streaked face made his heart ache, and seeing friends and teammates looking at him like he was dirt beneath their feet made his chest burn with white-hot hatred for Liza Gardner.

Chapter 33.

Stephen sat in the huge living room of the penthouse, the lights off, only the faint sun of a winter afternoon coming through the floor to ceiling windows provided any illumination. Beyond those windows, Boston Harbor was a bleak and gray expanse, matching his mood for the last week. He'd been living alone in his apartment since the first of the year, but the space around him had never felt emptier. He opened his cellphone for the hundredth time in the last two hours, checking his text messages. He'd sent Olivia a dozen messages since Saturday evening, asking her to please give him a chance to explain everything. Each message showed as read but she hadn't responded at all.

Stephen sighed heavily, leaning back into the plush couch, his head tilted back against the cushion as he stared at the shadowed ceiling. The ache in his chest was sharp when he first saw Olivia crying, like a blade slid between his ribs. Now it was a constant ache, a dull, relentless reminder of everything he'd lost in the span of a single, terrible night engineered by someone he'd once loved but who was now a bitter enemy. The betrayal hurt, but not as much as the loss of Olivia.

His thoughts drifted and he remembered back to those first few minutes in the reception hall and the chaos that erupted when he walked back in after collecting himself from the confrontation with Liza. Those murmurs and whispers, all of those eyes looking at him as if he were filth—all of that had been bad enough. But the sight of Olivia, tears streaming down her face as she fled the room, was the image that haunted.

He'd tried to follow her immediately, his heart in his throat and his stomach churning with nausea, but the crowd was on him like veteran defenders keeping him away from their goalie. Members of Randy's family—his mother and aunts, his father and a cousin—had swarmed him, demanding answers, asking accusing questions that he couldn't take the time to address.

"What is wrong with you?"

"You're sick!"

"Why would you show something like that here?"

Every second he spent fending off their questions felt like an eternity, and he could almost physically feel Olivia drawing farther away with each passing moment. When he was finally able to break free, he raced to their room, skipping the elevator, taking the stairs three at a time. He was far too late. Olivia's things were gone. Her bag, her coat, the little knitting project she'd been working on that afternoon—it had all vanished, like she'd never been there at all.

Panic surged inside him, dumping ice into his veins. He tore through the hotel like a madman, scouring the public spaces—the gym, the lobby, the bars, the shopping promenade—even the parking lot, hoping to at least find her car and know that she was still somewhere in the area, that there was a still a chance to fix this. But the car was gone. Olivia was gone, like she'd disappeared into thin air.

When Stephen returned to the room, defeated, desperate, unable to think about what all of this meant for anyone else, Kylie and Grandma Flora were waiting for him.

"Stephen," Kylie said softly, her usual playful tone replaced with an uncharacteristic seriousness. She sat perched on the edge of the bed, her expression both angry and worried.

Flora stood near the window, her small frame

silhouetted against the backdrop of the mountain's hugeness. She turned as Stephen entered the room, her face etched with concern. "Can you blame her, Stephen?" Flora asked quietly.

"Blame her?" Stephen repeated, his voice hoarse. "Of course I don't blame her!" he shouted. Seeing Flora wince, he felt a splash of guilt, and lowering his voice added, "I'm sorry. I didn't mean to yell, but I need to talk to her. I need to explain—"

"Not tonight, dear," Flora interrupted gently, her tone soothing but firm. "I'm… sure you have a good explanation, but Olivia's hurting. And right now, she doesn't want to hear from you. She needs some time."

Stephen sank into the room's one chair, his head in his hands. "I didn't do anything wrong," he said, his voice cracking. "That video—it's a lie. She has to know that. This is all Liza. She hates me so God-damned much. I never realized—"

"Olivia knows," Kylie said, her voice soft but certain. "Deep down, she knows. I'm sure she does, but Stephen, think about how it looked to her. She never told you how her last relationship ended, did she? She caught the guy cheating, like right in the act."

She stood, moved to where her brother sat, placing a hand on his shoulder. "Olivia's not just mad—she's hurt, she's embarrassed. You guys only just figured out what's what with you, right? It's all really new and then here comes that bitch Liza... she made sure this whole thing was aimed right at Olivia."

Stephen looked up, his eyes blazing with frustration. "I can't just let her believe Liza's lies—it's just some clever editing of a damned cellphone video. I can't let something like that be the end of—" His voice caught in his throat, preventing him from finishing the thought.

Flora crossed the room, placing a gentle hand on Stephen's other shoulder. "You'll have to give her space, Stephen. Chasing her now will only make it worse."

He had wanted to argue, to storm out and continue searching, but Flora's calm resolve stopped him. She was right. Olivia wasn't ready to hear from him, and forcing the issue wouldn't help. Kylie and Flora were the two people closest to him nearly his entire life. They cared about him deeply, and they wouldn't give him any advice unless they thought it would help.

The two women stayed a while longer, but there wasn't much left to say. Flora made Stephen promise to get some rest, telling him tomorrow was time enough to repair things with Randy and Amy and then he could think about how to approach Olivia. The rest of the night, he sat in the quiet of the darkened hotel room, replaying every second of the previous twenty-four hours in his mind, agonizing over the happy hours he and Olivia spent together, raging at the slaughter of his reputation and new relationship. He would go over those moments, allow himself to wallow in the pain and fury and then push them aside, trying to find a way to fix the damage. It was a vicious cycle that kept him awake all night and a week later, he was still lost in it.

Now, Stephen clenched his phone tightly, his chest tightening as he scrolled through Olivia's unread responses. He didn't blame her for shutting him out, not after everything she'd been through. But the silence was unbearable. He wished she'd just give him a chance, he only needed a few minutes to explain.

He thought of her laugh, her smile, the way her eyes lit up when she was teasing him. He thought of the quiet moments they'd shared, the connection that had felt so real and unshakable. He remembered her passion the night they spent together in the hotel. The ache in his chest was unbearable because all of that was slipping through his fingers, and he was powerless to stop it.

Stephen closed his eyes, exhaling deeply as he leaned forward, resting his elbows on his knees. "Olivia," he murmured to the empty room, his voice heavy with longing. "Please… just let me make this right."

Chapter 34.

Jack's kitchen smelled like fresh coffee, frying grease, and the warm, faintly spicy smell of tomato soup. Tomato soup and grilled cheese, two things Jack was pretty confident in his skill at cooking. He'd been making them as comfort food for Olivia almost literally her entire life, and when she came over late in the morning, he could sense it was one of those days when she needed comfort the most. Now she sat across the table barely even nibbling, hardly speaking unless he asked her a direct question. She'd only taken a few spoonfuls of soup, and a bite of the sandwich. No matter what was going on, Olivia was usually a good eater. Whatever was going on must have been pretty bad.

Jack wasn't the prying type. He respected his daughter's independence, and her privacy. Only very rarely had he ever pushed her to talk about things if she didn't bring them up first. Today though, she was more downcast than he'd seen her in years—maybe ever. Her shoulders were slumped and behind her eyes, she carried the weight of something incredibly heavy.

He stirred his coffee idly, simply for something to do, some movement to make, and watched his daughter as he mulled it over. Finally, unable to hold back any longer, he decided to ease into what he hoped was a fairly safe topic.

"So how was that wedding you went to with Stephen and the girls?"

At the mention of Stephen's name, Olivia's spoon clattered onto the rim of the bowl, tipping over the side, splattering droplets of soup across the tablecloth before tumbling to the floor with a metallic rattle. Her face crumpled and tears began pouring down her cheeks. She tried to cover her face with her hands, but the sobs came fast and hard, her shoulders shaking as emotion overwhelmed her.

Jack froze, stunned, at a loss. He hadn't expected such a strong reaction, but as realization dawned on him, he felt a pang of guilt. Clearly, he'd touched on the source of her pain without even meaning to—something to do with Stephen.

"Livvy," he said gently, sliding out of his chair and moving around the table to her side. He knelt beside her, wrapping an arm around her and pulling her close. "Hey, hey. It's okay. I'm sorry, sweetheart. I didn't mean to upset you."

Her sobs grew louder, and Jack stroked her hair, like he had when she was a little girl only just discovering the unfairness of the world. His voice low and soothing, he told her, "Get it out of your system, kiddo. It's okay. I'm here. Just let it out."

It broke Jack's heart to see her crying like this, to feel her body wracked with sobs. When she was a kid, crying over skinned knees or a broken toy, he knew how to solve her problems. Now he felt helpless, unsure of how he could make it better.

It took a few minutes, but eventually, her sobs quieted. Jack reached for a paper napkin from the pile in the middle of the table and pressed it into her hands. She took it, wiping at her eyes and nose as she tried to catch her breath.

"I'm sorry, Daddy," she said, her voice thick with tears.

"Hey, now," Jack told her, his tone firm but kind. He tilted her chin up gently so he could look her in the eye. "You don't need to apologize for anything. You're upset, and I'm sorry I touched a nerve. I really had no idea… but I wanna know what's got you so hurt." He tilted his forehead against hers, a gesture of closeness and affection. "I wanna help, if I can."

Olivia sniffled and dabbed at her face with the crumpled napkin. Jack could see she was thinking, deciding whether or not to tell him. The honest concern, the love, in her father's eyes decided for her.

"It's Stephen," she admitted finally, her voice barely above a whisper.

Jack nodded slowly, already piecing things together in his mind. "The hockey guy," he said, keeping his tone neutral.

She nodded, balling the napkin in her fingers, focusing her eyes on it instead of meeting her father's. "It's so stupid," she said, her voice trembling. "I thought… I thought we had something real. But at the wedding, everything fell apart."

Jack frowned but didn't interrupt, giving her the space to continue.

"I don't… really wanna say exactly what happened. You can probably find it online if you really want to know," she told him, her face flushing with shame and anger. That was a problem with being a celebrity she'd never really thought of until this past weekend—well, it didn't matter now.

"It was after we were… together," she said, embarrassed at discussing this sort of thing with her dad. Who else was there to talk to though? Dee had tried, sensing something was wrong at work her first day back, but as much as she loved Dee, she wasn't that kind of friend. She wiped at her eyes again. "And he said some really beautiful things to me before and after and then… well… there was some awful stuff that happened."

Jack's face flushed, both embarrassment and anger plain. "You know, I was never on the force down here, but I have some friends who were and we could make a visit. Teach this punk a lesson or two and—"

"No!" Olivia said quickly, shaking her head. "I don't want that. I don't want anyone to hurt Stephen. I don't know what I want… I mean, maybe it wasn't even his fault—what happened, I mean. I know he wouldn't have done anything to ruin Randy and Amy's wedding. He's not that kind of guy. But the other stuff…"

Jack's jaw clenched painfully. He didn't know Stephen well, but spending Christmas with the young man and his family, he'd gotten to like all three of them and he had a very good impression of Stephen in particular. He seemed kind and intelligent, and Jack didn't want to believe anything bad about him without hearing both sides of whatever happened, but just knowing Olivia had gone through some kind of hell was enough to set his protective instincts ablaze.

Still… there *were* two sides to every story.

"Have you talked to Stephen about this… whatever happened?" Jack asked after a moment.

"He's tried to reach out," Olivia admitted, her voice small. "He's texted me a bunch. His sister has too—Kylie. And Flora even left me a voicemail last night. But… I can't. I can't face him right now. It's still too much."

Jack sighed, brushing a stray strand of hair from her face. "Sweetheart, I guess I don't know the guy too well, but he seemed okay to me. And it sounds like you care about him a lot."

Olivia bit her lip, tears welling in her eyes again. "I do care about him," she whispered. "But—forget everything else—what if this is what it's always going to be like with him? What if there's always drama, always something or someone trying to ruin it? I mean, he's a celebrity."

Jack leaned back on his heels, giving her a thoughtful look. "That's a fair question," he said. "But life's full of drama, Livvy. With anyone." He chuckled. "I was a cop for thirty-six years. I know a little about drama. But sweetheart—Livvy, let me tell you life's about finding someone who's worth the trouble."

He placed a hand over hers, squeezing gently. "You don't have to decide anything right now. But if you really care about him, don't let fear make the decision for you. At least give him a chance to tell his side of things, okay? That's fair, isn't it?"

Olivia looked down at their hands, her heart aching. But she could hear the truth in his words. She hadn't let Stephen explain, and she really did believe he was a good person. Everything she knew of him, everything they shared in those few short hours they spent together, told her that much. The least she could do was listen to Stephen—if he still even wanted to talk to her.

"Thanks, Daddy," she said softly.

Jack smiled, the lines around his eyes crinkling, making him look even more like a comfortably stuffed old teddy bear. "That's what I'm here for, kiddo. Now, let's get this stuff cleaned up and go out for something sweet. Nothing a slice of pie can't fix, right?"

For the first time that day, Olivia laughed. It wasn't much of a laugh, but it was genuine.

Her phone chose that minute to vibrate with an incoming text. Her heart fluttered, thinking maybe it was Stephen—that some sort of kismet made him reach out again just at the moment she decided she'd listen if he still wanted to talk.

She fished the phone from her purse, feeling Jack's eyes on her. Maybe he had the same thought.

"It's Kylie," Olivia told Jack.

Chapter 35.

"You're still wearing the necklace," Kylie said, noticing the silver Scrabble pieces with Olivia's initials resting against the other girl's chest.

The sports bar was brightly lit, filled with the chatter of conversation and a dozen TVs all competing for drinkers' attention. The clink of glasses provided a counterpoint to the myriad voices. The air smelled of fried food and beer. It was the same bar where Olivia had seen Stephen on TV weeks ago, surrounded by her coworkers, where she'd first told someone about her relationship with Stephen Sloan—if that was even the right word. That night felt like a lifetime ago.

Olivia and Kylie sat in a booth near the back, Olivia twirling her straw idly around a half-empty glass of soda. Kylie offered her a beer or something stronger, but Olivia didn't want to become too relaxed. She trusted Kylie—they were friends—but she didn't want to let her guard down. Kylie obviously wanted to talk about Stephen and what happened, and Olivia needed a clear head for that. She still hadn't sorted out all of her feelings or decided what she wanted to happen next.

Kylie propped her chin on her fist and flicked another glance towards Olivia's neck. She'd helped Stephen buy that necklace—it was entirely his idea, and she was proud of him for it, but he was clueless about how to make it happen—and she thought it was a very good sign that Olivia was still wearing it.

Olivia's hand instinctively rose to touch the pendant. She hadn't even realized she'd put it on that morning, but now that Kylie had pointed it out, it felt like a spotlight was shining on it.

"It's a nice necklace," Olivia said after a pause, her voice quiet but steady. "It was a thoughtful gift, and… I do love Scrabble."

Kylie leaned back in her seat, taking a sip of her beer. "You really should let Stephen know that. It'd make him really happy."

Olivia's stomach tightened, and she glanced away, her fingers still brushing the pendant. "Kylie…"

"I'm serious, Liv," Kylie interrupted gently but firmly. "Just… let him know how you feel. And please," Kylie added, her voice softer now, almost pleading. "Give my brother a chance to explain everything that happened. It's really not what you think it is."

Olivia shut down hearing that, her face closing off as she turned her attention back to her drink. Even expecting this is what Kylie wanted to talk about, the conversation felt too close, the subject still too raw. She hadn't agreed to meet Kylie because she wanted to talk about Stephen—at least, not directly, though she knew it would have to happen. She just missed Kylie. And Flora. And the warmth of their family that had felt like another home for a few brief, wonderful weeks.

Kylie sighed, leaning forward and reaching across the table to take Olivia's hand. Her touch was warm, grounding, and Olivia reluctantly met her gaze. "He's as messed about this as I think you are, Liv…"

Olivia stiffened, but she didn't pull her hand away. "I don't know what to think anymore," she admitted. "That video… it was awful, Kylie. Everyone saw it. Everyone was looking at me like I was… pathetic. Like I was some joke." Her voice cracked, and she looked down, blinking rapidly to push back the tears threatening to spill.

Kylie's grip on her hand tightened, her expression fierce. "You're not a joke. And you're definitely not pathetic. That was—I don't even have the right words. It was a bitch-ass stunt that miserable witch Liza pulled to get back at Stephen, to make him look like an ass—to try to hurt you. But Stephen had nothing to do with it! I swear. If there's one thing I know about my brother, it's that he'd never do anything to hurt you or anyone else on purpose."

Kylie tilted her head, her eyes narrowing. "And besides, do you really think I'd let Stephen get away with anything if I thought for one second that he was lying about any of this? You know both of us better than that, don't you?"

Olivia allowed herself the tiniest smile. She did know Kylie—not for long, but long enough and pretty well after all the time they'd spent together. She knew Kylie's relentless teasing, her sharp and sarcastic way of talking, and her unflinching loyalty to the people she loved. But if Kylie was fighting on Stephen's behalf now, it wasn't out of blind loyalty, it was because she genuinely believed him.

"I guess you wouldn't," Olivia said softly.

Kylie's face lit up with a triumphant smile, but she didn't press the small victory. She leaned back, picked up her glass, taking a sip, then said, "He's miserable knowing how bad you were hurt. I've never seen him like this—not even when he first moved back into Grandma's house. All he does is hang around the penthouse by himself in his shorts."

Olivia's chest ached at the thought. She could picture Stephen so clearly. His body was so strong, and he was usually so confident, but he'd opened himself up to her that night in the hotel and she saw what a vulnerable, tender man he could really be. She already cared for him, but that night, it grew into something so deep. The memory of his face, the way he'd looked at her like she was the only person in the world the morning of the wedding, the morning after they made love, squeezed her heart painfully.

Her fingers went to the necklace again. She held it away from her throat, looking down at it. The small silver Scrabble pieces caught the overhead light, sparkling between her fingers. It was a simple, unassuming piece, but it carried so much meaning. Stephen chose it for her because he'd paid attention to what she loved, to who she was.

She missed him. Oh, God, she missed him.

"What the actual fuck," Kylie said, snapping Olivia back to attention. She'd never heard Kylie swear like that and it was shocking somehow, like hearing a sort of spicy but sweet little kid suddenly telling you to go to hell.

Olivia turned to see what had caught Kylie's eye. Her breath froze in her lungs. Liza Gardner.

Liza sat at a table near the middle of the bar, the center of a raucous group of young men and women, all of them hanging on her every word. Her platinum-blonde hair gleamed under the bar's dim lights, styled in loose waves that seemed to catch every flicker of neon, making it shimmer as she moved her head. She was dressed to a T, as always, in a form-fitting black top paired with designer jeans and stiletto heels that clicked sharply on the tile floor whenever she crossed her legs. Even in an average sports bar, she looked glamorous.

"What the fuck is she even doing here?" Kylie growled, sliding from her side of the booth.

"Wait, what are you—" Olivia began, but it was too late. Kylie was already making her way towards Liza's table.

Kylie stormed across the room, marching like a soldier off to war. Olivia shook off the stunned feeling at seeing this new side of Kylie and called out to her, alarmed, but Kylie didn't hear or didn't care.

Liza Gardner, seated like a queen in the middle of her court, laughed at something one of the other women said. Her eyes flicked towards Kylie and her mouth opened, but Kylie beat her to the punch, her voice cutting through the bar noise like a whip. "You miserable bitch, who do you think you are? What the hell were you doing at Randy's wedding? How dare you even show your face, knowing no one wanted you there? And then—*then*—you ruin Randy and Amy's special day with that stunt you pulled. Do you have any idea what you did to my brother? To my friend?" Her arm rose, pointing behind her in Olivia's direction.

The members of Liza's entourage shifted, unsure of what to make of this invader into their space. One of the men, a tall guy with sandy hair, stood up, stepping forward as if to put himself between Liza and Kylie. But Liza only arched an eyebrow, leaning back in her chair as if thoroughly unimpressed. "It's fine," she told him, gesturing for him to sit back down.

Turning to Kylie, she said, "Your brother brought that on himself. If he wanted to keep his skeletons in the closet, maybe he shouldn't have treated me the way he did."

She looked beyond Kylie to Olivia, standing behind her friend, completely at a loss as to what to do. She'd never been in a situation like this before—even in high school, she'd never been much involved in any drama.

Liza said, "As for the cow—"

"*Bitch!*" Kylie screamed as her temper exploded, lunging forward to grab a fistful of Liza's hair and yanking her out of her chair.

The table erupted into chaos. Liza shrieked, clutching at Kylie's hands as she tried to pry herself loose, while the young man who'd stood to defend Liza earlier dove forward, attempting to separate them. Drinks spilled, chairs screeched against the floor, and gasps rippled through the bar as everyone turned to see the commotion.

"You think you can get away with this?" Kylie shouted, dragging Liza a step away from the table as she tightened her grip. "You think you can ruin people's lives and just walk around like nothing happened?"

"Let go of me!" Liza screeched, clawing at Kylie's hands. "Get this psycho off me!"

"Kylie!" Olivia shouted, grabbing Kylie's right arm with both of hers. She pulled with all her strength, using her greater height and weight as leverage, and after a tense moment managed to separate the two women.

Liza stumbled backward, her hair disheveled and her face red with rage. "You're insane!" she spat, pointing a shaking finger at Kylie. "You're lucky if I don't press charges for assault!

"And you!" She turned her long-nailed finger on Oliva. "The day I need help from some fat, cow-titted, pig-faced nobody is the day I lay down and die. Mind your own God-damned business and keep your oinking to yourself!"

Olivia froze. The world seemed to tilt slightly, her vision narrowing as those words—*almost the exact same words*—dug into her mind and pulled her backward in time.

Stan.

The memory hit her like a freight train. She was standing in Stan's apartment, a place as familiar as her own home, her hands trembling as she stared at Stan and Sarah tangled in bed. Sarah had looked her dead in the eye and sneered, *"You God-damned oinker."*

It had cut her deeply, but she'd swallowed the pain, told herself to be the bigger person. She'd lashed out at Stan, but only because he'd tried to restrain her as she was leaving. Maybe even then she'd subconsciously realized that Stan wasn't worth fighting for, so she'd walked away—hurt and humiliated.

Now, Liza's words brought all of that boiling back to the surface.

Something snapped inside Olivia, a raw, fiery energy surging through her. Her hands balled and she rushed forward with speed that surprised even herself.

Liza's eyes widened, but otherwise she had no

time to react. Olivia's fist connected squarely with her jaw, making a deeply satisfying sound of bone on flesh. The force sent Liza tumbling backward, crashing onto the table behind her, and then over it. Plates, glasses, and silverware clattered to the floor with her, scattering in all directions.

The bar was already in an uproar, employees rushing towards the scene of battle, but now it fell into stunned silence. Every eye in the room was on Olivia, her chest heaving, her arm still raised from the strike.

Liza lay sprawled on the floor, unconscious, her hair a disheveled halo around her head.

"It *is* my business, bitch," Olivia said, her voice low and steady

Grinning, immensely pleased, Kylie took Olivia's arm. "Let's get out of here." She had already collected their purses and coats, so there was nothing to stop them from leaving—and no one dared to try.

Chapter 36.

"I think I could use a real drink now," Olivia said once they were outside.

A snow squall had blown up from somewhere while they were in the sports bar and a brisk wind whipped snowflakes around them. The cold was nothing though—it couldn't penetrate the heat from the fires still burning inside of Olivia.

"You are one sweet, rock'n'rollin' bad-ass bitch, you know that?" Kylie asked her.

Olivia looked at her hand. She still couldn't believe what she'd done. The adrenaline was just starting to wear down and she didn't feel it yet, but she knew enough about the human body to know that her hand would ache like hell soon. She laughed. "I guess so."

"I bet it felt good," Kylie smirked.

"Yeah. C'mon, I know a place."

She hailed a passing cab and directed the driver to a quiet little cocktail bar near the waterfront. It had a long, dark-stained bar along one side of the room, with a television mounted above it near one end. The other side of the room was lined with leather-upholstered booths. At the far end there was a dais with a piano, unused now. Soft music piped in from hidden speakers in the ceiling instead.

Once the women were ensconced at a table, each with a cocktail—a daquiri for Olivia, a peachy keen for Kylie—Kylie said, "She's had that coming for a loooong time." She reached across the table, squeezing Olivia's uninjured hand. "You feel better now?"

"Yeah." Olivia was not a violent person, but it had

felt good to take her frustration, her hurt, her anger out on something tangible. It helped that Liza Gardner was directly responsible.

Olivia smiled almost shyly. "I didn't know you or I had that in us."

Kylie didn't laugh, as Olivia would have expected. "I take care of my friends and family, Liv."

They were silent for a few moments, sipping the drinks. A daquiri wasn't exactly a winter drink, but Olivia wasn't really much of a drinker, and it went down smoothly, the rum settling in her stomach and spreading a faint warmth through her body.

Finally, Kylie said, "Are you gonna talk to Stephen?"

"Yeah," Olivia answered without hesitation. "Right now actually." She stood and moved off towards the unoccupied end of the bar, near the television. She opened her phone, scrolled to Stephen's contact and began typing when she heard a familiar voice.

"I'll take a few questions now."

Olivia's head shot up. Stephen was on the television screen, front and center behind a podium lined with microphones. The Warriors' coach and Randy Roberts stood behind and off to one side of him, and the backs of a number of reporters' heads could be seen in the foreground.

"A lot's been made about the fiasco at Mr. Roberts's wedding, Stephen. Care to comment?" a husky male voice asked.

"And what about Liza Gardner?" a female voice called out.

Stephen gripped both sides of the podium as if steadying himself. He looked directly at the camera and said, "Those two questions are related, so… sure, why not? Let's air some dirty laundry."

He took a deep breath. "Liza Gardner and I split up several months ago. I found she was having—well, there's no other word for it that I can think of, so let's call them what they were—she was having sex parties in my apartment while I was away on team business. I literally walked in on the middle of one when I came home early one day."

The crowd of reporters erupted, and a dozen questions were hurled at Stephen all at once. Even the bartender paused in polishing a glass and turned towards the TV screen. He lifted a remote and increased the volume of the set.

Stephen held up a hand for silence and when the furor died down, continued. "I broke up with Liza in no uncertain terms. She didn't take it well and she pulled that stunt at Randy's wedding, showing the edited video to try and smear me and ruin my friend's day." He turned towards Randy. "I've already apologized for that as deeply as I know how, but I want to say again how sorry I am, buddy."

Randy stepped up to the microphone, leaned in and said, "All good, man. Not your fault," and mugged a big Randy grin for the camera, tossing paired thumbs up. The assembled reporters couldn't help chuckling.

"So, that's that," Stephen said.

Olivia was awed. Stephen was so much stronger than she knew—so much stronger than she'd been. Maybe he had been moping around the penthouse, but when it came to Warriors business, he was right there, literally front and center, admitting to something embarrassing, even humiliating, and taking responsibility for it, even though it wasn't his fault at all. Her heart swelled with how proud she was of him.

If Stephen could be brave, so could she. She'd already stood up to and beaten—literally—Liza, the source of both of their problems. And for this, she decided, texting was too impersonal. Besides, she wanted to hear his voice so badly—the TV had only whetted her appetite for him. Wondering when this press conference had been recorded, since the Warriors had no games this week, she hit his contact icon and waited for the call to connect.

A moment passed, then the Stephen on the television took his phone from his pocket and glanced at the screen. She simultaneously heard his voice through the TV and her phone. "Olivia?"

He sounded both relieved and surprised—not nearly as much as Olivia was herself. The conference was live?!

"Stephen?" she said.

"Olivia, thank God!" Stephen said. She saw his face break into a smile on the screen, while the reporters began milling around, murmuring in confusion.

"Um, how are you?" she asked, feeling foolish, but not sure how else to begin.

"Better now."

"Stephen, who are you talking to?" one of the reporters called out.

"Is there someone new in your life?" the same woman who'd asked about Liza wanted to know.

Still holding the phone to his ear, Stephen looked directly into the camera again. "I'm glad you asked that, Ms. Jennings, because that's what I'm about to find out myself. I really hope there is."

Olivia's heart fluttered and then began to race, pounding in her chest. She glanced over, realizing that at some point, Kylie had joined her by the television. The younger girl looked at Olivia and her face split into one of the biggest grins Olivia had ever seen. Others in the bar had paused their own conversations and were now glued to the story unfolding right before them.

"Olivia? You still there?"

She turned back to the television. Stephen was staring directly into the eye of the camera, but it felt like he was looking into her own eyes. "I'm here."

"Olivia, I know we haven't known each other all that long—and a whole lot of crap has gone down—but I don't think this kind of thing depends on length of time or anything like that. It's about how you feel and—hell, I'm no good with this kind of thing. Olivia, I love you," he said.

It set off explosions inside of Olivia, like fireworks pinwheeling across her heart and soul, literally making her weak in the knees. She had to clutch the edge of the bar to keep her balance. Kylie hugged her and squealed, "Answer him! Answer him!"

Olivia glanced at her friend, then at the bartender and the couple nearest them at the bar. Everyone was waiting for her to say something, to respond to Stephen Sloan, one of Beantown's biggest heroes professing his love for her on what must have been national television.

She let out a shuddering breath and said, "I love you too, Stephen."

A cheer went up across the room and someone shouted, "Next round's on me!"

Up on the television screen, Stephen smiled and said, "See you soon." He stepped down from the podium and walked off stage, ignoring the questions hurled after him.

Epilogue

One year later

"Do you, Stephen Jonathan Sloan, take Olivia Ann Murray, to be your lawful wedded spouse? To have and to hold, to love and to cherish, in both sickness and in health, for better or for worse?"

The Mountain Crest Hotel was again a vision of winter elegance. Snow blanketed the mountain, and the pristine white peak sparkled beneath the brilliant blue of a crystalline January sky. Inside, warmth beckoned guests and travelers to join the celebration of life and love and dedication.

After what happened at the Mountain Crest during Randy and Amy's wedding, it might have seemed an unusual choice, but to Stephen and Olivia, this place was more than just a stunning venue, it was a testament to their resilience and the choice to not only reclaim their happiness but shout it out for all of the world to hear. Heartache had been inflicted on them here, but they were making it a symbol of their love and of a new beginning for their life together.

"I do," Stephen told the minister, turning a sidelong glance at Olivia. He was nervous, his guts were almost quivering, but he was so happy that the silly grin he wore had been plastered to his face all morning. Randy, his best man, gave him what he thought was a secret thumbs up, though the whole room saw it.

"And do you, Olivia Ann Murray, take Stephen Jonathan Sloan, to be your lawful wedded spouse? To have and to hold, to love and to cherish, in both sickness and in health, for better or for worse?"

White roses, eucalyptus, and twinkling fairy lights adorned the hotel's reception hall space, lending it a magical air with their soft glow. Rows of chairs, filled with family, friends, and teammates, marched away from the platform where the bride and groom stood with their bridal party.

Tears glistened in Olivia's eyes as she said, "I do." She didn't know it was possible to be this happy. Flora, Olivia's matron of honor, dabbed at her eyes with a lace handkerchief. She was flanked by bridesmaids Kylie, Amy, Jenny and Deann, who wept openly in happiness for her friend.

The minister went through the custom of asking if anyone wished to object, receiving only silence in return. He smiled at the couple. "I now pronounce you man and wife. Mr. Sloan, you may now kiss your bride."

Stephen leaned in, wrapped his arms around Olivia and kissed her, long and deeply and lovingly. The room exploded into cheers and applause.

When the kiss finally ended, Stephen whispered, "I don't know how I got so lucky."

"We both did," Olivia answered, and leaned in to kiss her husband again.

They linked hands and, turning to their friends and family, held them high. The guests roared in celebration again, fresh cheering and clapping filling the room. Olivia and Stephen squeezed one another's hands, each promising in their hearts that after all they'd been through to reach this moment, this was happily ever after.

The End

ABOUT THE AUTHOR

"Beth Anderson" is the joint penname of a veteran author of numerous novels of several different genres and a first-time author who loves romance novels.

This is their first work together.

Made in United States
North Haven, CT
24 December 2024

63382985R00137